Judy Astley was frequently told off for day-dreaming at her drearily traditional school but has found it to be the ideal training for becoming a writer. There were several false starts to her career: secretary at an all-male Oxford college (sacked for undisclosable reasons), at an airline (decided, after a crash and a hijacking, that she was safer elsewhere) and as a dress designer (quit before anyone noticed she was adapting *Vogue* patterns). She spent some years as a parent and as a painter before sensing that the day was approaching when she'd have to go out and get a Proper Job. With a nagging certainty that she was temperamentally unemployable, and desperate to avoid office coffee, having to wear tights every day and missing out on sunny days on Cornish beaches with her daughters, she wrote her first novel, *Just for the Summer*. She has now had eight novels published by Black Swan.

SEVEN FOR A SECRET

Judy Astley

BLACK SWAN

SEVEN FOR A SECRET
A BLACK SWAN BOOK : 0 552 99629 7

First publication in Great Britain

PRINTING HISTORY
Black Swan edition published 1996

7 9 10 8 6

Set in 11pt Linotron Melior by
Deltatype Ltd, Birkenhead, Merseyside.

Black Swan Books are published by Transworld Publishers,
61–63 Uxbridge Road, London W5 5SA,
a division of The Random House Group Ltd,
in Australia by Random House Australia (Pty) Ltd,
20 Alfred Street, Milsons Point, Sydney, NSW 2061, Australia,
in New Zealand by Random House New Zealand Ltd,
18 Poland Road, Glenfield, Auckland 10, New Zealand
and in South Africa by Random House (Pty) Ltd,
Endulini, 5a Jubilee Road, Parktown 2193, South Africa.

Printed and bound in Great Britain by
Cox & Wyman Ltd, Reading, Berkshire.

For Pauline Love Cornwell

Chapter One

It was Heather's twenty-fifth wedding anniversary, a landmark in life reminding her sharply that she could no longer pretend the 'over-forties', like Sartre's hell, were Other People. Silver weddings, she had always thought, were for those who had succumbed to growing old with grace, who truly welcomed presents of cruet-sets and cake-knives, and whose maturing insurance policies would comfortably finance a celebratory Mediterranean cruise complete with formation ball-room dancing. Her own generation had a long way to go yet.

It wasn't the wedding at which she'd married Tom – so far they'd now notched up eighteen years. (Success-fully? Well they were still together, when he was home.) This anniversary was the date of Heather's first wedding that hardly anyone knew about, was never talked about and was, as her furious mother had firmly decreed all those years ago, As If It Never Happened.

Heather remembered the twenty-five-year-old date while she was in her bedroom, looking for a pair of tights to wear to Kate's final speech day. It wasn't tights-wearing weather, being far too stuffily hot, and the school hall would be discreetly steaming with overdressed parents, but Heather's fingers scrabbled dutifully through her underwear drawer, searching for the right shade in seven denier. The weather had been the same all those years ago, full of birdsong, clear, hot, even in Scotland where she'd never been before and had somehow expected, fresh from recent geography O-level revision, frosty glens every morning and purple, snow-capped, deer-studded mountains even in July.

'Bugger!' she cursed to herself. The tights she was hauling up her legs were laddered at around mid-thigh, the kind of ladder that looked as if it was as inclined to travel downwards as up. Carefully, just as she had back in the days when a pair of tights had cost half a Saturday's pay in Woolworth's, she sealed the run with pale pink nail varnish. 'Won't show,' she murmured, pulling her navy silk skirt down and wishing she'd thought to use fake tan. Who'd notice? Well Kate for a start – there was nothing like a sixteen-year-old for seeing all and hearing all and making your short-comings public. Nothing like a sixteen-year-old, too, for demanding to be the most attention-seeking, shock-inducing creature on the planet, and then expecting her mother to fade seamlessly into the safe, dull background.

'Heather! You ready?' called a voice from the hall-way. Feet thumped heavily up the stairs and a woman's head, preceded by a soothing 'It's only me! House wide open to burglars!' appeared round the door.

'Good grief Margot, not a hat!' Heather blurted out with a giggle. The hat, squashed on to a mass of streaky blonde hair, was lilac straw with a big, bold, yellow chiffon flower on the side. It so exactly matched the mauve, cream and yellow flowered suit Margot wore, like a set of chintzy loose covers over her ample body, that it resembled one of those completely co-ordinated toddler ensembles that immaculate continental children wear.

Margot peered into the wardrobe mirror and patted at the hat, preening and smiling broadly at her smart self. 'What's wrong with it? Sets it off a treat, I think. Thought it was most appropriate, very PTA Committee.'

Heather grabbed her bag and shoved in half a box of tissues, just in case. It wasn't every day she had to watch

8

her elder daughter being presented with a school music prize, and, together with her leaver's medal, that might be just enough to set off a few tears. She pulled her cream silk jacket from its hanger, gave it a cursory check for marks, though she didn't know what she'd wear if she found any, and reassured Margot. 'The hat's lovely, really, just a bit unexpected; I've never actually seen you in daytime finery before. You look like a mayoress about to open a fête. Goodness, we're going to be late, let's go.'

'Finished my last dog at twelve, so I had lots of time to get ready,' Margot was saying as they got into Heather's Renault. 'Old boot wanted her poodle's back end shaved into one of those old-fashioned lion styles. In summer! Poor thing, it was a standard too, huge, white, panting animal – imagine carrying around all that fur at the front like that in this heat.'

Heather smiled, and glanced at Margot's own substantial front, wondering if she, too, found it a burden in the heat. 'Carries her tits around as if they're on a tray,' Tom had once said at one of the village Christmas drinks parties, when Margot's creamy cleavage, framed by a curved neckline of soft maroon velvet, had been displayed like a parchment scroll on a presentation cushion. Tom was always wary of breasts, it occurred to Heather as she nudged the car carefully out of the drive on to the main road. He'd never given hers much attention, as if they were too small and insignificant to require it. He was happy with her ectomorphic shape. 'Boy-shaped' he'd called her approvingly when they were younger, pleased at her angles and seemingly relieved that she didn't have great soft doughy pieces of flesh on her chest that got in the way, and assuming that they didn't need, well, kneading.

The traffic on the way to the school was unexpectedly heavy. The small market town they had to pass through was gasping with immobile fumes and almost pleading

9

for a by-pass. Where were all these people going in the middle of such a hot day, Heather wondered impatiently, why couldn't they all stay at home and sit under the trees in deckchairs? She stopped at the lights and looked around, sighing crossly and starting to feel tense. The woman in the next car was wearing gloves, little white cotton ones that flared out at the wrist. She sat at the traffic lights in her sparkling silver Rover, neat and still as a good child. Heather, checking her watch against the car's clock, could feel her heart starting to beat harder. They were going to be late. There would be nowhere left to sit and she (not Margot, who had a PTA Committee place reserved on the stage) would have to tiptoe conspicuously across the hall to the only empty seat, which would be just in front of the kind of father who was probably a high court judge. He'd be sure to give her that look, the one that announces, 'I'm extremely busy and important, and if I can get here on time on a Wednesday afternoon why can't you, a mere housewife, mother and part-time gardener?' Kate would tut loudly and make 'God, that's bloody typical' faces to all her sympathetic, smirking friends, and shy Suzy would peer at the floor, hide in her hair and hope no-one noticed that this grossly embarrassing mother was *hers.*

Heather revved the car and swore as another driver stopped in the yellow box just in front of her, so that when the lights changed she had nowhere to go. Any second the lights would be back to red again, and she would soon be cursing the way people unintelligently fill up the school hall from the doorway inwards, leaving only those odd seats right out on the far side. Couldn't they foresee the craven late arrivals needing some place to slide into in decent apologetic obscurity? Did they do it on purpose, smugly, as in: don't leave space for them, they don't deserve it? The woman in the next car sat still and didn't thrum her fingers on the

10

steering wheel. Heather would bet serious money on the probability that the Rover's ashtray contained nothing but one carefully folded Opal fruit wrapper. The neat white gloves reminded her of childhood clothes from approximately 1960. There had been something highly prized called duster coats, she clearly recalled, big cotton overall things in flowery fabrics like Margot's dress, rather resembling the kind of outfit the Queen Mother wore. She remembered wanting one so desperately, along with a matching cotton shirtwaister frock in candy stripes, like her friends Sandra and Janice had. 'Certainly not, they're from C & A,' her mother had sniffed, as if that made it absolutely out of the question, and forming in her suggestible eight-year-old daughter a long-lasting and extremely inconvenient suspicion of chain-store clothes.

'It's my wedding anniversary,' Heather, stirred by long ago memory, suddenly announced to Margot, as the traffic cleared and she put her foot down hard.

'Thought you and Tom had a winter wedding – all velvet and cute boots,' Margot commented.

'No, I don't mean him.' Heather opened the sunroof and felt a rush of cooling air, wondering which was the more exhilarating, that or her simple, unaccustomed statement. She'd never said it before, not about Iain. Every other July or so she thought about it, especially at the significant ones: five (wood), ten (tin) and fifteen (crystal). Right now, she could be organizing a major-scale silver wedding party, arranging appropriately pale flowers and supervising the cooking of salmon from one of Iain's own rivers – her rivers, too, they'd have been, of course. Half the county (the smarter half) would be there, and all Iain's clever writer/theatre/film friends would have become her friends as well. It was strange to have kept a secret for that long – really it should have been let out years ago. It reminded her of a sex offender grown too old and decrepit to be dangerous, but still kept imprisoned for no better reasons than habit and a sort of superstition.

'The first time I got married was twenty-five years ago today,' she went on.

Margot looked horrified, turning to give her a close stare as if she'd been wilfully misleading everyone about her age. 'Good grief, you must have been one hell of a child bride. Pregnant were you?'

'No, I wasn't actually. Well not then.' Heather felt a small cool shadow on the day but then laughed, and turned the car up into the school drive which was ominously lined with gleaming, well-kept cars. 'I was straight out of O-levels, just sixteen, barely legal,' she told Margot, peering past the cars and wishing that the affluent middle-classes could bring themselves to drive something smaller than Range Rovers and leave more space for tiny Renaults such as hers. 'Feels like a bit of a milestone, to be honest, even though the marriage didn't make it to twenty-five weeks, let alone years.'

'More like a bloody millstone I should think, if it *had* lasted. It's as long as a life sentence. Me and Russell won't make it that far,' Margot predicted dourly. 'Look, parking space, right by the door. Someone must have bolted before the start, and who can blame them?'

They weren't late; fresh-frocked mothers in low-heeled shoes, and office-suited, lost-looking fathers, were still filing into the hall. Among them Heather picked out Nigel from the plant nursery, arms folded, face thunderous. Someone had probably innocently enquired how his garden centre was doing, she guessed, imagining him making his usual outraged speech about absolutely *not* being a common peddler of plastic trellis, mixed summer bedding or cement hedge-hogs. She looked across at the rows of younger girls and immediately picked out Suzy's face turned anxiously towards her, the girl's expression switching to relief. Always so worried, poor child, Heather thought as she

12

waved to her. At thirteen, Suzy seemed to have an over-mature capacity for imagining disastrous scenarios: awful 'what-ifs', like school bus crashes, night-time sparks smouldering in the thatched roof, tiny but fatal water-vole-nibbled holes in her rowing boat, the sort of thing that was only supposed to go through the minds of over-protective adults. *Doesn't get that from me,* Heather admitted, vividly remembering herself at twelve, thirteen, right through to sixteen, sublimely unaware that anything planned could ever go wrong, and somehow assuming that tragedy and misfortune were items of fiction made up by newspapers and TV reporters, to provide a bit of vicarious grief for the rest of the world to marvel at from a safe distance. It was probably a reaction to her own mother's doomy warnings, punctuating her childhood with 'Don't touch', 'Mind the road', 'Watch your feet', 'Are those hands washed?'

It was hot in the hall, as Heather had known it would be. Parents gently fanned themselves with their programmes. The geography mistress, who should have thought of it earlier, was picking her way between the rows of seats with a ten-foot pole, trying to open the highest windows. Several awkward-looking fathers made small gestures towards helping her, half rising in their seats and holding out limp, indoor-pale hands towards the pole, but were fended off firmly by the stout, capable woman. Heather could smell school lunch, and heard clanking noises somewhere in the near distance. Did they still use leftover food to feed local pigs, she wondered, recalling how, when she was at school, the girls had scraped enormous quantities of uneatable food, plus the odd escaping fork, into vast metal bins, said to be destined for the nearest suburban farm. She felt a fleeting wave of nausea, remembering how she'd been completely unable to eat pork for years, sure that pigs were somehow made up of recycled old

13

lunches – spam fritters, mince, semolina, fish pie, jam sponge, butter beans . . .

'Kate's leaving then? Not staying on into the sixth form?' Heather was hauled back to the present by the question from the woman next to her, a co-parent from Kate's form. The woman indicated Kate's name among the prize-winners and leavers listed in the programme, and waited to hear the story behind her premature flight from school. Was it lack of money, her frankly inquisitive face wondered, or was there a secret, scandalous something that Kate had done?

'She wants to go to the sixth form college,' Heather told her. 'It's mostly because they don't do psychology here.' ('Bit of a fringe subject, don't you think?' the headmistress had judged sourly on the day Kate had presented her with her A-level choices.)

'They'll miss her in the orchestra,' the woman next to Heather went on.

'That's exactly what Mrs Franklin said,' Heather commented, grimly recalling that the headmistress hadn't actually acknowledged that Kate would be missed for anything else. 'Not really a team player' had been written on Kate's first-year report, with annual variations on the same disapproving theme ever since.

The school orchestra was sitting at the front of the hall, just below the stage, facing the audience. Heather knew better than to expect a welcoming wave from Kate, who sat among the violinists chewing a nail and staring moodily into space, with her hair hanging to the side of her head like a yellow flag. She was counting the seconds, Heather assumed, till she could leave the school behind for ever and escape from its three-page list of rules, greedy obsession with Oxbridge places and 'all those stupid bloody girlies', as Kate so scornfully put it. Heather's own last day at school had been speech day too, the difference being that her own mother hadn't had a clue that she was leaving school (and home). Only her delighted group of friends knew, sworn to thrilled secrecy.

'You aren't *really* going to do it are you, not *really*?' They'd all got her alone, accompanying her to the loo or cornering her in the playground, and asked in turn, terrified that she might truly be so much more brutally nerveless than they were.

'Yes, really. We love each other, we've got to,' she'd insisted, bewitched by romance, knowing two things only: the first, that she couldn't back down now, nothing would be more shaming, and the second, that having decided to go, she really had suddenly outgrown them all, become tired of childhood, wanting desperately the next thing. The next thing had been Iain of course, outside in the road, his seductive E-type revving noisily through the guest speaker's rambling, boring talk ('In my young days . . .') and pushing the excitement level of Heather's devoted group to fidgeting fever pitch.

There'd been so much delirious squealing later as Heather, still clutching her fifth-form English prize and a bag grabbed from the cloakroom, made her freedom dash from the school grounds, leapt into the glamorous car and roared away to Scotland, throwing her battered straw hat to the crowd like a wedding bouquet. The rest of her uniform was scattered up the length of the M1, which meant that she could never go back – in those days, Heather recalled, the only sixth form dress privilege meant not having to wear the school hat. She'd wondered at the time if this was how Wendy had felt, escaping through her bedroom window and flying away with Peter Pan. Like Wendy, she'd spared neither a thought nor a phone call for a distraught parent left behind.

The speech day proceedings took their usual long-winded course. Up on the stage, bright and jolly among the PTA Committee and sedate school governors,

15

Heather could see Margot's lilac hat nodding forward sleepily while an Old Girl (extremely old, the current lot of girls would consider her, at least 50) dragged from the back benches of the House of Commons as a symbol of what the girls should be aiming for, told stories of her schoolday misdemeanours. From the sighs of blank boredom and noisy scuffings of feet, the speaker should have recognized that the goalposts of bad behaviour had been moved since her time in the Lower Fourth, and that, apart from being unimpressed, everyone was far too hot to listen. But then, Heather realized, she was probably used to that in Parliament. Eventually the prizes were handed out, and to Heather's amazement, Suzy lined up to collect the second-year Achievement Award.

'Didn't you know?' the woman next to her asked in disbelief as Heather gasped with surprise.

'I'm afraid Suzy doesn't say a lot,' she told her, rather appalled at the lack of communication this proved about her family. But then, Kate was the one who communicated enough for six daughters, which didn't leave much room for unassertive Suzy to get a word in. Heather wished Tom was there to see her, to be proud of his younger daughter, but she was used to his absences. She didn't even have a clue, that day, if it was to Rio or Riyadh he was piloting a 747, and he was well-practised in experiencing home events at second-hand, with one or another of them shouting a précis version of family landmarks down the phone to him in anonymous hotel rooms.

Heather felt tense as Kate, defiantly sloppy in her uniform, with her shirt dangling below her sweater (even in this heat) and the ends of her sleeves chewed into holes, strolled casually up to the MP and collected her music prize. Somewhere in the back of her mind, she expected this to be a poignant moment. It went with the rest of the day – being old enough to have a silver

16

wedding anniversary, old enough to have a daughter who would, that afternoon, have left school and also old enough, she added to the list, to have a husband whose thoughts had lately turned depressingly towards accepting an early retirement offer. She wasn't sure she was ready for any of these, especially Tom's retirement – he'd be home all the time and expect to join in with the gardening, as if just anyone could do it. He'd hang around in the greenhouses and decide he could re-organize her paperwork. Probably he'd unthinkingly recommend deadly datura and laburnum for gardens where small children lived, and proudly root two hundred fuchsia cuttings that nobody wanted.

Heather started fumbling in her bag for the tissues as Kate listlessly took her place at the front for the solo in the last piece of music. She casually flipped her hair out of the way and started playing. Heather waited to feel the usual mixture of pride and anxiety as her daughter played, thinking, more like Suzy than she would admit, What if a string breaks, what if she faints? But, amazingly for once, the music made no emotional impact at all, and Heather was beginning to think she was becoming numb until Kate suddenly caught her eye as the piece finished and the applause began, and sent her a rare and radiant, heart-tweaking smile.

'I *saw* you. You were crying, everyone in the orchestra could see. You're an embarrassment.' Kate, loading her final batch of school possessions – art-work, folders of music, violin, books (most of which would have to be returned to the library with Suzy next term) – into the car, was accusing her mother. Heather didn't argue, it gave the girl something to occupy her while her friends did all their 'see you next term' goodbyes, in which Kate could not join. Her great friend Annabelle hovered uncertainly between Kate and the other girls, her

17

loyalties now divided. Celebratory tea in the school garden was still going on a few yards away, buzzing with conversation about planned holidays (the words Umbria and Algarve were trilled distinctly and frequently) and an undercurrent of speculation about how much the school fees were likely to go up next term. Demure hay-fever sneezes could be heard, and Heather's professional eye noted that someone could have been more thorough about controlling both green-fly and rust on the roses.

'Aren't you coming back tomorrow for the leavers' lunch?' she asked.

'Definitely not. I'm never coming back here again, not ever,' Kate stated decisively. 'Besides, it's really for the Upper Sixth. They all love it because they get told how wonderful they are, getting into the best universities and all that.' Kate shoved hard at her tennis racket, stuffing it into a corner of the car boot.

'What about the ones that aren't going to university?' Heather asked, trying to re-organize Kate's bags so there'd be enough room for Suzy's. 'What do they get told?'

'They just don't go to the lunch,' Kate said with finality, 'like me.'

Heather wandered off to look for Margot and Suzy, eventually finding Margot by the tea tent on the terrace, a cup in one hand and a strawberry tart in the other, and an expression of bewilderment as to how she was to eat it without a third hand. 'Russell's managed to get here at last, too late to hear Tamsin read her poem, of course, but there you go, I'm used to that. So we won't need a lift back with you, thanks,' she told Heather.

'Just as well, I think we're full. You should see the stuff Kate's bringing home. You'd think she was moving house.'

'I was wondering,' Margot said, looking around and finding a ledge for her tea, 'does she still want a job in

18

the kennels for a few weeks? It's just that I could do with the help, the place is going to be chaos. Russell and I and the kids are going to move into the old garden cottage. You've heard they're using the village to make a film?'

Heather had heard something about it; half the village had been complaining (in the pub) that the place would be full of trippers gawping around and getting in the way, while the other half wondered how much money they could make out of the venture. Margot had been one of the latter.

'Anyway, they want to rent our house for a whole month, so you can imagine . . .' She waited for Heather to say the right thing.

Heather smiled. 'Oh yes I can imagine,' she agreed, acknowledging yet another of those moments where the English, so politely, Do Not Mention Money.

'Anyway,' Margot continued, 'Simon is back from school on Saturday and I thought, if he and Kate could share the dog-walking, morning or evening, I don't mind which, they could earn themselves a bit of pocket money, couldn't they?'

Heather thought for a minute about the awful prospect of a pair of bored teenagers with eight idle weeks and not enough to do and agreed. 'Good idea. And they'll be company for each other.'

Kate smiled all the way home. She opened the car window wide and beamed crazily at startled pedestrians. She grinned at her sister Suzy, who immediately worried in case it meant anything sinister. 'I'm going to have a *wonderful* summer!' Kate declared, shaking her long pale hair free of dust, heat and five years of school. 'I've got *absolutely nothing* to do, and it's bliss. No revision, no essays, no maths.' Her face, Heather could see in the mirror, suddenly looked

19

ecstatic with realization. 'No maths *ever again*!'

'You might need to add up your change in a shop,' Suzy pointed out.

'Or calculate VAT,' Heather contributed. *Or plan a kitchen or work out a carpet area*— She stopped herself condemning Kate to future domestic tedium.

'*Boring*. I shall rely on honest check-out people and I'll *never ever* have the kind of job where I have to do VAT,' Kate retorted scornfully.

I used to feel like that, Heather thought. She half expected Kate, glorying in her early release from the seven-year sentence of school, to start flinging her uniform out of the car window, somehow feeling that perhaps it ran in the family. She'd have to stop her if she did – the chewed sweater might be a jumble-sale candidate, but the rest could hang in a cupboard till it fitted Suzy. Besides, she thought, slowing the car as they entered the village, Kate hadn't got in her bag a handy little purple satin Biba frock to change into as she herself had had all those years ago. Nor, she reflected thankfully, was Kate sitting next to a man of few scruples who was too old for her, believing without the slightest lurking qualm or sensible doubt, that he was whirling her away to a fairy-tale life of idyllic romance in his castle of perpetual delight. Kate, thank goodness, would never be that stupid.

Chapter Two

Friarsford, arranged prettily between the River Thames and the Chiltern farmlands, wasn't really a village any more. Heather felt conscious of this every time she drove through it; too many little collections of housing, overcoming token resistance from the Parish Council, had been tacked on over the years, to call it anything but a small town. The main road sliced through, dividing a chic and tiny Georgian high street that, unlike most rural communities, had actually added to its range of shops over the past ten years. These were stylish and tempting, but not of much practical everyday use, apart from the delicatessen, the inevitable Spar stores and a wily greengrocer who lured in customers, who'd otherwise defect to Sainsbury's, with six varieties of mushrooms and out-of-season asparagus. With antique shops, a hi-fi dealer, an interior design showroom and an eclectic gift boutique only a hundred yards from her gate, Heather could order from a choice of fifteen styles of sofa in the latest Designer's Guild fabric, but could not buy a leg of lamb. If she needed to, she could also pick up an early Victorian water-colour, a Senseless Things CD, a hand-embroidered Tibetan bathmat or a fringed cushion cover in three shades of unbleached raw linen, but had to drive five miles for a plug for the hairdryer.

Beyond the north side of the High Street was the functional section of the village: the green (with pond), primary school, church, cricket pavilion and recreation ground. A crescent of neat and weathered council houses, now mostly privately owned, faced the far side

21

of the green, giving the inhabitants an enviable view of the weekly summer cricket match, and a less attractive view of the bored and brawling youth of the village doodling obscenities on the bus shelter. Nearer the road, but tucked unobtrusively behind the High Street, was a small development of modern homes built in what Tom described scornfully as 'architect's rustic', with varying additions of wood cladding, dainty gables, local stone and a hardwood window option. Lonely women, whose fraught husbands commuted to London or Oxford, lived here, disappointed that the sacrifice of urban careers to bring up their children in a rural idyll had isolated them in cosy coffee-morning territory. More than one pined with miserable guilt for the bustle of Notting Hill, for the traffic fumes and multi-coloured people and the chance of a creative job only a couple of tube stops away. Raising funds to mend the roof of a church they did not attend couldn't even begin to compensate. In winter, villagers complained to each other how dreadfully quiet it was, and in summer, that you couldn't get in the garden of the riverside pub for tourists.

Between the road and the river, sheltered by spiky, burglar-resistant greenery and high, defensive gates, were houses such as Heather's – the Desirable Riverside Properties, treasured darlings of estate agents who shamelessly lined the High Street, like gathering vultures, with their BMWs and chattering mobile phones whenever there was a rumour of a potential sale. They would have described Heather and Tom's house as 'superbly-appointed', trusting that prospective buyers would become instantly besotted with the garden and not inspect the building too closely. The house was large, an overgrown Tudor cottage with sagging floorboards and no right angles, squatting under a huge, ancient roof of patched and creaking thatch, where war was waged on squirrels breeding in the attics. Outside, there was a swimming pool with a sly, untraceable leak and the little riverside dock, where Suzy kept her boat and where Tom intended one day to build a replica Edwardian steamboat. It needed a good deal of expensive shoring up, having been eroded by the wash of speeding hire-launches.

The garden, though, was Heather's exquisite success and obvious delight. It had to be, as she insisted to the family on long summer evenings when supper had to wait till she'd finished the mulching, it was her show-room, her workplace, her sampler. With well over an acre, plus the pony paddock, to play with, and all sloping down to the river, she had created a series of separate gardens-within-the-garden, outdoor room-sets linked by lawn paths. Potential customers, dithering over whether to call in Heather the expert, or muddle around with expensive garden-centre mistakes by themselves, asked around for advice. 'You should just see her autumn bulb garden' they might be told when wondering what to do when the summer bedding was abandoned to the compost heap. Or, 'If you're thinking about herbs, look at Heather's chessboard lawn.' New river-frontage residents, eager to make the most of the flood-area alongside the water, once they'd discovered that the river may not be tidal but that wasn't to say it didn't go up and down, were always sent to Heather to marvel at her deceptively wild marsh marigolds, water-buttercups, gigantic gunnera and graceful feathery astilbes. Unless they visited in the sodden, dreary depths of February, Heather didn't find it difficult to persuade them that in the long term, which was the only way, she told them, that gardens should be thought of, they would actually save themselves money by employing her to do their design and layout.

After the stifling formality of the school speech day, she was eager to be out in the garden, busy with harvesting courgettes and peas, not with her memories about Iain. Out in the late afternoon sun, she could hear Kate and Suzy shrieking and splashing in the pool, sounding more like a pair of toddlers than teenagers. She rushed to abandon the silk outfit in the cool, pale green bedroom, quickly pulled on her oldest pair of wash-faded linen shorts and a T-shirt, and strode through the vegetable garden to the home-from-home toolshed where she kept tea-making equipment, a portable phone and her gardening magazines. 'You look just like an old man on his allotment,' Margot had giggled when she'd come to collect her pre-planted hanging baskets in spring, and had caught Heather, complete with battered hat and old cane chair, taking a break between carrot-hoeing and lettuce-planting. Harvesting her own produce was a thrill that never palled. Somehow she found it was always exciting to dig carefully into the soft earth and find that, as if by nature's magic, at the end of all the plumey stalks there really was a bunch of carrots. Pea-pods always curled outwards slightly at the perfect moment of ripeness, as if offering themselves for the picking, and secretive strawberries always had just a few more fruit slyly hidden beneath their leaves. Courgettes, though, were sneaky, Heather knew as she fetched her trug from the shed and went to inspect the plants. However careful she was to pick them at the perfect, succulent six-inch size, there was always one under the leaves that was quietly escaping, growing secretly to the size of a prize marrow and greedily sapping the energy from the plant. Triumphantly, she bent and pulled one of these out from its hiding place, and was just wondering if there were enough of the flowers to make it worthwhile picking them for frying and then cooking in an Italian omelette, when the phone in the shed rang.

'You know what day it is?' Heather heard her mother ask.

'Thursday,' she replied stubbornly. It was years since

24

Delia had mentioned That Date. Heather wasn't prepared to revert to the days of her late teens when her mother had spent that particular day each year in tight-lipped silence and the strenuous revocation of the shame her daughter had once brought her. There was a vivid memory of her indulging in energetic housework, their chilly, thin-walled 1960s house full of the sound of the vicious beating-up of cushions. From every open doorway had flashed the darting, meaningful glances at her wicked daughter and the expectation that she should join in commemorating the great mistake. Heather had soon learned simply to absent herself for as much as possible of each 10 July, even if it meant sitting in the station café for three hours after college, staring at a cold cup of coffee.

'It was Kate's last day at school today,' Heather continued cheerily, making an effort to deflect her mother on to another topic. She couldn't, surely, have called just to wish Heather a happy silver ex-wedding?

'Can't think why she won't stay where she is till she's eighteen,' her mother said tersely. 'After all, it's not as if she's *got* to go to the college for her A-levels, like *you* had to.'

Heather sighed. There seemed to be no re-routing this conversation. It reminded her of other, even more unlucky, teenage brides of her youth, the hushed, delicious gossip – 'Of course she *had* to get married.' 'Was there a particular reason for calling, only I'm about to pick some vegetables for supper,' Heather asked, rather brutally.

'Oh, yes, well. It's your Uncle Edward: he's fading very fast. I've got him into the Millthorpe Clinic near you, so if it's all right, I'll need to come and stay for a little while. You won't mind, seeing as Tom's away.' Tom was always away, she implied, making it clear that this was the most satisfactory arrangement a husband could possibly make. Her own had long ago achieved this by dying. The 'you won't mind' was clearly an instruction, and Heather was at a loss to come up with a speedily convincing but kind reason as to why she definitely *did* mind. 'It's not as if you're going away anywhere,' her mother went on with disapproval. In her opinion, the school summer break was the only acceptable time to have a holiday. That's what it was for. Heather and Tom never took one then, there was too much going on in the garden, and generous air-fare concessions meant that Christmas or February in the Caribbean or Australia was preferable. Heather's mother was suspicious about this, considering winter holidays (except skiing, which she thought was healthy exercise, ignoring all the alcohol and the *après*) as somehow undeserved, the over-indulgence of the work-shy, pampered rich.

It was only later, while Heather was hoeing between the rows of strawberries, that she realized her mother hadn't said how long she would be staying. Presumably as long as it took old Uncle Edward to die. Tom, when she told him later, would call that a 'thin end, as in wedge, situation', and ask if his mother-in-law had put her house on the market and re-organized her pension arrangements for collection at the village post office.

What was it that was terminally wrong with Uncle Edward? Heather hadn't thought to ask. He and Uncle Harold had been strange, occasional presences throughout her childhood, the only links with her long-dead and never-known father. As his brothers, and as Heather's godparents, they'd done their duty by joining her and her mother two or three times a year for an unusually formal Sunday tea. Ham *and* salmon, she remembered, vinegary cucumber and gold-backed doilies. They must have visited over a period of at least twelve years, that she could remember, but she'd had no impression of them ever changing or ageing. Harold

26

always had the same tortoiseshell-framed glasses, Edward had the same thin grey-and-white moustache.

Oily Uncle Eddy, as she'd thought of him, used to stare at her in mock amazement and exclaim unfailingly, 'And *what* a big girl you're getting', before passing her a pair of sticky half-crowns. She remembered how she'd tried not to shudder as his leathery fist burrowed the money into her reluctant palm and he'd whisper closely, with too much flying spit, 'Just our little secret, eh?' Even worse was Uncle Harold, who liked to measure how much she'd grown from knees to knickers by squeezing his overheated hand none too gently up and down her inner thigh. She remembered wondering, interestedly, if he'd left damp fingerprints, and dashing up to the bathroom to check. She never reported him to her mother, that sort of thing came under the heading of rude and unmentionable, with the highly likely danger that her mother would dismiss it scornfully with, 'Don't be so silly, you're imagining things' – but after the age of twelve or so, it was tacitly acknowledged that Heather was never left alone with him, not even for a minute, somehow being called out to the kitchen to butter bread or fetch plates. When he'd died suddenly and unexpectedly, she'd briefly wondered if it was God's sympathetic judgement, and worked extra hard to come top in RE at school that year out of gratitude.

'Can I run down to Margot's and see about the job?' Kate's face appeared around the row of bean poles. 'Perhaps she'll let me do some dog-walking now. And pay me,' she said hopefully. 'And if I take them the other side of the rec where the woods are, do I still have to collect up the shit in little bags?'

'Probably not,' Heather told her, 'but you'll never get them to last out that far, you know dogs. Why don't you wait till tomorrow when Simon gets back, then you can negotiate a good deal together?'

Kate thought for a long moment, her wet hair trailing across her face as she used her purple-varnished thumbnail to slice open a ripe bean pod. 'I'll do better on my own. Simon's too drippy to battle about money,' she decided. 'He'd end up doing it for nothing – Margot would persuade him to do it out of mummy-love.'

Heather watched Kate's long tanned legs striding towards the gate and thought, probably accurately, that Margot could persuade Simon to help with the dogs just for a chance to gaze at Kate. I'll go round and see Margot later, she thought, after a swim.

Kate, in a tiny black dress no bigger than a man's vest, ambled along the main road towards Margot's house, reaching up now and then to strip leaves off over-hanging branches. Men in cars slowed and gave her low, appreciative whistles as they passed. And so they should, Kate thought, treating them all to scathing glances of teenage disdain. She was aware of a vaguely tense feeling of waiting for something momentous to happen. She'd left her school, exams were over, and the dreaded results were weeks away. Something had finished, so something else had to start. What was finished had been awful, so the next thing had to be brilliant. It was owed to her. Seven weeks of freedom just had to contain *some* thrilling event, especially now she was sixteen. Sixteen was what you waited for, the special age.

At the stifling end of the hot afternoon, Kate could feel her blood tingling all over the surface of her skin. She wondered if what she was feeling was connected with sexual desire, and if this summer would come up with any chances to find out. She did hope so; it was time. A hundred yards or so ahead she could see the school bus dropping off the village children who went to the comprehensive in town. The teenagers among them looked a more knowing lot than Kate and her own artistically fey friends. These girls wore short skirts which revealed firm and sturdy thighs. They dawdled around the bus shelter munching crisps and flicking their hair, posing with their trainered feet at challenging angles. Home-bound boys sidled past nervously or bantered flirting aggression. One of the girls was Lisa Gibson, daughter of her mother's cleaning lady. She was Kate's age, and had a reputation for certain oral skills, which was explicitly recorded ('Lisa G. sucks cocks') in red spray paint in the bus shelter. Kate only half regretted that she didn't know her well enough to ask if it was true, and what it was like.

'Grandma's coming to stay. Did you know?' Suzy yelled to her over the squealing of her mountain bike brakes, and Kate jumped nervously into a gateway.

'God, Suzy, stop creeping about like that! You almost scared me under a car.'

'Good,' her little sister said, satisfied. 'And I wasn't creeping. Well, did you know she was coming? And who is Uncle Edward? Have we met him?'

'Haven't a clue. Why, is he coming too?'

'No. He's waiting to die. But he's doing that somewhere else. I'm coming to Margot's with you so I can see Tamsin.' Suzy started to pedal away fast ahead of Kate then looked back over her shoulder and called with a sly grin, 'You should have put make-up on, Simon's home a day early. He must have passed you in his taxi.'

Kate scowled, picked up a handful of stones and hurled them at the bicycle's back wheel. The clattering sound as they hit mingled with Suzy's high-pitched giggle. Kate walked on and chewed the side of her thumb angrily. Suzy was getting so silly, so girls' school. Why ever would she imagine that Kate, who'd known Simon since they were both seven, would suddenly want to go out of her way to look extra-attractive for him? He was so clean, so nice-boy – she was pretty sure that she just couldn't fancy someone who smelt constantly of shampoo. Margot's pet dab-chick, she'd thought of him, ever since they were about ten and he had fallen out of his tree house in the orchard, landing surprised but unhurt on his back. Margot had rushed at him, flurried like a panicked hen, wailing, 'Oh darling angel baby! Is he hurt then?' Kate, from up in the ancient apple tree, had peered down at her in amazement. Privately the DAB acronym had stuck in her astonished mind – never had her mother or father called her or Suzy 'darling angel' *anything*. Just let them try, she'd thought, with an unusual stirring of appreciation for her parents.

Margot's house was the grandest in the village, with a garden almost big enough to be called 'land'. It had once been the rectory, built at the elegant end of the eighteenth century by a local overlord, who must have felt either a conscience-driven need to appease his God or that his personal clergy had appearances to keep up. Village opinion was that Margot and Russell were not (and never would be) the right people to own the house. Russell *sold* things for a living – the worst things imaginable – used cars. He sold a lot of them, almost every elegant local car had been through one or other of his many dealerships. This particular house, it was generally felt, needed the kind of traditional, discreet good taste that had evolved over generations rather than Margot's enthusiastic hobby of constant expensive refurbishment. Its panelled rooms, ornate ceilings and galleried hallway required heirlooms, furniture that wasn't simply shop-bought in the ordinary handing-over-of-money way, just somehow filtered in by ancient family osmosis. Julia Merriman, who chaired the Parish Council, had once claimed (wrongly) that she could smell Habitat in Margot's drawing-room, making it clear that an aroma of genteel decay and two-hundred-year-old woodworm would have been infinitely preferable to huge, lavishly squashy sofas covered in pale-flowered chintz, so indecently new it still had an unworn sheen on the fabric.

Heather liked visiting Margot. Fresh from her swim and only half an hour behind Kate and Suzy, she wandered along the road and in through their ever-open gate. The garden cottage, a house more than big enough for a good-sized family, into which Margot was about to move her own for the summer, was in the final throes of redecoration. Two battered vans stood by its door and the smell of fresh paint wafted out and mixed with the full-blown, early-evening glory of the honeysuckle that tangled its way to the cottage roof.

'Are you in there Margot?' she called, hearing a peal of cheerful laughter from somewhere inside.

'Come on in, I'm just having a chat with the lads!' Margot called back.

Heather carefully picked her way past the cans of paint, dustsheets and paint charts, evidence of more than one room's-worth of work. 'You're surely not re-doing the whole thing?' she asked Margot, whose generous–sized body was perched rather precariously on the new kitchen worktop.

'Might as well, while they're here,' Margot replied happily, grinning at her team of three workmen who, the day being just about over, were leaning around the walls swigging bottled beer. 'Wouldn't do to waste your talents, would it?' she said to the nearest painter with a naughty wink.

Heather flicked through a heap of fabric swatches and said, laughing, 'Any excuse, Margot – that "Inside Story" design place in the village must run entirely on profits from you.' She looked around and sniffed the paint-filled air appreciatively. 'I love it when you're re-decorating, it feels like I'm doing my own house by proxy, all the fun and no mess.' She held up a square of yellow-and-white checked watered silk. 'Wouldn't mind some of this for cushion covers in the sitting-room,' she said, then turned it over and saw the astronomical sum written on the ticket. 'Second thoughts, yes, perhaps I would mind.'

Margot jumped down from the work surface and led Heather towards the door. 'You're priceless, you know that?' she said, both laughing and telling her off. 'You spend an absolute fortune on best quality freshly-rotted horse-pooh for your precious roses and then quibble about the price of a couple of metres of material! Let's go up to the house and have a drink on the terrace, and I'll tell you all about my summer lodger and the megabuck movie.'

Simon, wondering in the rectory kitchen if his mother would miss a couple of bottles of beer from the gigantic back-up fridge in the larder, heard approaching foot-steps, grabbed four bottles in panic and slid out through the French doors and past the pool to the orchard, where Kate was waiting for him. Under the trees at the far side was the row of kennels, each with its individual run, where Margot fondly and efficiently boarded a steady turnover of dogs whose owners had gone for holidays, or bitches whose on-heat rapaciousness was easier dealt with by paying someone else to take care of it. Simon stalked softly across the grass, carrying his bottles, looking at Kate as if he was seeing a stranger. He slowed down and stopped under a plum tree, enjoying the moment, briefly fantasizing that she was waiting for him with passionate anticipation, waiting to fold her long limbs round him, inflamed by their term's separa-tion. If only, he thought.

She hadn't seen him, and was pacing slowly up and down by the kennels, deciding which dogs would be least trouble to take out first. Her hair was longer than at Easter, almost to her waist, even more gloriously barley-blonde than before, and it was a whole year, nearly, since he'd seen this much of her everlasting legs.

The summer before, perhaps even up to the spring, she'd just been Kate the neighbour, just the always-there girl up the road. Now she was suddenly Kate the Beautiful, Kate the Desired, Kate, God willing, the Holiday Project. She felt him watching, looked up and waved to him and he smiled his lovely mouthwashed smile rather sadly. Probably to her, he was still Simon the Stupid, Simon the Boring.

Overhead, peering silently down from the treehouse, sat Tamsin and Suzy, still and alert as wary rabbits. Neither knew quite what they waited for, but like little girls who'd absorbed too many mystery stories, they trusted that careful observation would unfailingly lead them to adventure: something to be solved, secrets to be stored and savoured. They watched Simon watching Kate and privately hoarded away the scene for later, with Suzy feeling, as well, her first tender tweak of adolescent envy.

Margot put the tray of drinks on the poolside table. The jug of Pimms was deliciously crammed with ice and fruit and hunks of mint. Heather kicked off her espadrilles, relaxed into the deeply cushioned swing-chair and wished that her own swimming pool changing room wasn't simply a garden shed with a bench, but like Margot's, a spectacularly vulgar, temple-like building with full central heating, two showers and practically a health club's-worth of warm fluffy towels. Bacchus and Pan watched over the pool's deep end like tall marble lifeguards. She smiled to herself, thinking again of the past twenty-five years of the kind of marriage she'd almost had. Iain wouldn't have approved at all of this kind of flamboyant opulence. He'd absorbed half a millennium of an inbred Scottish-aristocratic distrust of luxury. The small stone castle had been comfortless and,

33

disappointingly after the one hot day of their hasty wedding, freezing even in August, and Heather had soon learned not to bother mentioning the dank mist that lurked below over the lake and shimmied in through the stone wall. That kind of complaining had been simply incomprehensible to him. Sometimes the air was so damp, she'd wondered which way round it really was, whether the mist *was* actually coming in, or if it started way down inside the castle and seeped out over the land. How she'd shivered in her tiny, thigh-chilling dresses and skimpy, skinny little tops. The only room with any real warmth had been Iain's study, book-lined, tobacco-tinged and leathery like an ancient headmaster's den. A sooty fire was lit there every day by the doting Mrs Kirby, and Heather remembered tingling with embarrassment that a grown man not that far off thirty could still shamelessly call someone 'Nanny'.

'Not in here, Heather-Feather,' Iain had told her with babying firmness, when she'd crept into the study to get warm. 'This is the boy's room, for the boy's work.' His tiny red Olivetti Valentine typewriter, perched on the paper-strewn desk, had looked too like a toy for her to take seriously as the source of his work. Somehow she'd imagined his novels full of murderous horror (books for men, of course) came from a much more industrial origin than this cosy room and the pretty little machine. By now, judging by his major successes she occasionally read about, and could see for herself on any bookstall, he was probably well into the latest state-of-the art Apple Macintosh byte-blaster, and had become the sort of man who sat zapping out a couple of chapters on a Powerbook while waiting for the Edinburgh Shuttle. She took a long, luxurious sip of her drink and thanked Margot's statue gods for the sinless warmth of the Thames Valley.

'He's been expelled,' Margot told Heather, jerking

her head to where Simon was disappearing into the orchard. 'Can you believe it, on the last day of term? Drinking in the dorm or whatever they sleep in. Good God, who *doesn't* drink after their exams? I bet the teachers do. Boarding schools, I ask you, they're on another planet.' Margot lit a cigarette and inhaled deeply. 'Bet you anything we get a letter, come September, saying something like,' she pursed up her lips and put on a mock-snooty voice, ' "On further consideration we have decided to overlook, on this occasion . . ." etcetera. That's because they'll be wanting his sixth-form's worth of money out of us.' She stubbed the barely smoked cigarette out vigorously. 'Well they're not bloody getting it. He can go to the college with your Kate.' She chuckled knowingly and added, 'I've got a feeling he won't mind that at all. Another drink?'

'In a sec, when I've eaten all this fruit. Do you think the alcohol gets absorbed into it like a sponge?' Heather picked out a dripping slice of orange and chewed at it. 'It always tastes so deliciously over-strength. Tell me about the film. Is it a sort of historical drama? Is that why they need this kind of house?'

Margot thought for a minute. 'Not really, I gather they just wanted it because it's *big*, to be honest, the sort of place that could be an important embassy in the middle of a London park. It's a spooky spy thing I think, lots of dead blondes and Middle Eastern intrigue.'

'Not our sort of thing, really then. No laughs, no posh frocks, no witty repartee,' Heather said, laughing. 'More of a boy's film.' Even as she said the words, Iain, his lurid paperbacks and her banishment from his toast-warm study came straight back into her head. It was starting to get cool, she noticed, her toes were feeling chilled, and the shadows were dappling the pool's surface as the sun slid behind the clematis-twined head of the statue of Bacchus down by the temple changing room.

35

Margot continued, 'And it's not just the filming. The director or writer or someone is staying in Simon's rooms for the duration, which I don't at all mind. I'm happy to have someone on the premises during the nights,' she giggled. 'Russell would be hiring security guards otherwise. Even now he's talking about getting Harrods to store his precious model soldiers.'

Heather wasn't really listening, but waiting to ask, as calmly as she could, her next question, so she could get past hearing Margot's inescapable answer. She could feel her scalp tingling. 'So who is he, this writer, director, whatever? Have we heard of him?'

Margot reached forward and picked up the jug of Pimms, sloshing more, fairly accurately, across into Heather's glass on the table. 'Shouldn't think so, he's some Scottish laird or other, writes enormous block-busters, horror numbers with death and derring-do. Ivan someone could it be?'

'Iain,' Heather corrected, voicing the inevitable, 'Iain Ross MacRae.'

Chapter Three

It was a terrible thing, to wish a hasty death on poor old Uncle Edward just so that Heather could see her mother away as speedily as possible on to her homebound train. It was hardly the old man's fault if she and Delia were bonded by little more than an accident of birth. 'Do you know,' she told Margot on the phone, just before leaving to collect her mother from Reading station, 'I think that when God was dishing out the Things in Common between mothers and daughters, the two of us must have been gazing out of the window, having a serious lapse of concentration.'

'How sad,' Margot sympathized. 'I still miss mine. We were more like sisters, told each other everything.' This reminded Heather of her own schoolfriends' mothers, the ones who'd tried to recapture their own youth through their daughters, or hold on to being important in their escaping lives for as long as they could, insisting with teeth-gritted desperation in the face of sullen teenage self-centredness, 'Of course, we're best friends, you know.'

'I can't imagine Kate telling me absolutely *everything*,' Heather said, 'and I hope she'll realize, when the time comes – God if it hasn't already – that some things I might prefer *not to* know!' Who was it, she tried to recall, who'd said that when mothers and daughters are mistaken for sisters, it's only the mothers who are pleased?

'But surely you talk to your mother, you know, when things are going wrong at home?' Margot asked.

'Absolutely not. We talk about the weather and

what's for lunch and how the girls are doing at school and that's about it. Information is power with my mother. If I tell her I've had a row with Tom, perhaps over how much vodka he can put away, then six months later when Tom and I are four fights further on about everything and anything, she'll still be sending me cuttings from the *Telegraph* about AA meetings and counselling services in this area.' With Margot she could laugh about it, but Delia had a terrier-like tendency to hold on fast to snippets of personal information and re-use them against her, like evidence in a police court. She then thought briefly about Kate and Suzy and their spats of mutual hostility, realizing that, if she went by Margot's ideal standard, she certainly hadn't managed to produce a pair of even compatible sisters.

Heather had spent a resentful couple of days tidying the house to a standard not usually achievable during the growing season, even with Mrs Gibson's twice-weekly help, at the same time asking herself, also resentfully, why she bothered when there were beans to be picked and delphiniums to be staked and a garden in the next village to be redesigned. But she knew really. From forty-one years of experience, she knew how wearing it was to be on the constant wrong end of criticism. It was far more restful to eliminate the things that *could* be criticized. Back in her teens this had been organized by dodges like waiting till she had left the house and found a phone box with a mirror before applying her preferred full amount of make-up, ghost-white lipstick and sooty black Dusty Springfield eyeliner. Huge batwing false eyelashes could be whipped off as close back to home as the garden gate, with her mother having no clue that her daughter had spent the evening looking very much as if she'd been haunting the churchyard. 'Very high standards your mother has. It's being your only parent. Wants you to reflect on her with credit,' Uncle Harold had explained to her, with an extra helping of knee-squeezing, on one of the gold-doily Sundays when an appalling history exam result had produced a two-day maternal sulk, unmollified by otherwise excellent grades.

'Come to the station with me Suzy, I'm sure Gran would love to see you,' Heather pleaded cravenly, finding Suzy sprawled untidily on one of the sitting-room sofas reading *Swallows and Amazons*, and making notes in an old exercise book.

'Do I have to? I mean she'll see me when she gets here,' Suzy protested, reasonably.

'Yes but she likes to be *met*. It shows you're really looking forward to seeing her,' Heather cajoled, shoving Suzy's long bony feet off the freshly-laundered apricot silk cushions.

'But I'm not,' she heard Suzy murmur.

'Suzy!'

'Oh, OK, OK. I didn't mean it. It's just that she *picks*. Though maybe I could come if – would you buy me something? Please?' Suzy, the possibility of a reward making her suddenly compliant, leapt off the sofa, ran her fingers through her hair as her gesture towards making it look tidy, and tucked her Manchester United T-shirt into her shorts. 'It's only a small something, but I do *need* it.' Suzy produced a warmly persuasive smile. 'Just an oil lamp, for camping over on the island with Tamsin. They don't cost much.'

She made it sound very much already decided, Heather thought, wondering if this was something Suzy had made her agree to in one of the absent-minded moments between an early evening vodka and tonic and the cooking of dinner. She plumped up the sofa cushions and took a last look round the unnaturally tidy room, trying to see it with the sharp eyes of her mother. Books on the shelves were all neatly spine-out and lined up, and videos were filed away in the cupboard instead

39

of lying abandoned across the floor. The curtains, lavishly patterned with enormous foxgloves, were prettily scooped into their silky rope tie-backs and fluffed out at matching angles, and surely *no-one,* not even Delia, could find fault with the glorious view from the French windows, down across the sloping lawn past the swimming pool and box-hedge-bordered herb garden, to the river with the willows and fields and hills beyond the opposite bank. The carpet still showed tracks from Mrs Gibson's loyally fervent vacuuming, and the air smelled deliciously of the rich cream-and-yellow roses picked that morning from the pergola that sheltered the cars. She hoped, suddenly, that her mother wouldn't ask what the names were, realizing that some kind of serendipitous accident had led her secateurs straight to both 'Wedding Day' and 'Schoolgirl'. She stifled a chuckle that would have had Suzy thinking she'd gone crazy, and turned her attention back to what her daughter had said.

'I'm sure this is the first I've heard of camping, and a lamp does rather imply night. I don't like you being on the river in the dark, you know that,' Heather pointed out as they headed for the Renault.

'But we wouldn't be,' Suzy argued. 'We're going to row there in daylight in the afternoon and sleep in Tam's tent. We'll have a little fire, cook something, like being in the Scouts. It's all arranged.' Her voice rose, seeing her plans threatened, especially now she'd stupidly mentioned the trigger-dread word 'fire', about which even she had her usual fearful qualms, and she just knew that her mother's veto would invoke Tamsin's shaming scorn. Tamsin could do anything she liked, she'd bragged, Margot *never* made rules. Heather drove slowly along the High Street, avoiding a group of ambling day-trippers.

'And the island is only *yards* away. You could probably hear us if we shouted, or I can take your mobile phone,' Suzy continued.

Heather's attention was wandering by now, as she noticed the yellow-and-white fabric that she'd admired at Margot's cottage, draped over what looked like a rusty old iron spear, but which must surely have been a highly chic curtain pole in the window of 'Inside Story'. Shame how being part of a window display somehow diminished its desirability. Everyone in the village would have seen it. She could just imagine Julia Merriman, round for the Help the Aged envelope (conveniently at the gin hour) banging noisily at the new cushions and booming, 'Wasn't that hanging in the shop for *simply ages*? You got a jolly good ex-display discount I suppose?'

'I hope she doesn't bring Jasper,' Suzy said later as the car pulled into the station car park. 'He bit me last time, and Gran didn't believe me. She said I was imagining things.'

'I'm afraid she's always said that,' Heather told her with a sympathetic smile. 'I think it's something of a habit. It was her generation's way of stopping us all being feeble. When you think of the war and what *they* could have been wimpish about . . . Anyway, tell me if the dog tries to bite you this time and we'll suggest it might be better if Margot puts him up in her kennels.'

Delia didn't like the way her heart raced when she gathered her luggage as the train pulled into Reading. It wasn't just the heat, she was sure. Her coat was a light summer one, though smart (Delia believed in dressing well for travel – even though she'd only come from Putney via Paddington), and she was hardly conscious of her hat, her favourite cream straw with a pair of pink roses. She'd worn it so often that it had become cosily shaped to the outline of her pale grey curls. Had it always felt like this, this babyish fluttery panic that the train would pull away before she'd had time to get off,

41

that she'd leave her bag behind, or the dog, or not be able to open the door? For the last minutes, even while she'd looked out as usual for the landmark of poor Oscar Wilde's gaol, she had felt a real anxiety that she would be the only one getting off, and that no-one would help her, or notice her struggling, the old being so *invisible* somehow, and she'd be trapped in the train all the way on to Bath. Perhaps she should have travelled on the other line, the shabby suburban stopping train that called at every dreary station along the endless wasteland behind Heathrow airport before terminating at Reading. That way, safely up against the buffers, there'd be plenty of time to organize herself. But then there was the risk of rowdy home-bound schoolchildren. It was so hard to resist telling them off for their appalling language and litter habits. When she did, they just swore. And they were so huge, which she put down to fast-growth hormones in all the chicken everyone ate these days. She told herself briskly not to be so silly, forcing herself not to try getting to the door while the train was still moving and risk being cata- pulted by a sudden stop into the lap of the oily young man with the phone sitting opposite. As usual, though, half the passengers seemed to change at Reading and the oily young man kindly carried the wriggling Jasper down the steps to the platform. Jasper, a jumpy West Highland terrier, yapped over-excitedly and Delia hoped that the greenish smear on the man's jacket was not the dog's fault. Smears like that, along with generous moultings of white fur, so often were.

'There's Gran' Heather said, pushing forward through the exit-bound crush.

'And Jasper,' added Suzy glumly.

'Suzannah! How lovely! Kiss for Grandma?' Delia enfolded slender Suzy to her ample bosom like a great bear gathering up its tiny cub. To Heather she simply said, 'Hello dear, looking quite well, aren't you.' Smiles

42

but no hugs, no kisses; neither could quite remember when that kind of thing had actually stopped, and they weren't now likely to start reviving an easy intimacy where they could begin analyzing it. 'Her hair could do with a cut. It'll get all split-endy,' Delia said, looking at Suzy as they walked to the car.

Suzy, tugging the reluctant Jasper's lead, shook her head and glowered. 'I want it as long as Kate's. And then I'm going to dye it even blonder than hers,' she declared, 'or maybe pink,' she added, looking back at them and grinning provokingly. Heather, unlocking the car, gave her a warning glare across the Renault roof.

Delia caught the look and smiled knowingly. 'It's all right, I know what she's up to, heard it all before haven't I?' Both Suzy and the dog growled quietly and Heather flopped into the overheated car. Oh this is going to be such fun, she thought, all it needs now is for Tom to come home for a bad-tempered jetlagged stopover, and we'll all have a *really* jolly time.

Tom dashed through the staff immigration channel at Gatwick, running away from a member of the crew who had turned him into an object of adoration, a position Tom was needing time to wonder if he could get used to. Sometimes, jokingly, as he left for a work trip, Heather would say, 'Don't go making any new friends!' almost like a witchy charm to ward off possible adultery. So far the incantation had worked. The thought of leaving Heather and the girls to set up home with a comely purser within kerosene-sniffing distance of Heathrow made Tom shudder at the upheaval that would be involved. Sex with a stewardess would be career-suicide. She'd be crowing down the phone to Heather before the damp patch had dried; those who hadn't been snapped out of First Class by Texan oilmen all wanted to marry pilots, in the same way that nurses were all assumed to aim to end up as Mrs Consultant.

Tom always liked to escape from an airport as quickly as possible. If he wasn't flying the things, he didn't want to hang around close to aircraft. It had started with a repulsion for the smell of the planes themselves. Somehow inside them there was always the underlying hint of vomit in the air, even on brand-new planes. He wondered if it was something deliberate in the cleaning fluid, if it was sprayed on to the carpets to reassure queasy passengers that it was all right, absolutely fine, they weren't the first to feel sick. Maybe they even sent a severely drunk stewardess on ahead to throw up on the upholstery before the planes were put into service. It was the same smell he'd noticed in the kind of country-club hotels that did a lot of wedding catering, with cheap overnight rates for those who couldn't quite make it to their cars without falling over, and who turned out to be incapable of quite making it to the bathroom too. Not an atmosphere you wanted to linger in.

And then there were the air-crashes which, rare though they were, he knew perfectly well, happened most often on taking off or landing, and he had recently started only to feel comfortable at least twenty miles from Gatwick or Heathrow. He was absolutely fine up in the sky – like most people with a car they're driving, it had somehow never occurred to him that a plane he was piloting could actually fail to get safely to its destination, however distant, however hazardous the clear air or the lightning. It was other people's skills that worried him. Watching the planes juddering ready for take-off while he waited in his car at the traffic lights on the perimeter road, they seemed lumberingly huge. There was so much and so many packed into each and every one. One of them, full to bursting with Tenerife-bound holidaymakers, or four hundred sales executives off to a conference in Cyprus, could land on him, shatter its overloaded weight up there just above Crawley, and scatter suitcases, seats, sickbags and stewards all over the county. He collected his car from the staff enclosure and drove fast towards the motorway and away from his admirer, trying not to look at the nearby runways, and certainly not glancing up at the sky, not even to see what the weather was doing.

'Nigel from the nursery phoned, said your camellia order was in!' Kate called to Heather as she got out of the car, then she added, welcomingly, 'Hi Grandma, you're looking very summery.' She was at her smiling teenage best – clean hair, ripless dress, a faint fresh perfume of Body Shop roses.

Delia beamed at her and stretched out her arms for a hug as Kate strolled across the gravel from the front door. 'Lovely Kate, getting so beautiful. How were the O-levels?'

'It's GCSEs now, Gran,' Kate corrected gently. 'And they weren't as bad as I'd expected, which probably means I'll have done really terribly. I think they're meant to be hard.'

'Nonsense, clever girl like you . . .' Delia was saying as they all went into the house

Suzy, glad to be left alone now her grandmother's attention was on the adored Kate, dashed into the kitchen and pulled her new oil lamp from its box. Tamsin would be so jealous, it looked just like a real hurricane lamp. She held it up and swung it, imagining it hanging and swaying from a tree above their camp, lamplight flickering wildly and making lurid shadows in the bitter wind, wind that was blowing harder, much stronger, swirling the water and whipping up waves – impossible and too dangerous now to row home . . . She shivered and prayed quickly for a still, calm night for

45

their camping. It was such a curse, always imagining the worst.

Her mother's head was this way and that, Heather could see from behind her on the stairs, taking in the new pink paint – National Trust's Ointment Pink, on strict 'in keeping with the property' instructions from Marco at 'Inside Story' – that had been chosen to warm up the hallway, and she wondered how long it would be till she caught her peeking under the Kelim rug to see if something had been fixed to stop it sliding on the dangerously polished wood floor. I don't like myself thinking like this, Heather realized, trying to see objectively that the person she'd brought to her house as a guest was not just a parent with a lifetime's excess baggage of wilful misunderstanding, but an ageing, slightly nervous woman, becoming frailer and reluctantly conscious of it. If we don't resolve the past soon, though goodness knows how, it will be too late, Heather thought sadly as she carried her mother's case into the spare room.

'Not too much sun in the morning I hope, dear,' Delia said, looking anxiously out of the mullioned window and searching the sky for the direction of the sun.

'Same amount as last time, Ma,' Heather told her. 'You said you liked it then.'

'It wasn't high summer then. It's been quite a time since my last visit,' Delia countered. 'Still, these curtains are properly lined, I expect I'll be all right. You don't sleep as well when you're older. You'll find that yourself one day,' she predicted, not without satisfaction.

Tom walked into the kitchen during supper, not particularly surprised that he didn't seem to be expected. 'I left a message on the machine,' he told Heather as he kissed her. 'Any lasagne left?' he asked, suddenly starving for real home cooking. That was another thing he was tired of: flavourless hotel steak with shake-on Bar-B-Q essence. Airline dinners reminded him, even the first-class ones, of mini-portion baby food. He picked at Heather's salad: the home-grown rocket, mange-tout and cucumber.

'You didn't say Tom was coming home,' Delia accused Heather, as if she might not have come to stay if she'd known.

'Well he does, you know, most weeks, if only for a couple of days,' Heather told her patiently, just as she had many times before.

'Hong Kong and back doesn't take that long. We've come a long way since eighty days was a fast time for round the world, and everyone sat in wicker chairs and got put to bed on the upper deck with pure linen sheets,' Tom joked, unsuccessfully, at his mother-in-law who stared coolly back at him.

'Did you bring me anything Daddy?' Suzy cut in, smiling at him, then prodded at his guilt as the constant family absentee, 'Seeing as you missed Speech Day.'

'I heard you got a prize. Well done Suze. I've got a couple of those baggy silk shirts you like in my bag – you and Kate can squabble over which ones you want.'

Heather relaxed, started to enjoy her food and let Tom take over as the centre of the family. Her mother brooded over her supper, picking the mange-tout out of her salad, saying had she meant to include a vegetable that should be served hot with butter, not cold with vinaigrette?

'Tell me about Uncle Edward. What exactly is wrong with him?' Heather asked.

'Age, I suppose. He had a bit of a stroke and recovered quite well about a year ago. I rang and told you, remember?' Heather did, but only vaguely. She'd have sent a get well card for more than 'a bit of' a stroke, so it couldn't have been too bad. 'And now he's got a

47

collection of various ailments. With leukemia on top. There's no treatment of course, not at his age.' Delia sighed, perhaps feeling too uncomfortably close herself to 'his age'.

'Why not?' Kate, who had been dreamily munching her food suddenly demanded. 'Surely they can do something? Has he told them not to?'

'He's not really in a position to tell them anything,' Delia told her. 'You aren't, with doctors, are you? Besides he doesn't really know what he's got, what's the point at . . .' she sighed again, 'at his age?'

Kate was frowning, trying to work out what she'd heard, if it was as bad as she imagined. 'He doesn't know? Has no-one told him? Why not? *I'd* want to know.'

'Well not everyone's like you, Kate, perhaps Uncle Edward would prefer just to slip away without a whole lot of drug side-effects to cope with,' Tom explained to her quietly. Delia was getting twitchy, twisting her fork round and round, and her eyes flickered quickly from Tom to Kate.

Heather felt grateful to Tom for his unusual gentleness – it had taken him years not to rise to Delia's baiting antagonism which mostly stemmed from her being simply unaccustomed to sharing a house with a man. 'I've never remarried,' she would state proudly to uninterested bus queues, post office counter staff, and anyone else who'd listen, when Heather was a little girl. 'It wouldn't be right,' meaning it wouldn't be convenient, unconsciously way ahead of her time in deciding men were nuisances round the house, making the lavatories smell, folding the newspapers the wrong way and polishing their shoes with the newly-washed dusters.

'And if he *did* get better, who is there to look after him?' Delia went on. 'I can't, I've done my best, visiting him on and off, and bringing him pies and casseroles.

The best I could do was get him into this clinic.' She looked at Heather, appealingly. 'It's what your father would have wanted for him, I'm sure.'

Kate, feeling there was an issue here worth wrestling with, couldn't let it go. 'Have I got this right? You mean he's going to die because he'd be a problem if he lived? And because he's old he's not allowed to make his own decisions about treatment? Is that it?'

Delia thought for a moment and then squared up to Kate with the defiance of long experience, 'Yes, if you put it that way, that's about the size of it. And you know, one day you'll be saying all this about me. I shan't mind.' A note of challenge was rising in her voice.

'Uncle Edward might though,' Suzy said quietly.

Heather, rather hot from her shower, opened her bedroom window wide to the late night sounds and the soft cool air. Out on the river, ducks and moorhens scuttled, splashed and squawked gently, settling and roosting. 'Stay safe,' she whispered to them, fearful of prowling foxes and hungry water rats stealthily creeping up on the floating nests, vulnerable among the reeds and bank-grasses.

'What are you gazing at out there?' Tom asked, coming quietly into the room. She listened to him fussing about behind her, unpacking his ever-present flight bag. It occurred to Heather that he had clothes that seemed to be permanently in transit, either between continents or between the bag and the washing machine. At least the clothes didn't get jet-lag, she thought, remembering Tom on his last trip home: he had decided it was high noon at 3 a.m., just the moment for cooking a much-missed full English breakfast, complete with toast burnt enough to set off the smoke alarms. She wondered if she should worry that, for her, Tom occasionally resembled a rather difficult house guest. Perhaps, though, it was a good sign that, so far, she wanted to resist that feeling. The thought of what it would have been like still being married to Iain crossed her mind. Presumably he had, as he had then, an office wherever he was living, so that, in a sense, he'd always be 'home'. She'd never get to sleep blissfully alone, never have to deal completely by herself with frozen pipes, blocked drains, garage mechanics who tried to con her that it would cost her at least *this* much for new brake pads. How peculiarly alien such cramped togetherness would seem.

'I'm not really looking, just listening,' she told Tom. 'I can hear family life out on the river – the wildfowl kind, not human, though somehow it doesn't sound that much different. Parents worrying about their children's safety, the getting comfortable for a peaceful night, if they're lucky.'

Tom went into the bathroom to make space on the shelves for the contents of his sponge bag. Mrs Gibson always reshuffled everything during his absences, spreading toiletries over the shelf-space as if he was unlikely ever to return. There followed the sounds of brushing teeth, the downpour of the shower and the loo flushing, and still Heather leaned on the window frame, inhaling honeysuckle scent. Lucky plant, she thought, to be blessed with two such lovely names: honeysuckle *and* woodbine. She smiled as she thought briefly of Nigel from the nursery, who saw plants in terms of italic-script Latin tags. 'Oh yes, *Lonicera caprifolium* – perfoliate woodbine or goat-leaf honeysuckle to the *hoi polloi*,' she could hear him declaiming, reducing the magic to the level of an index.

'I suppose their family structure is just like ours really.' Tom, Asia-bronzed and naked, joined Heather at the window and peered out through the blackness towards the river. Flashed glimmers of reflected light showed its progress past the end of the garden.

'What? Oh the birds. Yes, except we don't starve our weakest ones.'

'I mean they breed, worry about their babies, fuss over them and then trust they'll survive when they've flown the nests.'

'Big difference, though.' Heather turned back into the room and peeled off her satin robe. 'Their young don't seem to turn full circle in middle age and start worrying about their parents.'

Tom lay heavily on the bed, frowning. 'I never realized before how much you and your mother were two of a kind. You complain she's always wanted to know what you were up to so that she could have a managing stake in your life, and now you want to interfere in whatever deal of death she's got going with your Uncle Edward. Don't forget you probably don't even know the half of it, just like you've always said about her.'

She regarded Tom coolly. Her own body, reflected in the mirror on the open wardrobe door, looked as if it still wore a light-coloured swimsuit. Tom's was evenly tanned all over, as if he'd been turned slowly on a spit. He had a very grown-up body, long and solid and well-covered, with large, confident movements. Last time she'd seen him, it had been English-pale and a little flabby, but now he looked as if he'd been making good use of the hotel gyms and tennis courts. It was such a pity he'd made that pompous little speech, just when the surprise of how attractively unfamiliar his body was looking had started to interest her.

'Mind you,' he went on, 'I wouldn't like it. We should promise each other that if we ever get anything terminally awful wrong with us we'll *tell*. I think we'd both rather make our own informed decisions about the end, wouldn't we? God, no wonder they call it the second childhood, all your hard-earned adult rights taken away.'

51

Heather relaxed and snuggled next to him on the duvet, watching with slightly less distant interest as his penis started to uncurl like a waking animal. She wished, suddenly, that it didn't remind her of a David Attenborough wildlife programme she'd once watched about the rather repulsive underground life of the naked mole rat, a wrinkled, bald, ugly creature with loose pink skin just a couple of sizes too big, that squirmed blindly but with fervent purpose in tunnels beneath the earth.

Tom reached across and put a heavy arm around her, stroking her left breast quite tenderly, though she knew he'd rapidly move on. The mole rat was livening up, quietly expanding to fit its skin. 'Of course we're not like that generation,' he murmured into her neck. 'We don't keep secrets from each other, do we?'

Chapter Four

Something invasively loud, ducks squabbling on the river, or the approaching careless racket of distant dustmen, woke Heather at about 6 a.m. and she got up and went outside to water the herbs before the scorching sun got to them. Silver slug trails patterned the path, twined and twisted like Spaghetti Junction viewed from the space shuttle. Heather checked quickly that they hadn't been feasting off her sorrel, then wondered what it was, this time, they had decimated. She fixed the sprinkler in place, glanced up at her mother's window and noticed that the curtains were firmly hauled together, blocking out even the tiniest intrusion of light, then she took off her robe and slid quietly into the swimming pool. Silently, in the steam that wafted gently up from the water into the cool air, she breast-stroked up and down for twenty muscle-toning lengths, thinking about the whole truth and nothing but the truth. In her head was a nagging little refrain from the first days when she'd met Tom: 'You don't have to tell him everything about yourself, you know,' her mother had hinted heavily.

Heather, twenty-two and still childishly baitable, had risen angrily like a hooked trout. 'If I ever *do* marry again, I don't intend to have any secrets,' she'd replied loftily. Her mother's raised eyebrows and pursed mouth had signalled her favourite 'Well we'll see about that, won't we' expression. Of course Tom had known she'd been married before, Heather had told him quite early on. It wasn't a problem, just something to report to the registrar's clerk when arranging the wedding. It was true there hadn't been any secrets, just maybe a slight omission of the complete facts, which, according to her mother, wasn't the same thing at all.

'Some things they'd rather not know,' Delia had insisted, so Heather had decided she was being kind, not dwelling on what was past. If she tried, she could make it entirely his fault that she'd been hazy on the details – he should have shown more curiosity. Her marriage to Iain had been brushed aside as 'just an early mistake, all over long ago' and neither she nor Tom had ever mentioned it again. There had been no need. Heather turned over and swam lazily on her back, watching flakes of cloud trail across the blue above her. But *why* hadn't he wanted to know more? Why had they never had one of those cosily drunken late-night, true-confessions conversations in which Tom admitted something shocking like catching clap on a school trip to Hamburg and she countered amusingly with a briefly-told little story about being a runaway teenage bride with her school photo in all the papers? Why had she never pointed to the best-seller racks at the airport bookstall and said, 'Good grief can you imagine, I was actually married to the man who wrote that stuff'? Perhaps Tom had also had a mother who'd given him firm instructions Never To Tell All; there could be so much she didn't know (perhaps wouldn't want to know) about him, too.

While Heather floated, the village seemed to be waking up more busily than usual. From the main road, though still some distance away, she became aware of a rumbling, rolling sound which turned into the steady, slow thrum of an approaching convoy. Probably, nothing more thrilling than an early bulk delivery to the local Waitrose, she thought. She climbed out of the pool and was on her way back into the house, warming herself in her bathrobe, when Kate, who probably hadn't seen this time of the day since she'd been waking

54

for four-hourly feeds, suddenly rushed out of the back door, brushing her hair.

'Kate? Where on earth are you going?' Heather asked, amazed at the sight of the girl, in full going-out make-up and a wispy metre or so of a silky floral dress. She must have been up at least an hour, Heather estimated – no hint of the puffy-eyed, baby-bird-look that Kate usually presented to the breakfast table. It suddenly occurred to Heather that she couldn't be a hundred per cent sure that Kate had even been in that night and been to bed. Perhaps teenage girls really did need an armed guard in the corridor outside their rooms.

'It's today! They're all arriving today! All the people for the film. I've got to get there. They might want extras, Simon said.'

Heather could hear, no further away than the recreation ground, truck-brakes squealing and huffing, a settling and parking batch of sounds. 'But they won't want them yet, will they? These will be just catering and props and things like that, I expect,' Heather said, not really having a clue whether she was right or not, but with a motherly instinct that Kate should at least have some breakfast before she went to find out.

'Yes but at least if I'm *there* . . .' Kate reasoned, backing towards the side of the house and the gate to freedom.

'Go on then, but don't come back all deflated because there's no-one there but the equivalent of road crew, will you?' Heather warned her.

But Kate was gone, running down the road, chasing an exciting life.

'Ooh you don't want her getting involved in films, anything could happen.' Delia, asking about Kate's absence at breakfast, had expected to be told that she was still lazing in bed, at which she could have tutted contentedly and told Heather the girl was over-indulged. This, though, was probably better. 'Artistic people,' Delia sniffed, 'nothing regular in their lives.'

'Surely that's the whole point,' Heather told her as she crammed thick wholemeal into the toaster. 'What teenage girl with any spirit wants "regularity" in her life?' Except with their periods, she added silently to herself. 'I expect she's looking for something more thrilling than walking a kennel-full of pampered dogs for Margot.'

Delia scowled, expressing deep distrust of anything that might be judged to be 'thrilling'. 'Doesn't she have any school work? Or what about a nice little holiday job in a shop?'

Heather gave a spluttered laugh. 'Oh Mother, really! Can you imagine Kate interested in a "nice little" anything? If she was, she'd have stayed at her "nice little" school, with all those "nice little" girls! Some grow up faster than others, some want nothing but a typing diploma and an engagement ring at her age, but most, those with imagination, hope there's some magical, fantasy life-drama in which they can be the star. In Kate's case, literally – you don't think she just wants a spear-carrying part or whatever, do you?' Delia looked mystified and Heather banged around the kitchen, crashing cups on to the table. 'She's probably imagining that the director will be helplessly overcome by her looks and her legs and all that golden fairy-princess hair, and offer her an immediate starring role. In her head she's not even *here* any more, she's probably in Hollywood at the Oscars, wearing a Vivienne Westwood and sitting next to Keanu Reeves.' She paused for breath and caught sight of her shining eyes in the little star-mirror on the dresser. She'd been shouting, she realized; the kitchen seemed to be full of diminishing echoes. Coffee gurgled in the percolator, an apologetic, rather comic sort of noise, like a nun with indigestion.

Delia was watching her, bird-like eyes bright and darting, her whole face keyed up to choose the right words. Here they come, thought Heather, reaching thankfully into the cool fridge for milk. 'I never realized how much she took after you,' Delia said quietly.

Heather took a deep and calming breath and forced herself to smile, 'Well we all take after someone don't we?' she said. 'I wonder who my rôle model was?'

She'd gone through a phase in her early teens when she'd wanted, needed, to know about her father. It was a mystery, and she'd hoped there was some glamour attached to this, anything to make her a source of envy to her friends.

'He died. Complications,' was all she'd been told. 'Complications' had sounded enough like a terrible disease in itself to be quite adequate an explanation for a very young child of limited vocabulary. Heather at eight had been awed by the number of syllables — obviously that made it *much* worse than mumps or measles. It was as big as the mysterious scarlatina, which sounded as if it should be the name of a dazzling gypsy dancer in a frilled skirt. But by the time Heather had got to the second form at the grammar school, it was nowhere near enough for her to know.

'Complications of *what*?' she'd asked her mother over one of their comfortable winter-night casseroles.

'Something he got during the war. He was never the same.' Delia had looked lonely, suddenly, which alarmed Heather at the time – mothers were supposed to be strong and powerful. Hers was an admired survivor, battling alone with bureaucracy that still, in the 1960s, demanded a father's, not just either parent's, signature on a child's passport application, and a detailed written explanation if that signature was unavailable. At the end of each summer term, when copying her own address on to the large brown envelope that would contain her end-of-year report, Heather had been the only one in her form who couldn't address it to Mr and Mrs. She sat, now, in her maple and mint-green kitchen, listening to watery sounds overhead as Suzy splashed about in the bath. She'd never found out about those 'complications'. She'd given up trying after several secret sessions, under the far table in the school library, with her highly inquisitive friend Barbara and a selection of unhelpful history books.

'Trench foot? Mustard gas?' Barbara had suggested eagerly, flicking through tatty pages illustrated with ancient Punch cartoons.

'Wrong war, I think,' Heather had told her dispiritedly.

'A lot of them caught diseases of the ... of Down There.' Barbara had slithered up close to her and whispered with a sly, giggly grin. 'Off the French girls. All that can-can.'

'I expect it was shrapnel,' Heather had replied curtly, reluctant to speculate on her father's sex life, as well as being pretty sure that if he had been diseased Down There, she herself, who was made several years after the war ended, wouldn't have been born at all.

'Could be shrapnel,' Barbara had conceded reluctantly. 'Perhaps it got lodged Down—'

'In his head somewhere. Then it moved and he got ill and died. Probably,' Heather had decided, and slammed shut the fattest history book, gathered the little heap together and filed them quickly away on the bottom shelf in the wrong place. How ridiculous it must seem to every generation that their parents *do it*, she thought. And in turn, she thought, all these years later, looking at her mother who was neatly folding the last crust of toast into her mouth, how outrageous it must seem to every generation of parents that *their children* should get round to a sex life, too. I've got it all to come, quite soon, with Kate, she thought, feeling a sneaking sympathy for her mother as she was twenty-five years ago, coping with the chaotic hormones of a teenage daughter, with no man around to deal with her own.

Outside, a magpie started its aggressive, football-rattle sound. She looked out and saw the pushy, spiteful bird, bullying robins away from the bird table on the terrace. It was past the season when magpies were in pairs, and superstitiously she muttered, 'Good morning Mrs Magpie, I hope your family are well,' to stave off the bad luck.

'Is it one for sorrow?' Delia asked from the table.

'Yes, frightening the robins away,' Heather told her. 'Magpies are such pretty birds, I always think,' she went on, carrying cups to the sink. 'You wouldn't think something so lovely could do such damage, stealing baby birds and eggs from nests. I've seen them out there taking on a whole treeful of sparrows and trampling quite ruthlessly through all the nests after the babies. The poor parents were frantic.'

Delia started rinsing plates at the sink, somehow sure that dishwashers didn't really get things properly clean. 'They remind me of mackerel, just the colours of them, all that gleaming bluey-black and the pale underneath. Smoothly turned out, good-looking and dangerous.' She paused for a moment, the water running unnoticed over her wrists, then added with an expression of miles-away thought, 'Like men in evening dress.'

Kate had to admit to disappointment. She'd got there well ahead of Lisa Gibson, who probably wasn't even awake yet. Lisa, when she wanted to be noticed, would be loud and unmissable, wagging her double-D tits at whoever glanced her way. Kate looked forward to pointing out that being on film was well known to add at least 10 lb to one's appearance. Out by the cricket pavilion, the early signs had been good, all those trucks arranged in a circle like a traveller's illicit convoy, at the edge of the recreation ground, on the rough area where the mothers always parked to collect their children from the pavilion playgroup. The lorries and buses reminded her of a circus. They weren't like ordinary goods trucks, there was that slight otherness about them, just like romantic fairground wagons, that made you wonder where they spent their off-road time. No-one saw vehicles like these actually travelling around, using motorways like any old Pickfords furniture truck or an ordinary Habitat van, they just appeared where they weren't before, like fairy rings on the grass in the early morning. There were converted buses with shabby curtains, luxurious magenta coaches with racks and racks of clothes, a catering wagon with the kind of fold-out flaps and cleverly built-in equipment that would, if it was in miniature, make a small child satisfied that they'd been given the perfect good-value toy.

A semi-circle of six or so men sat around on upturned boxes with mugs of tea, eyeing a cavernous bus-load of lighting as if putting off the moment when it must be unloaded and dealt with. Kate hovered shyly outside the ring, her eagerness wavering now that she didn't quite know what to do, who to approach, how to ask if she qualified as star material. Couldn't the right person simply take one look at her and *realize*?

'Cup of tea love?' one of the men called to her. He looked like one of Margot's builders, with baggy jeans slung under a beer-belly and a grey T-shirt that looked as if it had been used to clean a fly-smeared windscreen. Kate hesitated, wondering if this was a gathering she should, as she normally would, avoid – they reminded her of the workmen who'd taken three whistling, leering weeks to mend a small hole in the school fence. Yet one of these smirking, slurping men could be just the one to help her towards fame and fortune. Perhaps film directors were like rock stars: impossible, till you got a full dose of their ego, to tell them apart from their entourage.

'Two sugars please,' she then said suddenly, catching sight of Simon emerging from his gateway. When he found her, she would already be an old hand, sitting among these early-morning men as if she'd travelled with them, she thought with happy satisfaction.

Simon was dithering on the pavement, looking up and down the road as if searching for something. Kate, perched on an upturned plastic crate inside the men's magic circle, watched him covertly. She felt very much as she had as a small child playing at camping in the pony paddock. Once inside her tent, or in winter under the shelter of the huge old viburnum that sprawled against the stable wall, it had been as if she was keeping watch on the rest of the world, from a hidden one which was entirely her own. Beyond the cricket pavilion she could also see Julia Merriman walking her labradors and staring with frank curiosity at the collection of strange vehicles.

'Bit of local colour,' commented one of the men, indicating Julia who, as if dressed for the part by an over-efficient wardrobe supervisor, was wearing the Compleat Countrywoman outfit of Barbour, green wellies and a misshapen tweedy fishing hat of her late husband's. There was probably, Kate guessed, a pair of unravelling string riding gloves screwed up in the pockets, too, stuck together with congealing Kendal Mintcake.

'Good morning!' Kate called to her, trying to keep natural insolence from her voice.

'Oh! Oh it's you Kate!' Julia shouted back, startled. She took several hesitant steps towards the group, looking round for the support and protection of her uninterested dogs. 'I thought . . . well goodness you are up early! Should you, er, be here?'

'Mum knows, it's OK. These are some of the people

who are doing the filming.' Kate felt rather grand saying this, as if she was not only one of them but actually in charge. The men muttered greetings and the one with the fly-spattered T-shirt actually stood up and offered a plump hand for Julia to shake. 'Brian – nice to meet you, and you are . . . ?'

She took the hand with her automatic good manners overcoming what looked like a tremor of secret horror, 'Er . . . Merriman,' she conceded.

'Is your house one of those that we'll be using?' Brian asked. 'Are you going to be totting up the tax-free after we've gone?' He winked at her, and Julia backed away.

'No. Absolutely not my sort of thing,' she answered coolly.

'Money is most people's sort of thing,' he replied with a knowing grin, returning to his mug of tea. Julia returned to her circuit of the rec as Simon crossed the road and joined them.

'I thought you'd be here,' he said to Kate, scuffling his feet awkwardly, his hands half-thrust into jeans pockets that were too small to take them, waiting to be introduced.

He's so clean, she thought, gazing at his damp, freshly washed hair. On anyone else she would be suspicious that the dampness was really grease, but with Simon it was out of the question, for without fail he would have Washed and Gone. She could smell oatmeal soap on the breeze. Even at this hour he must have had a shower and taken time to choose the right clothes. She'd done the same, she admitted to herself, but that was different, that was quite an exception, a special occasion. Perhaps Simon had become so thoroughly conditioned by his boarding school that he couldn't even contemplate starting a single day without a complete all-over scrub.

'Are you coming to our house?' Simon asked the men, giving up on Kate and introductions. 'We're renting it out for a few weeks, Mum said. And the man who wrote the script is coming to stay, too.'

'Aha. You'll be Margot Carpenter's son then,' Brian said, grinning at Simon. 'Now there's a lady with no objection to a bit on the side, as it were, in the cash sense I mean, of course. We'll be along to you later with all this lot – just across there isn't it?' He gestured towards the far side of the road and the dense greenery that protected the houses from casual view. 'You're in for a spot of upheaval.'

Kate was bored by the lack of activity. During the morning a few people arrived in the village by car and went either to the pub or to see Margot. The early morning men she quickly dismissed as mere crew and of no real use to her at all. Hanging around on the rec, she began to feel like a nosy child, and she worried that she'd be noticed in the wrong way – to be laughed at. Even Lisa hadn't shown her pink-and-white face. Obviously the people to see hadn't yet felt the need to arrive. So fed up was she that she found herself agreeing to accompany her mother and grandmother on a visit to the dying uncle later that afternoon.

Heather was amazed. 'There's no end to how much they can surprise you when they're completely and utterly bored,' she told Tom, who barely glanced up from the Test Match on TV.

Heather had an idea that Uncle Edward wouldn't have changed a bit, that she'd have no trouble recognizing him. He'd seemed old enough in her childhood for there to be no scope in the process of ageing for him to look any greyer or frailer. He wasn't in a hospital, it was more of a nursing home with medical facilities added on, perhaps in much the same way as the sauna and spa option in a luxury hotel. She wondered if he'd remember her; the last time she had seen him had been at her wedding to Tom, when Delia had rounded up as many relations as possible to bulk out their side of the family and make the register office seem respectably full. Delia had spent that day beaming determinedly at everyone with an expression underlying the smile that challenged its startled recipients to dare, just dare, to mention Heather's elopement. She'd overheard, at one point, the words 'unfortunate mistake' and she'd had to be firmly reassured for a good fifteen minutes that the speaker was referring to a guest's choice of hat. Delia felt that Iain had been present at Heather and Tom's wedding like Banquo's ghost, and she was only truly happy that day when she packed them both off to New York for the honeymoon.

Heather remembered Edward's slithery, liver-spotted hand on her wrist and his wetly whispered comment at the time: 'Not in white then?' – as if his brother Harold had bequeathed him the rôle of leery old goat in his will. It was far more likely that Edward wouldn't recognize her. That morning she'd stared carefully into the mirror and wondered how much of the schoolgirl-Heather was left that Iain, if they should chance to run into each other in the village, would remember. She'd been happy to decide that there was very little: her hair, which had been as long and golden as Kate's, was now fringed, bobbed and streaked with the kind of metallic highlights that were a hairdresser's tactful preparation for a client's seamless transition to grey. She was still slim, but on the larger, more comfortable scale that was to be expected in her forties. She wondered briefly if Twiggy, with whose ironing-board flatness of front it had been bliss to be compared before the days when anorexia was to be feared, had also filled out a bit. She reckoned she could, with luck and some careful avoidance, get away quite safely with living unidentified a few yards away from her ex-husband. But there was the dangerous presence of her over-inquisitive mother to consider. Keeping Delia ignorant and uninterfering was going to be tremendously difficult.

Heather, whose knowledge of hospitals was gained from only a couple of visits to casualty with Suzy's broken collar bone and Kate's febrile convulsions, had expected the nursing home to smell of cabbage and urine. She sniffed cautiously at the air as she, Kate and Delia went in. She could smell polish and air freshener but neither lunch nor pee. 'Smells OK,' she commented, surprised, looking round at the reception area that wouldn't have been out of place in a good country house hotel. The peachy striped wallpaper was fresh and clean, no torn edges or discoloured patches. The caramel-coloured carpet had no mysterious stains to challenge a squeamish imagination.

'So it should at these prices!' Delia retorted, clutching both hands around her bag as if expecting Uncle Edward's fees to be snatched from her the moment she crossed the threshold. 'Do you know,' she went on, 'Edward's had medical insurance since way before it was the thing to do. He must have been one of BUPA's first customers.'

Heather was surprised; the pair of uncles had seemed so pre-war somehow, as if they wouldn't either know or be bothered with such late twentieth century calculations. She remembered how they'd grumbled when *The Times* took their personal column off the front page. But then, she remembered, they were also part of the pre-welfare state generation, perhaps with the notion that using the National Health Service was like a shameful acceptance of charity.

'Never a day's illness till that stroke. He wasn't the type to bother the doctors,' Delia said, admiringly.

'You're supposed to bother the doctors,' Heather told her gently. 'Especially at that age. Perhaps they could have prevented the stroke if he'd had regular check-ups.' Not to mention done something about the leukemia, she thought, which reminded her, the leukemia was exactly that; according to instructions, not to be mentioned.

'No green paint,' Kate commented as they were led by a pink-uniformed nurse to Edward's room. 'I've never been to a hospital with no green paint.' She was clearly impressed and asked in a tone of hope, 'Have we got private insurance, Mum?'

Heather was still wondering about the germ-trapping qualities of the clinic's lavish soft furnishings when they were shown into her uncle's room. It had a cheering, non-hospital lack of embarrassing parapher-nalia – no badly disguised commode, no odd-shaped cardboard pee-bottles, no drips, kidney bowls, catheters or privacy-destroying bowel-movement graphs. Was Edward even ill at all, she wondered, or just having a supervised vacation? Among the generous, non-institutional furniture – the bed, sofa, TV, table – she didn't at first see him. Then came a shocked moment of recognition – the paper-coloured man, who quavered thinly from deep inside a navy-blue paisley dressing-gown on the edge of a rose velvet armchair, was a shrunken, desiccated version of her old relation. He looked as if all his body fluids had been drained away, as if in premature preparation for embalming, leaving him looking like an empty leather duffle bag. He'd once been so very big, she'd been certain. How else could his leathery hand have pre-vented her, as a strong, feisty child, from escaping its grasp? Surely, too, he had had to stoop to whisper in her ear, or had it just been that he'd liked to get close? Then there was his hair. 'Grey' she'd always imagined, was a terminal, unchanging old-age colour. It was what you went, with no deterioration, hair-wise, beyond that. Now she realized that in her childhood Uncle Edward had sported a fine, distinguished shade of deep badger, no trace of which now remained, all pigment having gradually leaked away, leaving a few limp, bleached-out tendrils.

'Hello Edward,' Heather said, giving a social smile and deciding she was far too old to call him 'Uncle'. The old man's speckled blue eyes, pale mottled as the surface of a duck egg, looked at her with beady interest and a very slowly gathering recollection. 'Jack's little girl,' he at last said huskily, his long pearly finger shaking out towards her after only a few moments thought. His yellowed, half-bald head nodded slowly, on and on as if, once started, he had no power to stop it till the action wore itself out.

'Well this is nice,' Delia said, bustling her way to the sofa and looking around the room taking in, with satisfaction, the way the flowers she'd sent had been prettily arranged. 'And this is Kate. You've not met her, she's your great-niece,' she told him, grabbing Kate's hand and pulling her rather forcefully to stand in front of Edward for his inspection. Heather held her breath, praying for Kate to be polite – she didn't at all like being pulled about, wriggling out of hand-holding even at the most dangerous road crossings as a small child. But Kate beamed down at the old man, and his rheumy eyes glittered back at her with appreciation.

'Like your mother,' he said. 'Just like your mother round about the time she went off and got married. I don't remember much, but I remember that.' He gave a crackly snigger and turned to Heather and his voice strengthened along with his memory. 'Where is he then, that chap you ran off with?'

'Shall we go and have tea in that nice conservatory? The nurse said we could . . .' Delia interrupted, fussing awkwardly for her bag under the sofa. 'It's about the right time.'

Heather helped to raise Edward from the chair. Should hospital chairs be this deep and squashy, she wondered distantly, seeing how difficult movement was for elderly patients. 'Tom is at home, watching the cricket,' she told him firmly as they left the room.

'Tom? Who is Tom? In the *News of The World* they didn't call him Tom.' Edward chuckled.

Chapter Five

'Why did he say all that stuff about Dad?' Kate asked in the car, as Heather had known she would – Kate would never let a comment like that pass unquestioned. All through the conservatory tea, during the stroll to admire the clinic's flowerbeds, the pause for Edward to rest on the terrace bench, she must have been waiting, keyed-up with curiosity, to ask. Heather was concentrating on pulling out into a busy stretch of rush-hour motorway, which unfortunately left Delia to seize the moment and get in first.

'Just an old man's muddle dear,' she cut in firmly, with a long, hard warning stare at Heather by way of the rear-view mirror. Heather glared back, though at the same time thinking that at least her mother hadn't replied with the 'Never you mind', with which she'd answered so many of Heather's own teenage questions. Kate wouldn't have put up with that; such a tantalizing brush-off would have been a challenge to her. Kate immediately lost interest, preferring to stay fastidiously ignorant of unpalatable senile failings, and was slumped over with her head vibrating against the window, trying to see her reflection in the wing mirror. Delia liked to sit in the back of the car, from where she could give imperious directions and prod at the driver's seat as she changed her mind about which way to turn.

Heather felt irritable. If she and Kate had been alone, this could have been just the moment to tell her all about the earlier marriage, about the journalists who'd rushed to photograph the Squire and the Schoolgirl, and pestered furious Delia for photos of Heather in her school uniform. Such stories had appeared quite often in those days, though theirs was a variation on the usual Wild Heiress And Her Garage Mechanic. They could have giggled together about the silly romance of it all, at the starry-eyed pre-feminist fantasy of it, at the same time making sure that Kate knew that the rules about instant Gretna Green weddings had been changed since those days, in case she was tempted to turn it into a family tradition. She could have laughed off the whole ridiculous marriage as 'no more than the length of time you might stay interested in a boyfriend'. Kate would have been terrifically amused, probably dashing off to phone Annabelle with this crazy tale of how wackily fallible, amazingly so in fact, hippy-generation parents could be. Now the moment had passed, and finding a quiet time to talk about it would seem too deliberate, give the story an importance that she'd spent twenty-five years denying to herself it had, as if it had been so delicately special she'd had to wait all this time for both Kate and herself to be ready for the telling of it.

Back at home, Tom looked as if he hadn't moved all afternoon. Only the untidy collection of lager cans on the table in front of him showed that he'd got up occasionally to visit the fridge. Slumped across the sofa with his bare brown feet dangling over the arm, and the cushions squashed to shapelessness beneath him, he still gazed at the cricket on the television, with the sound turned down and the radio commentary on.

'Not doing so badly,' he murmured as Heather came into the room. 'How was the old man?'

'Old,' she said, falling onto the other, neater sofa with a depressed sigh. 'Very old. And I know what they mean by *wizened* now. Strange place, though. It seems to be full of ill people without any of the trappings of illness. It's so discreet. It's as if you pay all that money just so no-one has to acknowledge that your insides are turning into a mush. There must be rooms somewhere,

70

where they keep medical equipment, and things that relate to functions, but I didn't see any. I wonder what they do with the really decrepit ones? There are probably floral-patterned incontinence pads knocking about . . .' She stopped and looked from the television to her husband. Tom was dozing as the final wicket fell, and England were all out for 268. He hasn't heard a word I've said, she realized. How interested would he be in old Edward forgetting he existed? In the old man recalling only his briefly there and never met predecessor? Probably not in the slightest, she decided, and not surprised either.

Suzy and Tamsin sipped ice-cold Coke in the treehouse and wished they had boys with them. Lisa Gibson had two moodily attractive brothers, one of whom was fourteen and newly returned home from Care, on the condition that he stopped vandalising cars. He had acquired an exotic glamour from his enforced absence, one that affluent village boarding-school boys such as Simon couldn't even begin to match. Shane Gibson strutted about the village green and terrorized the recreation ground as cockily as if he'd just completed a full-scale outward bound course, or yomped bravely across some empire outpost, liberating it single-handedly from invaders.

'I saw *him* this morning,' Tamsin told Suzy. 'And he *looked at* me. Right at me, in that way he does, you know.'

'Yeah, I know!' Suzy lied, as she was expected to. She didn't know. Shane had never, ever noticed her that she could recall, not treated her to one single, accidental acknowledgement of her existence. Not even a withering, lip-curling, 'What d'ya think you're looking at' sneering glance. Tamsin, who was ten months younger than Suzy, had a figure developing at an amazing rate and would quite soon not need the help of her adored black Wonderbra to give her a cleavage to rival her mother's. She looked forward to Becoming A Woman, which should, they both thought, happen any day now.

That morning, she had sneaked them both past the film security men into the rectory to show the highly envious Suzy the collection of sanitary-wear she'd already amassed in her bathroom cupboard, each packet selected after careful advertisement research, from the Feminine Hygiene section at Boots in Oxford. She had pads with wings, pads without, tampons with flushable and unflushable applicators, and teeny mini panty-liners ('for the lighter days') in gift-wrap packing that was supposed to make it a matter of jolly, unembarrassing fun if they fell out of your school bag on the bus.

'I'll just keep trying them all till I find the ones that suit me best,' Tamsin had told her, while Suzy was envying not only the collection but also the fact Tamsin had her very own pretty pink bathroom, complete with a lightbulb-surrounded make-up mirror, just like a theatre dressing-room. The effect wasn't unlike being inside a My Little Pony plastic grooming parlour, a toy which Suzy would not quite yet allow to go to the church jumble. 'And you can have all the leftover ones I don't like,' Tamsin had continued with an attempt at kindness, but adding, unforgivably, 'When you actually start, that is, if ever.'

Suzy tolerated Tamsin's jibes with quiet stoicism, simply overlooking such comments as if she'd never heard them, and calmly practising the adult skill of Rising Above It. There weren't that many girls of her age in the village, or, she admitted, of her type; everyone from the comprehensive hung mockingly and loudly around in the terrifying bus shelter. When she passed by on her slightly too-small pony, they tended to call out to her in mock aren't-we-posh voices, or run up behind shouting 'Gee up Neddy'. No-one ever treated Tamsin like that, and Suzy had already worked out that that was because Tamsin was a different kind of rich, the flashy and glamorous sort the others all wanted to be. She reflected that her own family, rather sadly, believed in being careful with money, and that flaunting it was vulgar. Tamsin had something else to provoke envy and keep Suzy slave-like as a friend, something to which Suzy secretly dreamed of having unlimited access – her brother Simon.

Heather saw Iain a couple of days later. She was sure it was him when she spotted the car, and it made her insides lurch in a way that unsettled her breakfast toast. She was in the Renault, waiting at her gateway to pull out into the main road on her way to Nigel's nursery, when the stream of traffic up on the High Street slowed to a stately pace, like a royal procession, led this time not by a black limousine, but by a cherry-coloured Mercedes – the sort of thing that Russell would give pride of place in his flagship showroom. It was probably the biggest you could buy, Heather thought as she waited, tapping impatiently on the steering wheel for the thing to pass her gate. In the very next second it occurred to her that it could only belong to Iain. He'd always used his car as a kind of personal selling point, she remembered. It had been as if, having displayed, like a strutting cock-bird, his Granny Takes a Trip velvet suit and hand-made Deborah and Clare shirt, casually mentioned his forthcoming first novel and his to-be-inherited title, the bright pink E-type snug against the Chelsea kerb would be a sure-fire into-bed clincher. Heather watched the scarlet Mercedes hesitate opposite Margot's gate before turning into it. She was sure she had been right, and she pulled out into the traffic, driving quickly away from the village towards the anonymous safety of Nigel and his plant-filled poly-tunnels.

The early summer party, where she had met Iain, was going vividly through her mind as she drove. Barbara, who at school claimed to have some terminally fashionable extra-curricular friends that would have been the envy of the fifth form, had they not suspected she'd invented them, had invited three chosen schoolmates to what she promised – swore – would be the party of the year. It was in London, to start with, not just 'quite near' as in, vaguely up the Southern Region line towards the the Richmond direction from dreary Staines where they lived, but with a proper postal district: SW3 to be exact, the one they'd all heard of and yearned to exist in. She guaranteed them the presence of a Rolling Stone at the very least, possibly even a Beatle, though that was actually less appealing to Heather. Heather had secretly felt quite certain that if she got the opportunity (and Barbara didn't *always* lie) she would gladly forget about such a momentous occasion being ideally one of true love, non-school knickers and foregathered contraception, and enthusiastically donate her virginity to Mick Jagger. This she promised herself, even though she was still under age and so fearful of committing crimes that she never even tried to get away with half-fare on the bus. It was a long way to go from Staines, to be disappointed, especially after complicated telephoning to make sure that each set of parents thought the girls were innocently staying the night somewhere else, and the four of them were thoroughly determined to enjoy themselves and act as if they were too sophisticated to care or notice that neither a Stone, Beatle nor even a humble Herman's Hermit was present, or likely to be, in the cramped, gloomy attic flat just off (very off, really, by several streets) the King's Road.

'That bloke over there looks like Peter O'Toole,' Barbara had whispered to Heather, 'don't you think?'

Heather looked at him. 'Not really,' she'd said, not quite truthfully, because he did have an actorish sort of face, but determined not to let Barbara off the hook for the complete lack of celebrities present. She wasn't going to allow her to get away with merely producing people who might just very slightly, perhaps in a deeply darkened room, *resemble* the fashionable famous. She herself had ironed her wavy blonde hair so flat that she rather expected to be mistaken for Marianne Faithful, but it wasn't far off midsummer and, in spite of indigo tie-dyed drapes all over the walls, not quite dark enough.

She'd sipped her cider and pouted uninterestedly in the direction of the Peter O'Toole character, while Barbara composed her face into her well-practised 'I'm definitely a lot older than sixteen' smile, at the same time arranging her feet so that she looked cutely pigeon-toed and appealingly baby-dollish, the way she'd seen Patti Boyd modelling in *Honey*. Much too old for me, Heather was thinking, mentally comparing him unfavourably with the attractions of a widely fancied local bad boy, currently suspended from the grammar school for having his hair permed *à la* Jimi Hendrix.

'He's coming over, look, no don't look!' Barbara hissed excitedly beside her, nudging her so hard with her elbow that Heather's cider, on its way to her mouth, splashed all down the front of her new plum crêpe Bus Stop dress.

'Allow me,' a smooth, deep voice had said.

Did people *really* say that? Heather, now driving along the rough track to the nursery, wondered. She was sure that he had, just as she was sure that it had been a reassuring voice that sounded accustomed to being very much in charge. These were, she recalled, the days when no-one watched James Bond movies for their comedy value. She was also sure that Iain, who'd introduced himself to her but not to the envious Barbara, had produced a pink-and-mauve spotted silk handkerchief from his velvet pocket with an extravagant magician's flourish. She'd treasured it since that night, right up till months later when it had been the only thing available on the train home from Edinburgh with which to mop the blood as her barely-formed baby had started its fall from her body. How naïve she must have been to have felt so impressed by him, by the fact that he didn't take the opportunity to dab and swab at her cider-soaked breasts but had handed the handkerchief over to her with what she sweetly took to be gentlemanly restraint. Boys of her own age wouldn't have done that. They'd have prodded and rubbed and taken a crafty look round to make sure that their envious friends were watching.

Heather pulled up on the gravel outside the largest of Nigel's greenhouses with that awful feeling that she couldn't in the slightest recall how she had got there from home. I could have run over a cat, or a child, she thought as she climbed out, appalled at her lack of concentration. She couldn't remember at all whether she'd taken the lanes behind the recreation ground and past the primary school, or driven through the new houses behind the High Street. It would have been Iain's fault if she'd crashed, she decided unreasonably.

Nigel was at the far end of his big greenhouse, hidden away, attaching 'special offer' signs to unsold specimen clematis, and blending in perfectly in blurred muddy colours of woodland. His Barbour pockets overflowed with twine and casually gathered weeds, and were stiffly corrugated with the dried blood of slaughtered wildlife.

'You always wear camouflage green,' Heather complained cheerfully as she picked her way across a tangle of hoses. 'Do you enjoy making it hard for customers to find you?'

'Of course I do. Hiding from the frightful masses is part of the fun,' he told her; emerging from a row of Nelly Mosers. 'In order to find me they have to search through my entire stock. That way, they often come across just the thing they've been needing to fill that little gap by their horrible mock-Regency double garage. I want their cash.' He rubbed his earth-covered hands together greedily and smiled welcomingly at her. 'But customers like you I treasure, of course – you spend such a delicious lot of other people's money. I've got your camellias. I hope they aren't for Julia Merriman, her garden is far too chalky. Coffee?' Nigel strode ahead of Heather towards his office.

'Thanks. They *are* for Julia, as it happens, but she wants them in great big pots on her terrace, so no problem.'

Nigel flitted about his untidy room, moving the cash box from where the kettle needed to be, and the kettle from where a pile of receipts and bills awaited his reluctant attention.

'She would. Why can't people accept what is and what isn't growable in the earth the good Lord in his wisdom has put in their gardens, and not keep nancying about wanting something *else*? I blame all those glossy gardening magazines. Every one of the chattering classes from miles around comes running in here, demanding *exactly* the myrtle they've just seen featured in the RHS mag, and they never know its proper bloody name, either. Their gardens will all one day be identical and I shall be able to lie on the sofa ordering all my stock based on the weekend columns in *The Times* and *Telegraph*.'

Heather moved a large, bored black cat from the window seat and sat patiently waiting for the end of Nigel's ranting. He was always like this, furious that he was in *trade* for a living, and furious that, having battled with his grand family to establish his nursery on the

77

edge of their crumbling estate, he'd discovered he truly loathed having to deal with the ignorant public and with their grubby money. 'Born to be idle and to potter, that's the real me,' he'd once told her on one of his previous tirade-days. She felt quite cool in the office that had once been part of a stone stable block. The floor was cobbled and covered by an unravelling old embroidered rug worn so thin that it moulded itself over the shape of the floor, forming ripple patterns like ebb-tide sand. Nigel seemed to glory in untidiness, as if it was an art form he had spent many years perfecting. Seed catalogues were piled on the floor next to the telephone, plant labels – some written on, some not – were scattered across the papered surface of his desk as if he'd started to work on them months ago, and then forgotten what he was supposed to write. The top drawer of the desk itself was open, revealing a stapler collapsed into two halves and a large bag of Everton mints spilling empty cellophane wrappers out onto the floor.

'Chaos,' Nigel murmured, by way of description rather than apology, catching her glancing round as he handed her the coffee. 'Fancy a mint?'

'No thanks, Nigel. And I'm not deceived either.' Heather grinned at him. 'I know it's all an act and that your computer is stuffed with every possible business-aid gadget. You never let your fax machine run out of paper, and I know that you know exactly where to get any plant I want *and* where it will and won't grow. All this muddle is just so people won't realize you're making a hefty profit out of them every time you so kindly discount a boxful of winter pansies.'

Nigel pouted then smiled, acknowledging her perception, then flounced rather camply over to the fridge for more milk. That was another little piece of deceit, Heather considered, the fact that he tended to *mince*. She remembered when she'd first met him at the school, collecting his daughter from an after-hours hockey match, and had been surprised that he actually had a family. She'd assumed he lived with a male interior designer in the kind of exquisitely restored cottage ('found the Adam fireplace in a builder's skip, *so* lucky') that rates a five-page feature in *Country Homes and Interiors*.

A friend who had once visited the nursery with her had said afterwards, 'Oh he's married, is he? Well you do surprise me.' Heather secretly suspected his campness was both a ruthless pursuit of the pink pound and left over from having been rather a tart at his public school: he must have been extremely pretty in his early teens. Even now, when you could get him to forget his cantankerousness and smile, the weather-tanned edges of his deep blue eyes crinkled into sunrise lines and his teeth gleamed stunningly.

It crossed her mind that Iain had probably been rather attractive to the other boys at his own, decidedly rugged boarding school. Perhaps, she thought, that was why he had pursued not only her, but later a widely-reported series of young impressionable girls, rather than real, grown-up women who would have expected to be on less adoring, equal terms. The last one the gossip columns had mentioned had been only eighteen, with Iain now, she reckoned, being well into his fifties. She didn't need to wonder how he did it, fame and fortune had their own pulling power, and no-one would deny the erotic quality of a title. 'Sir' wasn't quite on the same quasi-orgasmic level as 'Earl' or 'Marquis' but it was enough in most susceptible girls to cause just a touch of internal dampening.

'Have they asked you to do plants for this movie that's taking over the village?' Nigel asked.

'Shouldn't think they'd need me, surely, they're more likely to want a florist,' Heather replied, rather reluctant to show much interest in case Nigel recommended her

79

and she was forced to come face-to-face with Iain over a hastily pot-plunged bed of full-bloom Madonna lilies.

'Don't be so sure,' Nigel said, wagging his composty finger at her. 'I should get in there if you've got the chance. Who knows where it might lead? Even if it's just to some bone-idle co-star who can't be bothered to rearrange their own patio, it's all work.'

'Well why don't you go along and leave a few business cards with the right people, locations managers or whatever they are and then *you* can do it,' Heather suggested, pretending she was being generous.

'Not me, deary. Got enough here to keep me going,' he gestured round the tip of a room, 'even if it's just a spot of tidying up. You're the one with the design eye. Get Margot to suggest to the director that her garden's Lacking Colour, most gardens are by August. We have all suburban England thanking God for *Anemone Japonica* and the appalling ubiquitous *Lavatera Barnsley*.' Nigel's blue eyes twinkled craftily at her, and he said, as if he'd only just thought of it, 'And of course, everything you might just happen to need, you can get from me – can't you?'

Kate wished she hadn't chosen to take the Afghan hound for a walk. She daren't let it off its lead, because she knew it would disappear and chase rabbits in the wood, or steal chickens from someone's back garden hen-run. A note pinned to its kennel had warned that it was 'lively', which she took quite rightly to mean that, given its freedom, it would take off, deaf to any commands, and turn up two days later on the other side of Oxford. She'd chosen it because it was so pretty, its fur was flowing and blonde, brushed to gleaming show-standard under Margot's doting care. Secretly, as she was hauled energetically round the village pond while the dog attempted a hopeless chase of the ducks, she thought the pair of them made a rather gorgeously complementary couple: both long-legged and slim, both with flowing golden hair. Perhaps Shane Gibson's older brother Darren and his less attractive, jeering mates would realize how stunning she was, and in a desirable class way above the slaggy bus-shelter girls. Unfortunately, Darren was nowhere to be seen that day, and by the time she'd strode several times round the council estate, through the woods (nervously, in case of stray lone men) and across the recreation ground, where he might be smoking on the swings, she and the dog were both trailing their feet and drooping their flaxen heads.

'Rather a stunning pair of blondes,' A smooth, appreciative (at last) voice could be heard saying in the orchard as Kate unleashed the dog and sent him, exhausted, to the water bowl in his kennel. Kate shoved her hair out of her face and smiled up at Margot and the man with her. She assumed he must be one of the actors – he had the craggy, over-large features that look so good on the screen. She could just imagine him playing the sort of rather dated ruthless spy who never failed to lure beautiful women to his bed. She could feel herself glowing under the smiling warmth of his all-over scrutiny of her, as he looked her up and down in a frankly sexual way. He was too old, way, way too old, even the fully ripe Margot looked quite spring-chickenish beside him, but she was happy to have him inspecting her like that, as if he could spread her on toast and nibble her like an expensive, savoury delicacy. The most she could have hoped for from Darren was a brooding glare from under the shadowy peak of his baseball cap. She thought of this as good practice for later – learning how to react without either girlish simpering or a tarty reciprocal leer.

'This is Kate – she lives along the road and comes to walk the dogs for me. Little holiday job till school starts again,' Margot explained.

Kate thought that was catty, but managed not to scowl with fury and retort, childishly, that she wasn't going back to school but on to college. Margot might then explain that it wasn't *real* college, just sixth-form, for A-levels – or at least she would if, as Kate suspected, she fancied the man herself. And who, of that ancient age group wouldn't, she thought condescendingly.

'She'll be coming to your party, won't she Margot, if she's a neighbour? I do like to have the young ones around on social occasions, so enlivening,' he said.

Kate squirmed with glee, loving being discussed as if she was a pretty piece of desirable confectionery.

Margot grinned at her. 'Of course. And her parents, we're great friends – you must meet them.'

Kate skipped off home feeling that all her insides were tingling. Too letchy and old, practically grand-fatherly, she thought, not what I'm looking for at all. She stared in useless hope across the rec to see if Darren was lurking. Surely he'd notice how *glowing* she was feeling? How lovely, how delicious to be noticed, she thought.

Chapter Six

On his way to the kitchen Tom wandered past the phone, looking at it sideways and willing it to ring. He didn't want to call Hughie, that would look eager, but he very much wanted to know if Hughie was still interested enough to call *him*. Really, this sort of thing should be kept for the stopovers – he had never before overlapped work sex with home sex. Really, he knew quite well and with delicious guilt, this sort of thing should stop. There shouldn't *be* a double life. I'm too old, he thought, glancing in the mirror and trying to decide which was his best side as he filled the kettle. There were deep lines running from the edge of his nose to his jaw. The grained-in tan that went with his job was beginning to look falsely tawdry; the view in the mirror was like unexpectedly seeing an ageing television presenter in real life, whose off-duty face still has studio pancake unevenly plastered over it, and powdery hair. He looked all right at work, the uniform demanded an effort at glamour: the passengers expected it still, even in these blasé days, needing to feel they were being flown by someone more super-human than an airborne taxi-driver. Hughie was too new in the flight crew to look anything more than Home Counties pale, and was still tending to be quietly nervous with the passengers. Tom was far more used to hearty, confident stewards swanning like Julian Clary up and down the aisle, competing for giggles from the passengers. ('Silly me, you weren't the chicken were you, far too *bovine*. Another juicy big steak here please, Carol!') They hid behind the bulkhead, greedily gobbling too much of the plastic food and then complained about putting on weight. Tom didn't like that; the whole desirable point about their bodies was the skinny hardness of them. The moment they went soft and girlish, he had no interest. Hughie had a body so slender that, exposed to Holiday Inn air conditioning, it went as goose-fleshy as newly plucked poultry. Even in the hottest climate, his shivery body distrusted the luxury of the sun. Tom, lazing away a Hong Kong afternoon on a lounger, had watched enthralled as Hughie dipped a wary toe into the waters of the hotel lagoon, as if fully expecting the disheartening chill of an English municipal outdoor pool. Experienced crew never did that – they knew full well that you got what the airline paid for, and were confident that they would always plunge into at least 80 comfortable degrees.

When the phone did finally ring, Tom felt a startled panic, like a teenager longing for a first-love's call. He skittered nervously across the hall rug, chased by the yapping Jasper, rushing in case Heather or Delia got there first, and wondered who on earth Hughie was, had they met him, was he local, was it work – all the usual women's questions.

'Oh you're home!' Margot trilled into his ear.

'I live here, Margot,' Tom reminded her patiently.

'Not often you don't. Always arrivals and departures.'

'Goes with the job—'

'Yes, I know, I'm sorry. We always seem to have this conversation, don't we? Anyway I'm glad you're here, tomorrow is party time and I'd like you all to come. Children too, seeing as it'll be outdoors mostly, weather permitting, of course, as usual in England. Been meaning to do this ever since Russell had that barbecue thing built out by the pool, and of course we've got our house guest and lots of interesting people for you . . .'

Tom thought it sounded as if Margot intended to cook

84

the house guest along with all the interesting people. He imagined them threaded on skewers, separated by the tools of their trade: musical instruments, easels, cameras, books, Formula One racing cars like hunks of lamb alternated with onions, tomatoes and mushrooms. Margot was still in full flow, having moved on to describe the seductive warmth of her pool and how wonderful the garden was looking (thanks to Heather). He interrupted. 'Margot, we'd love to come, but we've also got Heather's mother—'

'Oh do bring her! All the Parish Council Committee are coming, I'm sure they'll have lots in common, well at least their age-group, I mean. They all do golf and church flowers, or whatever it is you have to be over 65 for these days . . .'

'Well of course you want to go! Don't be silly!' The two sentences were familiar to any parent persuading a shy young child that they really would enjoy a friend's birthday party. Coming from one adult woman to another, they sounded bossy and inappropriate. Heather had last used the formula-words herself when Suzy was perhaps seven, scared to go to the circus in case the clown picked *her* to be the one who was bounced in a blanket, or made her balance on the slithery back of a Shetland pony. Heather and her mother faced each other across the kitchen table, where Delia was opening a can of dog food and releasing from the tin an odour so awful that Heather had trouble breathing, which made it very difficult to come up with the necessary spot-on lie for a reply.

'But Margot's your friend!' Delia continued, just as she would have done thirty-five years before. She was puzzled, peering into Heather's eyes for a clue to the real reason why she'd claimed casually that she didn't really feel particularly partyish, would rather stay at home with a tuna sandwich, could feel a headache coming on, why didn't they all just go without her. Instinctively, Delia was no more inclined to believe her than she had when Heather, aged eleven, had complained of earache every Thursday morning in an attempt to get out of a bone-chilling hour of lacrosse. Jasper jumped and snarled around their feet, anxious to be fed.

'What party? Who's going to a party?' Suzy came into the kitchen and grabbed an apple from the bowl, ignoring the tension in the air between the two women.

'We all are!' Delia said, beaming at her as she forked out the dog food. 'Even your old gran! Isn't that nice?'

Heather recognized the tone in Delia's voice, a small but distinct crow of victory. They would all go to the party – Delia would not now have to plead that she couldn't possibly go with just Tom and the girls, not knowing anyone, that she didn't get out much these days . . .

'Oh yeah. Oh you mean Margot's barbecue,' Suzy said between apple-crunches. 'Kate told me about it, she said Margot's trying to bribe the village into not minding about these people filming all over the place.'

Later, Heather wallowed in the bath, trying to work out which aspect of Margot and Russell's party bothered her the most. Unless Margot had somehow scooped up the film's leading man, Iain would undoubtedly be there, being towed around the terrace and introduced to all and sundry as if she'd won him as first prize in a raffle. She could just imagine him being charming to every female over four years old. Russell would get drunk very early, complain merrily about how much Margot had spent and then later magnanimously urge everyone to eat more, drink more, life's too short etcetera. She could probably avoid Iain somehow, if she stayed wary and kept a safe distance between them; there would be a big enough crowd to hide in, and with her hair tied back and an indecently sparse amount of make-up, he was hardly likely to recognize her.

Women, luckily, had so much more scope for changing appearance than men did. Last time he'd seen her, she was pretty sure she was still at the stage of painting on thick, black fishtail eye-liner and cute dolly-freckles across her nose. Delia was the big problem, she decided, as she scrubbed earth and compost out from under her nails. Delia had never actually met Iain, but she had his name, so she had once theatrically claimed, burned into her brain, like a red-hot stake carving into brimstone. Someone might mention his name within the boundless range of her hearing – a sense that seemed to have developed a highly tuned acuteness in old age, as if it was God's apologetic compensation for fading eyesight and uncertain balance. But even then there was a chance of getting away with it. Iain, Heather knew, wrote as Iain Ross, not using the family name of MacRae. Delia knew nothing about the lurid books he wrote, but would have been satisfied, if she did, to find that totally in keeping with her so long-held opinion of him.

'That Terrible Man, that Deceiver!' she had ranted, years ago, at Heather after her inglorious return home.

'But I wanted to go. He didn't kidnap me, I could've said no,' Heather had protested, insulted that her mother thought her quite incapable of having chosen the elopement option all by herself.

'You were led,' Delia had insisted. 'You always were easily led,' she'd continued damningly. Heather hadn't bothered to argue – to argue properly, you needed a worthy opponent, one whose mind was capable of change, otherwise it was completely exhausting, like trying to fend off a raving Rottweiler with a sock full of cotton wool, a waste of effort. You might as well lie still and play dead till the savaging finished.

*   *   *

87

'You can invite a friend or two if you like, we don't mind, you know.' Margot, her face gleaming with rejuvenating cream, hovered in the doorway to Simon's room and tried to cheer him up. Through his bedroom window, she caught the highly satisfying view of caterers arriving to do expensive organizing out on the pool terrace. Simon had thought of asking Nick or Alex from school, but wanted neither competition nor a sniggering audience in his pursuit of Kate.

'S'all right,' Simon replied, 'everyone's too far away to organize this late. It'll be so much better when we can all drive.' He looked up from playing computer snooker and grinned at her.

'Oh will it?' Margot replied. Of course Simon would get a car – Russell would make sure his showroom at Upwardly Mobile had in stock just the right racy little girl-pulling GTi job round about the time of Simon's seventeenth birthday.

'You spoil that boy,' he kept telling her whenever Margot bought him something new. The last thing had been the leather jacket, a lovely scuffed-up soft one from the Harley Davidson shop in Chelsea. 'You could have got one like that on the market,' he'd moaned, when he caught sight of the receipt stuffed not quite far enough into the kitchen bin, forgetting that the day Margot married him he'd bragged that she need never worry about bargain-hunting again. Giving Simon a car would be justified as 'a sound marketing decision'. 'Spend a bit, make a *lot*,' he would say, the idea being that all Simon's friends, turning seventeen, would be able to tell their parents what a terrific deal they could get, investing in a trouble-free little motor from Russell's high-status dealership.

'What shall I wear?' Heather murmured as she gazed into her wardrobe.

'Do you really want an opinion, or is it just rhetorical as usual?' Tom said, grinning at her from the bathroom doorway. 'Whenever you've asked me that before, you've always completely ignored what I've suggested. Women do, and I know I'm not supposed to say that.'

Heather laughed at him. 'I just mean, do you think it's going to get really cold later, which means layers, or is it worth risking it and wearing something strappy in which I might freeze?' She didn't mean that at all. Her fingers were trembling slightly as she examined possible outfits. She wanted to look good, but not overdone – it was a casual sort of party. But if she *was* recognized by Iain, she felt a healthily vengeful urge to stun him, to make him think he'd really missed out on something all these years, wasted something special. In the end, while Tom was climbing into linen shorts and a wash-faded T-shirt, she chose a short black skirt and a long white collarless shirt. She tied her hair back with one of Kate's big velvet scrunchies and added a pair of silver hoop earrings. Shoes had to be the flattest she could find, so she could be as short and unnoticeable as possible. She considered wearing her reading glasses too, but thought that might result in her tumbling theatrically down Margot's terrace steps and rather defeat the object of passing unnoticed.

'You'll get barbecue sauce all down that shirt,' Tom warned her as they went downstairs.

'You sound like my bloody mother!' she warned him back.

Delia liked going to mixed-age parties. The great consolation for her age and frailty was that she felt like the queen arriving. Often she was the oldest guest, which gave her a satisfying *gravitas*, but if there turned out to be a glut of pensioners present she felt a mean little stab of pique. People tended to be kind, take an elbow to lever her over small doorsteps, make sure she had somewhere comfortable to sit, knew where the loo was and had a constantly topped-up drink. They felt this was the best they could do, and she accepted that and was content with it. No-one knew how to speak to old people; she was accustomed to being treated as if her mental faculties had died off ahead of the rest of her and as if English was only her second language – second, presumably, to fluent geriatric ga-ga. There was plenty of solicitous courtesy and a regard for comfort, but little chance to exercise her powers of conversation, as if by living a long time she was likely to have exhausted both vocabulary and opinions. She didn't mind this at all, having long ago decided that age conferred a restful right to be entertained by others rather than being burdened with doing it herself. Party small-talk was a waste of time, and watching people, especially if they showed signs of potential mis-behaviour, was far more rewarding. Often, at neighbourly gatherings in Putney, she and her friend Peggy clucked like ancient gossiping extras from a BBC costume drama, lined up against a wall with an extra-large Amontillado each, allowed to witness pre-adulterous goings-on, on the grounds that surely they were too old to have all their wits, add two and two and make it a judgmental four. If there had been a guillotine, they would have happily knitted beside it.

Delia sat on a thickly padded chair at the highest vantage point on Margot's terrace and watched groups of people arrive, collect drinks and identify acquaint-ances to chat to. Kate, she could see, was perched on a low wall by the changing pavilion, drinking a tumbler of something fizzy that could have been Aqua Libra (she'd seen bottles of it on the way through Margot's kitchen) or could have been the champagne that she herself was enjoying, once the bubbles had settled. She also noticed that Kate was giggly, talking to Margot's handsome son, but always with her eyes darting just past him as if waiting for someone else.

'Get on very well don't they?' Tamsin murmured to Suzy, looking across the pool to Kate and Simon. Suzy felt tortured – why wouldn't Simon come and gossip about the guests with *her*? She just knew Kate was simply being talked *at*, was having to make no effort at all herself simply because, in her tiny little baby dress, she looked too good to have to entertain. She herself, well she could tell Simon all sorts of deliciously malicious things about the village residents. She'd bet a month's allowance that he hadn't read the comments in the bus shelter about Lisa Gibson. Lisa was being employed to serve drinks, wearing a white, tight, low-cut top and a skirt that was hardly more than a waistband with a couple of layers of added frill. Suzy watched her going up to men with her champagne bottle, looking impudently into their eyes and asking pertly, 'Fancy some of this?' brandishing it at breast-height so they couldn't miss her best asset. Her heavily lipsticked mouth was pouted into a bored smile and she made sure that when she served the women she poured the drink slightly too fast, sending bubbles splashing carelessly over their hands and wrists. Lisa's brother Shane was round at the front of the house, supervising the parking arrangements.

'I believe in giving people a fair chance,' Margot was telling Heather, who had pointed out that with Shane's record, such a responsibility was just a bit of a risk. 'If he's in charge of the cars, he'll feel too responsible to do any damage, won't he?'

'Well, it's one theory,' Heather told her with a hesitant smile, wishing she shared Margot's habitual optimism.

Margot watched the aproned caterers expertly wielding giant barbecue tongs over the children's hamburgers. 'Feels like the last supper,' she confided.

'From tomorrow, we have to stay out of the way and leave the Great Writer to rattle round this place all by himself now that the actual filming is going to start. I'm beginning to wish I hadn't said yes, but they were so persuasive.'

Heather was quietly wondering about the exact size of the cheque they'd been persuasive with, when Margot broke into her thoughts. 'Of course you must meet him. Absolutely charming. And did you know he's actually a *Sir*?'

Heather took a too-fast gulp of her drink and spluttered instead of replying. Of course she knew. That was something else she'd done wrong, according to her mother. Having disgraced them both (irrevocably) by running off with Iain, she had then failed yet again by completing her divorce just three months before he inherited his title. 'Could've been *Lady* MacRae if you'd only stuck it out a bit longer. And you wouldn't have had to drop the title just because the marriage was over, you know,' Delia had grumbled to her as she finished reading out old Sir Cuthbert MacRae's obituary from the *Telegraph*. 'Then you'd have had something to show for all that trouble.'

'You mean *you* would!' Heather had retorted. 'I can just see you, showing off to all those witches down at the Townswomen's Guild.'

Heather was glad they hadn't arrived early. Plenty of people mingled noisily in Margot's garden, the film technicians looking completely at home and falling on the food as soon as it was ready. There was no sign yet of Margot's pet guest. With any luck it would be dark before he appeared. Perhaps, though, she suddenly thought, he was there all the time, as unrecognizable after twenty-five years as she herself hoped she was. She inspected all possible men closely. Iain must be in his mid-fifties by now, the romantically luxuriant hair that had reminded her of a portrait of Shelley might long ago have disappeared down shower plugholes, Heather realized, as she caught herself appraising men who were still years short of a mid-life crisis. He could have run to fat, be wearing glasses, or have lost a leg for all she knew. In spite of his fame, she had never seen him on TV; his wasn't the kind of literature that rated a South Bank Special. Melvyn Bragg would not salivate over titles like *Death Rattle*, the cover of which Heather had seen, featuring a half-clothed woman doing something bizarre with a snake.

Most of the men in Margot's garden she recognized from around the village: the young harassed husbands who lived behind the High Street, the improbably red-haired short one who ran 'Inside Story', the cricket team, Nigel from the nursery who had brought his beautiful, artfully tousled wife with him. There seemed to be an entire cross-section of the village population, probably because Russell and Margot were somehow unclassable. The impoverished land-owning régime, who enviously trashed them as swanky and vulgar, were not too proud to accept the chance to be so generously catered for, and everyone else was thrilled with the opportunity to drool over their decor. Julia Merriman happily accepted a third glass of champagne from the convivial Russell and then just as happily whispered to her companion that it was rather *de trop* to serve The Real Thing at an informal barbecue. 'Not sure about you,' she then commented to Heather, 'but I find barbecued food quite frightfully sticky.'

Heather smiled. 'But don't you just love licking all the gloopy bits off your fingers without it being considered appalling manners?' she asked. Julia frowned and looked uncertain. Heather grinned to show she was teasing, but Julia was looking at her as if she suspected finger-licking to be highly pornographic.

'Come and get some food,' Tom said to Heather, appearing suddenly after an agreeable maligning of the

England selectors with a computer analyst from the new estate. 'I thought you might need rescuing from Julia. I could see her revving up to ask you whether she should prune in March or October. It must be like being a doctor where people think it's all right just to ask a quick one about an iffy bladder.' They made their way past the pool's diving board to the pavilion, where the buffet and barbecue were spread under a yellow-and-white striped awning. Small children were leaping in and out of the water, shrieking at top volume to each other.

'They'll get cramp, swimming so soon after eating,' Tom remarked. He could see a gasping six-year-old with deflating arm bands struggling to the steps at the shallow end, swimming along with his mouth open in the way Tom imagined whales ingest plankton. 'Is no-one watching them? Where are their parents?' he wondered aloud, feeling that he'd done his stint as a diligent lifeguard when Suzy and Kate were little, and that he should be let off responsibility duties now.

'Oh around. And I don't expect they've eaten much anyway. They were probably all thoroughly fed before they came out. You know what people are like, a whole evening can be blighted if they get to a party and the only thing picky little Tarquin is tempted by is the dreaded forbidden Mad Cowburger,' Heather replied, relieved that someone at last was hauling the child from the water and wrapping his shivery tiny body in a huge Snoopy towel. 'Don't forget how it was when ours were little: somehow you're keeping an eye on them, even when no-one thinks you are.'

'Even blind drunk?' Tom said, helping himself to spare ribs, chicken, salad and garlic bread.

Heather watched Lisa shimmy past, with her arms precariously full of empty bottles, on her way in to the kitchen. Her older brother Darren was trailing sullenly behind her, unhelpfully burdened by just one bottle, as if afraid to compromise his cool-rating. The girl smiled at Tom, a smile full of habitual promise, even if it was only that he would be next when she brought another supply of full bottles out. He backed away, nervous of her décolletage and rounded hips. Heather's were slim and bony, and contrarily she'd always wished for a pert, rounded bottom. She watched men watching Lisa wiggle her way through the throng and up the steps towards the house, and thought how sad it was that Lisa had probably already been conditioned into watching her weight and honing away her captivating curves.

She could see Delia sitting up on the higher part of the terrace, under a hanging basket planted in shades of cream and yellow, surveying the scene like the queen on a state visit to somewhere interestingly primitive. She looked as if she was relishing a display of tribal dancing. Next to her was sitting a woman who could easily have passed for well over a hundred – Heather wondered if it was a trick of the fading light, or if her deeply tanned skin really was practically reptilian. She wore a magnificent lime green cartwheel straw hat tied under her chin with a scarlet chiffon scarf. Delia had on a soft crocheted beret in apologetic beige and was probably, Heather guessed, deeply suspicious of the other woman's panache.

'That's my ancient mother,' Nigel declared, arriving next to her with a newly opened bottle of champagne, which Heather assumed he had easily charmed away from Lisa. 'Yours doesn't seem to be listening,' he observed, taking note of Delia's bird-like darting eyes as he refilled Heather's glass.

'No, well she's watching, that's why. In the morning she'll be able to re-run this party like a video, telling me who said what to whom, and knowing exactly who disappeared into Margot's orchard with someone they hadn't arrived with.'

Nigel laughed. 'Yours might be the more eagle-eyed,' he conceded, 'but mine has got by far the best hat.'

'I can't argue with that,' Heather agreed. 'It's a colonial masterpiece. She looks as if she's just come back from ruling Burma.'

'That's the single advantage of having skin like a tortoise – it gives an impression of imperialism. That's from a lifetime of hunting seasons and pruning roses in the midday sun, much as she'd love it to have been from running a tea-plantation.'

Just then Kate emerged from the kitchen and stopped to talk to the pair of old ladies. She was lit from behind and her golden hair shone, Heather thought suddenly, like the aura on the picture of Archangel Michael that she remembered pasting into her Sunday School attendance book when she was about six. Immediately she could smell the dusty room above the vicarage and the stale mustiness of the piled-up, spidery jumble ready for the next bout of fund-raising. She wondered if Delia would want to go to the local church while she stayed with them, and if she would complain about the vicar's wife accompanying the hymns with her jolly banjo.

Kate was no longer talking to her grandmother, Heather then realized, but was standing, staring at one of the guests who had walked past her down the steps towards the pool. Heather watched him, too, curious to see what interested Kate about him. Behind him, the two old ladies had their heads bent together for intense conspiratorial whispering. Like Kate, they were looking at the man who by now was being accosted by Lisa with her drink supply. Heather's insides took a very uncomfortable lurch as he moved out into the light of one of Russell's row of garden flares. She recognized him. His hair was still intact, as she should have guessed it would be, and he walked with the same confident lope she had found hard to keep pace with all those years ago. She moved gently backwards to the far side of Nigel, relieved that Iain was striding along the far side of the pool towards the pavilion. It was quite dark now and she felt sudden enormous gratitude that her mother preferred early nights and would provide an excuse to leave soon.

Kate also recognized the man, Iain she remembered his name was, the one with Margot, who had said he hoped she would be at the party. He must have seen her, but had walked straight past, which irked her. She decided that she'd wander down the garden and lure him into conversation about the film – surely he would be able to secure a part in it for her. It was tempting to stop on the way and think of something sensational to say to Darren. He'd finished helping Lisa on bottle-duty and was now leaning on the low wall by the barbecue, looking bored and scruffily out of place, and pulling tiny plants out of the cracks. He looked as if he needed cheering up. Kate had drunk several glasses of champagne and was feeling whirly in the head. She also felt brave and adventurous, and in need of being thoroughly noticed. Lisa, now off-duty, was strutting her high-heeled stuff by the pool and also heading for the man, probably with the same career prospects in mind that Kate had. She was walking, Kate thought, like one of the girls she'd seen during the time-outs on American boxing matches on TV. She should have been carrying a placard, 'Round 3.' One stone, two birds, Kate decided, casually missing her footing and tumbling into the softly floodlit water.

'Oh God, it's Kate,' Tom said to Heather. 'Do you think she's pissed?'

Kate was swimming elegantly to the pool's edge, close to where Darren was opening a bottle of beer with a piece of the wall he sat on. Just too late, but mindful of priorities, he carefully balanced his beer between an anthemis and an aster, and got up to offer a rescuing hand to Kate. He was too slow. Instead she was hauled out of the water with gallant strength by her alternative quarry. Iain, still protectively holding on to her hand, even though she was now out of the pool, was among many who admired the way her dress had collapsed off one tanned shoulder and clung over the contours of her body. She looked, Heather thought, like one of those dreadful wet T-shirt competitors, and she pushed her way through the throng to cover her with Suzy's damp towel.

'What on earth are you playing at? Can't you even walk straight?' she hissed crossly to her daughter who stood casually wringing out her long hair and smiling triumphantly at Lisa.

''S'OK Mum,' Kate said with her best smile and her eyes shining. 'Just slipped.'

'This lady is your mother?' Iain said, looking at Heather for the first time. It was too late for Heather to get away. Iain was now gazing intently at her face and she cursed herself for hoping that he had become short-sighted enough not to be counting her wrinkles. 'Hello Feather,' he said very quietly. 'Such a very long time.'

Chapter Seven

A quick getaway from Iain and the party was easy; Tom was flying the next afternoon and getting tetchy for the want of a forbidden drink, and of course there was the need to take Kate home and get her warmed up. Margot quite understood that there would be nothing she could offer from her own extensive wardrobe that would come close to what Kate would deign to be seen alive in. Walking along the road to home, Heather decided it was time to tell all to Tom. It was just a matter of choosing the right words, perhaps jokey ones as they climbed into bed. She thought about her underwear – beneath the big shirt she wore an uninspiring plain white body, chosen with the intention of minimalising Visible Panty Line rather than for the purpose of fun and games. She linked her arm comfortably through Tom's and mentally rifled through her knickers drawer, choosing something more sensuous to put on for bed. Tom had an erotic fondness for silky textures, which he attributed to the comforting nightly stroking of the pink satin eiderdown which had covered his childhood bed. Heather, when she first discovered this, had realized she was very fortunate Tom's mother hadn't been a devotee of candlewick, and that she hadn't had to mail-order a collection of tufted knickers in carbuncle-pink. The two of them were trailing the dripping but delighted Kate, followed by a complaining Suzy ('Why can't I stay the night? *Why?*') and tired-out, slightly muzzy-headed Delia.

'I'll go straight up to bed dear,' Delia said as soon as Heather unlocked the front door, allowing Jasper to rush out and do some urgent leg-lifting against the terracotta pots. 'All that excitement, and tomorrow I must go and see Edward again.' Delia hovered in the hallway. 'Come on Jasper,' she called to the scuffling dog, 'that's surely enough for now.' She wouldn't look at Kate, whom she strongly suspected of showing off.

Heather recognized the pointed Ignoring of Drawing Attention Ploy, and wished her mother was the type of woman who would have conveniently forgotten everything by the morning.

Miraculously on the walk home, neither Tom nor Kate had mentioned Iain the gallant rescuer. Leaving the party, neither of them had piped up with 'Who was that man? How does he know you?' Being as totally self-absorbed as only a teenager could be, Kate had probably not even been listening. Heather had dreaded either of them talking about him in front of Delia. If his name had just chanced to slip out, Delia might possibly have gone into a faint, or even, it occurred to Heather, dropped dead. Now that *would* have been the ultimate in Drawing Attention, she thought. As she got undressed it also occurred to her that her mother's instant (painless of course) death would make her own life a whole lot simpler. She touched wood, crossed herself and blushed with sickening guilt at the sinful thought.

Tom was saving his opinions for the privacy of their bedroom. 'So who was that oily creep? The one who pulled Kate out of the pool and then stood there oozing lechery at her?' Tom's reference to 'oily' reminded Heather of Uncle Edward; that poor man seemed to have had all his own oil sapped from every pore to the point of crispness. The TV adverts for the reputedly healthier sorts of cooking fat sprang to mind as she cleaned off her make-up: great colanders full of French fries having their grease shaken off. Perhaps we are all simply chips sizzling in the great deep fat fryer of life, just waiting our turn to be scooped out and drained . . . I must be drunk, she decided, her train of thought making her feel queasy, but she carefully dolloped a double measure of lubricating moisturiser on to her face to stave off the awful fate.

'Old enough to know better, gruesome old goat.' Tom was rattling on half to himself as he padded around the room. 'Dribbling at a young girl like Kate.' Heather regarded him calmly. Somehow his attitude didn't make her feel he would be terrifically interested in her scarlet frilled underwear – clearly it was hardly worth opening the drawer. 'And he seemed to know you. Where would you have met a jerk like that?'

The sweetest and most tempting answer would be 'Darling I married him'. Heather considered, wondering if she could raise the energy for devilment. Tom was being hostile and challenging. She certainly didn't feel awake enough to enter into an explanation that would, given his mood, become inevitably defensive. It would simply be easier to keep the information to herself. It would only lead to derision, to disbelief and to an exhausting late-night bout of self-justification. What's another twenty-five years, she thought, if I can possibly get away with it? 'He's just someone I met years and years ago,' she told Tom, then added, 'long before you.' It wasn't quite 'Mind your own business', but close enough.

'Knew him well, did you?' Tom wasn't looking at her, feigning only half-interest as he nonchalantly tapped at the keys of his Psion organizer, already half-absent, checking out the next day's flight times.

Heather smiled at him as she brushed her hair in the mirror. It was a trick question and they both knew it. He was asking if she'd slept with Iain, but she mulishly refused to identify the code he was using. 'I didn't know him terribly well actually, and not for very long,' she told him instead. Well at least that much was true, she thought, switching off the light.

*   *   *

Simon decided it would be safer to go by river. Even if no-one saw him climb over the wall, and he managed not to spear himself on the dense invader-deterring barrier of holly and hawthorn, there was still the danger that their security lights would go on, revealing him creeping round the edge of the herb-lawn like a stealthy burglar. The rowing boat made no noise as he gently dipped the oars into the flat black water, but moorhens flapped like abandoned bin-liners as he passed them, and the rats and voles scuttled and rustled into holes in the bank. Night-time noises were so exaggerated, he thought, as an owl took off from the oak tree with a tremendous commotion. He was hardly daring to breathe in case lights went on and shotguns came out all over the village.

Simon rowed round the back of the little island to lessen the chances of the bankside residents wondering what a lone, unlit rower was up to so late at night, and he approached the almost derelict dock from downstream. As he looked at the house, crouched silently in the boat while he shipped the oars and tied a rope to a rusty iron ring, a woman appeared at an upstairs window and briskly closed the curtains. His heart boomed under his leather jacket and he needed quite suddenly to pee. It felt all wrong, having a pee behind the willow overhanging the dock in Kate's garden, somehow sacrilegious, as if he was in a graveyard, defiling the dead. He hadn't dared direct the flow into the river in case the noise in the silent night cascaded like Niagara. He tried to think of it as marking territory like a lion, pissing a pattern of his initials up the tree bark to avoid the thunderous sound of splashing on the grass.

Afterwards, he edged past the paddock, terrified that Suzy's podgy pony would canter across to him, whickering for a midnight feast. Next he crept along the wall of espaliered fruit trees, alarmed at how, in the gloom, their skinny crucified limbs made him think of a row of torture victims. Simon's breathing was juddery and shallow as he finally reached the house and stood quaking under the window that he'd identified as Kate's. Ideally, he knew, she would have a balcony like Juliet's, twined with night-pungent jasmine and easy to climb up to. (A set of steps would be helpful, he thought, feeling he had exhausted his adventurousness for one night.) Unlike Romeo, though, Simon had no illusions that Kate would welcome his nocturnal visit. For one thing, she was not posed above him in a see-through nightie gazing languidly at the stars and wishing he, and only he, would appear. Her light was out. She was probably fast asleep, he realized dejectedly, dreaming of that gross nerd Darren, or the smarmy git who'd pulled her out of the pool. Simon lurked under Kate's window and wondered rather drunkenly what he had hoped to achieve. He'd been imagining she would be wandering about in the garden, having realized Darren was a complete crud and that older men drooling over teenage girls were nothing short of sad vampires looking to leech off young blood.

Bored and tired, he kicked carelessly at a stone on the terrace which clattered against an earthenware pot. Immediately a dog started a hectic yapping, and Simon fled, terrified, down the garden, pursued by lights that went on at three windows and spread their beams down the garden. On balance, he thought as he lay uncomfortably flat in his boat beyond the willow till the commotion died down, it would be cooler to be caught burgling than romancing.

*   *   *

In the morning, Tom was preparing to be on the move again. Heather woke up unnecessarily early and in need of aspirin, to hear him clattering noisily in the bathroom. The shelves were emptying once more. The familiar flight bag was out, being reloaded for another trip, this time a double, taking in Singapore and continuing for an extra couple of runs from there to Australia. He could be gone for up to three weeks, but she didn't ask when he expected to be back, having got used to vagueness of answer over the years. When the girls were little, she'd disappointed them too often by geeing them up into a state of excited tension, promising, 'Daddy will be home on Tuesday, definitely.' Then, after baking a cake and cooking a welcome-home supper, she'd find that there were delays and he'd wander in two days late. They'd always blamed her, of course, being the one on the premises, accusing 'But you *promised*. You *promised*.' This was so often followed by a sulk and a declaration (usually from Kate) of eternal hatred, that she'd long ago adopted a casual indifference to Tom's schedule, and they'd soon learned to do the same. It was, anyway, difficult to keep up a heartfelt atmosphere of celebration for the return of someone who kept coming and going during eighteen long years. It was like wearily applauding too many curtain calls at the theatre – all strained smile and a need to get on with something else. All Heather could manage to feel about his forthcoming absence, that slightly hungover morning, was a hope that he wouldn't pack the John Frieda shampoo.

Down in the kitchen, Delia made the kind of fuss that implied Tom was leaving to defend Queen and country rather than to ferry a few hundred executives to enjoy corporate hospitality in one of the world's best shopping centres. 'It's important to have a good breakfast when you're going to travel,' she was telling Tom out on the terrace, as Heather slopped drowsily into the kitchen. Tom had walked through, leaving the room pungent with aftershave which he wore only for work, feeling it was part of the uniform. Delia was grilling bacon, many slices of it, along with tomatoes and mushrooms. 'Would you like an egg as well?' she called out to Tom solicitously.

Heather immediately felt a need for comfort food. 'You don't need six slices, do you Tom? I quite fancy a toasted bacon sandwich.'

'Oh it's not for you!' Delia told her sharply. 'It's not as if you're going anywhere.'

'Why do I have to be going somewhere?' she asked, inspecting the contents of the fridge. There was no more bacon. 'Here, let me do that,' she said, moving to take over from her mother who seemed to be finding the grill heavy to handle.

'No. I'm doing it,' Delia insisted, shoving at Heather with her elbow. Heather noticed the arthritic mounds on her mother's fingers and understood the old lady's stubbornness. This obstinacy must be the old-age manifestation of the strength she had had in her youth. Pity for declining powers prevented Heather from childishly wresting the grill-pan away, and she contented herself with making toast and then going outside and surreptitiously stealing a slice of bacon from Tom's overloaded plate.

'She's trying to kill me,' he muttered to Heather while Delia clanked the crockery in the sink.

'Only with kindness,' Heather whispered.

'What's the difference? Dead is dead,' he said, nevertheless eagerly piling mushrooms, toast and a deftly folded slice of bacon on to his fork.

'What was going on in the garden last night?' Delia asked, bringing her coffee out to join them on the sunlit terrace.

'No idea,' Heather said, 'probably just a fox mooching about.'

Delia shuddered. 'They're wicked, nasty things, foxes, we get them coming along the railway embankment at home. They scavenge at all those fast-food places. I'm sure they spread disease.'

'Here they just pick off the ducklings,' Heather told her, wishing that fifteen years of riverside living had made her feel tougher towards murderous wildlife.

'Perhaps they could scavenge among Heather's old boyfriends,' Tom joked through a final mouthful of bacon. 'Plenty of those about.'

'Just the one, darling,' Heather hissed sweetly, flashing him what she hoped was a menacing smile, 'for now.'

In spite of misgivings about his arteries silting up, Tom was finishing the last of his breakfast, a piece of speared toast was circling the plate, mopping up leaked mushroom juice. Heather picked up her coffee cup and went back in to the kitchen, not looking at Delia, not wanting to know whether her mother's curiosity-radar was in full working order or not. Her insides tensed as she heard music starting up in Kate's room. Oh God, she's up, she thought. How long before Iain's name is actually mentioned in front of Delia? Feeling cowardly, she retreated upstairs to get ready for the day, calling back to her mother, 'I'll give you a lift over to the clinic later if you like. I've got to go that way to Julia's, to plant her camellias.'

'Thank you dear, I was rather counting on it.'

'Kate, if you want breakfast, the kitchen canteen is about to close,' Heather called to her as she passed her bedroom door.

'Mum?' Kate's head appeared round the doorway, followed by a body wearing only an ancient tie-dye T-shirt and a pair of tiny black knickers. 'Has anyone phoned for me this morning?'

'No – are you expecting someone?' Heather asked.

'Not particularly.' Kate's brown legs were fidgety, a

sure sign that she was being only half truthful. Probably that boy Darren, Heather thought, wondering why each generation of teenagers unfailingly imagines that their parents don't notice anything. She knew quite well, with the enlightenment of hindsight, that he, lumpen and undeserving as he was, was the reason why Kate had so gracefully tripped herself into the pool. How infuriating it must have been for poor Kate to have ancient Iain thinking he was doing her a favour by pulling her out.

'Look, I'm going out later after lunch, taking your gran over to the clinic again and then on to Julia's. Why don't I give you a lift into town and you can go and see one of your school friends?' Kate wrinkled her nose with a distinct lack of enthusiasm. 'Not even Annabelle?' Heather asked. Kate and Annabelle had been inseparable for the past six months. Only weeks ago, Heather had dreaded the ringing of the phone, because it would then be monopolised for at least an hour while Kate curled up on Heather's bedroom carpet and giggled and whispered about all the things they'd already giggled and whispered about all day at school. As she flurried about in her bedroom putting last night's abandoned clothes away so that Mrs Gibson had space to do her cleaning, it occurred to Heather that the phone had been distinctly quiet ever since the end of term.

She went back out on to the landing. Noises of reluctant bed-making came from Kate's room. 'Has Annabelle gone away?' she called.

'No, why?' Kate asked, padding out of her room and rubbing last night's mascara out of her eyes.

'Just that you don't seem to see as much of her, and the phone's been so quiet,' Heather said.

Kate was tangling the end of her T-shirt and looking uncomfortable. 'Well, we don't really see each other so much now. I mean we won't, will we, with me being at the college next term and her still being at school.'

'Well you could still be friends, surely. And it's the holidays – so what difference does it make where you're going next term?' Heather asked. She felt a vague unease, something horribly familiar from a long time ago, like the remembered sparks of an oncoming migraine or the first twinges of going into labour.

Kate started going slowly down the stairs and then looked back with her face full of painful honesty. 'I suppose it's because I've left and moved on. It's as if there's a gap. It's not just Annabelle, I've got it too. Not like I'm older than all that lot or anything, just further on, just, well, different. I've made one more choice than they have so far – they won't have to decide anything that important till they get their UCAS forms way on into next year. You know?'

Heather knew. She took refuge in the airing cupboard, sorting duvet covers that were already perfectly in order as Kate went down to mess up the kitchen and get in Delia's way. Goodness, how she remembered that feeling, that isolation. She'd had hers after that summer, the married summer. By September she was, in spite of her mother's warnings that she wouldn't be welcome, humbly home again and somehow assuming, with blithe teenage optimism, that if she went back to just how things used to be, everything would fall comfortably into its old place, and her 'old place' would still be there, as if she'd only gone off for a practice run at real life.

The first shock was not being allowed back into school. There had been an interview with the headmistress. She remembered waiting with her mother outside the door on which there was the little set of miniature traffic lights. You knocked on the door and the appropriate light came up: red for go away and return later, orange for wait and green for enter. For years into adulthood, Heather's stomach had given a tiny reflex flicker while she waited in her car for real traffic lights to change. It was just before term-time, and the corridor had the oily smell of its new fruity green paint. Another, more sickly smell wafted from the main hall where the parquet floor gleamed richly chestnut with new polish, in preparation for another year's pounding from regulation Clark's shoes filing in for morning assembly. The school had been dustily deserted except for the head and a couple of office staff, but the light system was still in officious use. Amber had flashed for at least five nerve-wracking minutes after she had knocked, and on green for enter her mother had pushed her quite roughly ahead of her into the gloomy room. No-one else had come out, paper-work had been getting priority.

Pre-computers, there had been a huge whole-school timetable, a muddle of different biro colours, taking up a whole wall. Heather had looked at it briefly and realized suddenly that she was wasting her time. There could be no room for her now, not even with her nine good O-level passes. She was going to be made an Example – going to the bad was neither to be condoned nor forgiven. The brief, but flashily public, upheaval caused by her running away had been smoothed over, patted down, and there must be nothing left to show it had happened. It reminded Heather now of the secret burial of a small child's hamster, the ground carefully levelled by conscientious parents so the child wouldn't know where to be tempted to dig.

'I don't run a school for married women,' the headmistress had told her, her heavy black fountain pen still in her hand from dealing with something so much more important than mere pupils. Heather, with a subversive urge to giggle, had been willing her to proclaim 'You've made your bed, you must lie on it . . .' so that she could relish her realizing too late that she'd clichéd herself into a near *double entendre*. Instead she had stared coldly before suggesting, 'Have you thought of evening classes?' while Heather calculated if she was actually trying to be constructive and kind. 'You could perhaps learn some basic cookery . . .' she'd continued with calculated spite. How callously she'd almost managed to reduce Heather to tears with that. Clever girls at her school, girls like Heather, weren't allowed to take cookery lessons. They were reserved for forms like 5C (Commercial) who alone were allowed the delight of taking home Hungarian goulash and apple strüdel instead of 'A' grades for Chaucer essays and zoology dissections. They'd talked mysteriously about RSA and Pitmans, back-combed their hair rigorously and left the school at sixteen to have giggly times in typing pools. While Heather's clever friends haggled with parents to be allowed out later than 10.30, the Commercial girls would be sipping Dubonnet over steaks in Berni Inns with men who were being ruthlessly assessed for their potential Mr Right-ness. So the headmistress had lumped A-stream Heather in with these.

'Spinsters!' Delia had spat the word scornfully as they waited for the bus home from that interview. 'Shouldn't even have bothered going. Shouldn't have given her the satisfaction of turning you away.' It was the only time Heather had known for sure that her mother wasn't the opposition. Later, from the local College of Further Education along with other Bad Girls, public school throw-outs, ambitious second-chancers and quiet, new-start former victims of school bullies, she had watched her former friends still banding together and, like the school itself, seamlessly closing over the space where she had been. They wore uniform, she didn't. She worked with boys, they only giggled and flirted at them. She wore make-up, as much as she wanted – they were given childish detention for the slightest trace of mascara. Being married became only the smallest part of the difference between them – she couldn't even blame Iain for this one.

She remembered now, as she keenly felt Kate's isolation, how much of school friendships depended on the simple presence and small daily patterns of the school itself. Kate would be left out because she *was* out. 'You know Kate, it'll all be over by Christmas,' Heather called down to the kitchen.

'What, like the war?' Kate shouted back up.

'What war?' Delia asked as she opened the front door to take Jasper down to the rec.

'No war,' Kate told her. 'Just, well, stuff.'

'Oh, "stuff",' Delia said huffily, sensing it was no good expecting to be informed.

'You'll have a whole lot of new friends by then,' Heather told Kate as she came back up the stairs. 'And the old ones who matter, you'll still have them too if you make the effort.'

She'd gone too far. Kate scowled. 'Look Mum, it's OK. I've got things to do, I wasn't complaining. You asked about Annabelle, I told you. End of story, and I'm fine. You don't have to worry. In fact please don't.' Her door closed and music started again.

Heather felt dismissed. The phone rang minutes later and Heather wandered into her bedroom fully expecting it to be Annabelle, on the talk-of-the-devil basis.

'Hello Heather-Feather, you certainly know how to give a man a surprise,' Iain's voice purred down the phone. She could almost picture his lazy smile, could see his mocking eyes narrowed, cat-like. She imagined him sprawled across Margot's chintz sofa, his bony fingers playing with a cigarette as he spoke.

'Why are you calling?' she asked him abruptly, infuriated by his use of the old pet-name.

'Hey, sorry!' he laughed as if she was being childishly aggressive. 'Couldn't I just be calling to ask after your daughter? Has she recovered from her soaking?' Heather said nothing. 'You do remember I rescued her?' he went on, slightly less fun in his voice.

111

'Of course I do. She's fine. She swims breast stroke for her school team and had a county gymnastics trial, so her balance is spot-on. She jumped in on purpose and didn't need pulling out. But thanks anyway.'

'Uh-oh, sarcasm I sense. It's *sooo* long since I've had girls throwing themselves into deep water for me,' he continued.

Heather suppressed a shriek of fury. 'Good grief, you don't imagine it was *your* attention she was after do you?' she said with a burst of laughter, wishing immediately she'd been a little less emphatic, that she was capable of simple cool disinterest.

'Actually Heather,' Iain became more business-like, abandoning the drawling banter, 'actually, I thought that as fate seems to have thrown us together for a few weeks, perhaps it would be nice to have lunch and do a spot of catching up.'

Heather gasped. 'You want to do twenty-five years of catching up over *lunch*?' she asked, incredulous. 'Why on earth do you think I'd want to see you?' She could hear Tom down in the hallway. Any minute he'd be up making enquiring faces from the doorway and trying to find out who she was talking to. She pulled her dressing-gown tightly around her and wished she was fully, defensively dressed.

'Curiosity?' Iain suggested.

'About what?' she snorted back.

'Oh come on Heather, it would be such fun, just for old time's sake. Perhaps I could meet the rest of your family; *they* must be curious about your old ex from the past, even if you're not.' Such arrogance, Heather thought, as if she'd rushed home like an over-excited child from the party and talked about nothing else. She hesitated; it would perhaps be useful to talk to him, to see if he had developed a better nature she could appeal to, in the little matter of her family knowing nothing about him. 'OK lunch tomorrow then,' she stated. 'The

112

Beetle and Wedge at Moulsford, 12.30. *Don't*, whatever you do, mention it to Margot – or anyone.' This necessary request made her feel vulnerable, which she detested.

Iain laughed, misunderstanding. 'Don't worry, it'll be our secret. Just like the old days, huh?'

'No Iain. It isn't at all like the old days,' she replied, then hung up.

Chapter Eight

Maddening man. Heather was still fuming about Iain when she drove Delia (with Jasper) to the clinic. He'd got the better of her, just as he always had when she was a silly and impressionable teenager. He'd made her feel so daring then, persuading her to lie and defy her mother's curfews, and dally the hours away in bed with him. He hadn't been the one who'd had to invent whoppers about staying the night with a friend who needed homework help ('a whole Wordsworth project, honestly it'll take *hours*'). He hadn't been the one who'd then had to get up while it was still dark to rush back to school on unreliable trains, dashing in after assembly, signing the late book and pretending excuses about alarm clocks. In his Chelsea flat, she recalled vividly, he'd had the first duvet she'd ever seen. It had been called a Puffin Downlet, an exotic piece of bed-furnishing at a time when no-one knew how to pronounce 'duvet', or had yet decreed that the term 'continental quilt' was destined to become obsolete. This was an era when people used their wedding present bedlinen till it wore out, and replaced it with pastel sheets only if they were really artistic and daringly experimental with colour co-ordination. The only function of beds was to accommodate sleepers in inhospitably chilly rooms, so Heather knew instinctively that only the dangerously louche and decadent made their beds into such tempting nests as Iain had. The room had been the warmest in the flat, and there had been covers for the duvet in stylish maroon and chocolate colours; his cleaning lady had hated changing them, struggling to match corners with corners and complaining that the the zip-openings had been too small. There'd been one cover in dizzying op-art black-and-white squares on which Heather was terribly sick when she'd drunk too much vodka and orange juice. At the time he'd asked her, with perverse amusement, 'Did you feel it was lacking colour?'

'I'm surprised you wanted to come out. I'd have thought you'd want to spend Tom's last day with him,' Delia's voice trilled across from the back seat.

'Tom's always having "last days", Mother. We don't make a big song and dance about it, it's just his job. And anyway I've got mine to do; if I don't get these plants delivered to Julia Merriman, it'll be all round the village that I'm just a dabbling amateur.'

'Men like someone to fuss,' Delia warned. 'If they can't get it at home, they'll look for it somewhere else.'

It would have been decidedly cruel of Heather to ask what Delia could possibly know about it. Perhaps she was a bit casual about Tom, but surely better that than a tearful goodbye and frantic welcome every time he went to work and returned safely. As a family they weren't fractured and helpless without his daily presence – it wouldn't exactly make him happy to imagine they were. While he was up in the sky making the tricky descent into Hong Kong, he shouldn't have to worry about whether his wife was capable of ordering the right heating oil, or unblocking the sink. And wouldn't a massive last-supper goodbye rather imply that his job was unacceptably dangerous and that it was a constant miracle that he returned at all? Sometimes he was only gone three days – how could anyone keep up the necessary level of emotion over the years that her mother thought appropriate?

'At least he was there for your friend's party,' Delia said with a sigh, as if the event would give Tom fond thoughts of home to comfort him during lonely foreign nights. 'It was quite fun really, wasn't it? I do like to see a good *mixture*,' she added, making Heather, who was trying to overtake a lurching minibus, think immediately of a rich fruit cake.

'I saw you having a chat with Nigel's mother,' Heather commented, praying to get the party covered without mention of Kate's rescuer.

'Oh yes, I liked Clarissa. Now she *is* a lady,' Delia said with a satisfied sigh. 'You could tell by the hat. Do you know, she's invited me to Slingsby Court to have a look at the roses.'

Heather smiled at her through the mirror. 'Well that will be lovely, the roses there are wonderful. Some are centuries old . . .' but Delia had a faraway look and her hand was up, gently patting at her old straw boater.

'Perhaps I should pop into Oxford and get a new hat . . .' she was murmuring.

Just as Heather assumed with relief that they were safely past the subject of Margot's party, Delia's attention flashed back over it like a radar beam. 'By the way, dear, is it wise to let Kate have alcohol? Is that why she needed pulling out of the pool? And who was that man?'

The barrage of questions rained over Heather from the back seat, and she almost felt she should cower for safety, like the child of jokey parents who shout 'duck!' when driving under a low bridge. 'Hey, one thing at a time!' she said, forcing a laugh. 'Kate wasn't *that* drunk, she could easily have climbed out by herself. And . . .' she chose her words carefully, 'I couldn't tell you who he was. Just someone Russell and Margot know, I suppose. Something to do with the film.' Of course she couldn't tell her mother who he was, not unless she wanted to see a demonstration of instant apoplexy.

'Looked vaguely familiar, I thought. One of those tricky sorts of men. I don't know where I've seen him before, but it'll come to me, you mark my words,' she warned.

Heather managed another brittle laugh. 'Honestly Mother, if everyone *had* "marked your words", as you put it, over the years, we'd all have seen the complete failure of decimal currency, Concorde wouldn't have got off the ground and Margaret Thatcher would never have got off the back benches.'

Through the mirror, as Heather sped down the last straight stretch of road, she could see Delia frowning, deep in thought. 'Hmm, we'll see,' she was saying, nodding ominously.

They were approaching the clinic. Heather turned the Renault off the road and onto the winding, laurel-lined drive. It reminded her very much of the entrance to a crematorium: discreet and leafy, one's final destination not revealed till the last possible moment, just a soothing pathway decorated with clumps of inoffensively subdued bedding plants, as if to distract gently from the awful reality and keep it well hidden from those whose turn it wasn't quite yet. The view could hardly make any difference to those whose turn it *was*. She wondered if this ever crossed the wandering minds of new residents to the clinic as they arrived – that their next journey could be the one for which this was so like a dress-rehearsal, even to the extent that old and sick people were always put in the back of the car, as if they were already half-corpses on whom a front-seat view would be wasted.

'You'll just pop in, won't you dear, just to say hello,' Delia said to Heather as she climbed out of the car. 'Stay there, Jasper.' The dog growled crossly. Delia looked nervous, as if half dreading that she was about to be met by a sorrowful nurse waiting to tell her that Edward, sadly, had just that moment passed away, but there was no reason why she couldn't just come and see him, looking so peaceful as he was . . .

Heather looked at her watch. 'I'm supposed to be at Julia's . . .' she started saying. Also, could she trust the dog not to get fractious and start chewing at the camellias which were crammed into the space behind the back seat?

'He'll be so pleased, you know. At that age, there aren't many left to visit.' Guilt won her over easily and she locked the car, sighing. Delia adjusted her snug pink hat and smiled contentedly at Heather as if she might, after all these difficult years, seem to have the makings of quite a dutiful daughter. *I'm nowhere near assertive enough*, Heather thought as she walked in through the clinic's main entrance hall. But then, there wasn't a lot to be assertive about. How stingy could she be with a mere ten more minutes, after all?

Uncle Edward was in bed this time, with a nurse checking his pulse. She wore a more starchily traditional uniform than was nowadays seen in National Health hospitals, rather as if acknowledging that private patients were paying for a return to old standards. She did not have a name-tag with 'Sandra' etched on to it, such as Delia had been so furious about when finally making her painful way up the waiting list and achieving a few hours in the Day Surgery unit in Putney, to have her veins done the previous year.

'Mr Phelps is feeling a little tired today,' she explained quietly with what her mother's smile told Heather was the right amount of deference. She heard a slight sharp exhalation from Delia and recognized that she had been holding her breath, waiting to see if the nurse committed the terrible chummy sin of addressing her patient by his first name. Worse even could have been 'Eddie', Heather thought, glad the nurse had passed the test.

She looked at Edward, shrunken and skinny in the ice-white bed. The curtains were only half open, and the pale sparkle of his eyes looked dulled. *How much worse can he get?* she wondered with pity. What a long drawn-out process a diseased end of life was. What sort

118

of state must his insides be in, if his outer appearance was so ravaged and frail? Had his bones powdered away their strength, shedding scales of worn-out calcium like flakes of dandruff? Were his organs crinkled and drained, like his skin? Heather tried not to shudder at the terror of fading vitality.

Startling her, Edward's eyes turned suddenly towards her, and his hand shot out quickly and grabbed her, strong as an owl's claw, just as she remembered it from her childhood. He grinned, showing toothless, pale gums. 'Bring the little girl again for me?' he asked, child-like, almost a whine. 'Little Heather,' he said, before drifting back into half-life.

'Won't be long now, I dare say,' Delia said to Heather outside Edward's room. She sounded very matter-of-fact, less as if she was talking about imminent death than as if she was waiting for a train and had just seen the level crossing gates opening at the end of the platform.

'Ssh, he'll hear you,' Heather said, moving them both away towards the reception area.

'Will you bring Kate again for him? He'd love that, you know. And Suzy too, he should see her,' Delia asked.

'I don't know. It's so depressing for them. And he doesn't really know them. He thinks Kate is me.'

'Well let him. He was happy back in those days. Why not let him pretend a bit?'

'I'll ask her,' Heather conceded. 'And now I really must go. I'll collect you later. What about the dog?'

'Oh I can't have him here dear, you take him with you – he'll enjoy a run in your friend's garden. And don't worry about me, I'll arrange for a taxi home. I shall like that.' She patted Heather's arm, then gave her a small but forceful push before turning back to Edward.

Heather felt as if she'd been sent out to play. Oh good grief, she thought, how did I get stuck with the awful

Jasper? He sat panting eagerly on the back seat waiting to be praised for having caused no plant-damage. In spite of having left all the windows open, she opened the car door to a newly resident smell, non-specific but definitely of dog – a mixture of Jasper's foul breath and flatulence. More of the qualities of ageing, Heather thought with depression. She felt superstitiously that her daughters should be kept safely away from the dying old man, as if decay was catching. It wasn't as if Edward had something that could be usefully warned against, as if he'd been a sixty-a-day smoker brought to premature decay by his own foolishness. Then she could have said to them after a dispiriting visit, 'There, now you know what happens if you smoke', and let it stand as a warning. In his case, all she could say would be, 'There, that's what happens if you're lucky enough to have a long life.' Better to let them believe in immortal youth.

Suzy knew who had been in the garden the night before. She knew even before she found his Zippo lighter on the grass by the dock. When Jasper started barking in the middle of the night, her light had been the first to go on, almost as if she had been waiting for Simon. She'd caught just the briefest sighting of him in his delicious leather jacket, sprinting down the lawn, past the paddock until he'd disappeared by the willows. For just one fleeting, thrilled, half-awake moment, she had imagined that he'd come for her. Now, in the midday heat she led her hot and dusty pony into the shade of the paddock oak tree and started to give him a thorough brushing. She worked hard, trying to eliminate by sheer mind-numbing physical effort the hopeless stupidity she'd felt after that blissful millisecond, when she realized exactly who Simon had come looking for. When, oh when, she pleaded to the guardian angels of adolescent girls, would she get a body like Kate's? Surely Kate, at very nearly fourteen, hadn't looked so like a juvenile stick-insect? Suzy leaned her head against the pony's chunky withers and wished she could weep dramatically. However hard she squeezed her eyelids and thought of the Ginger's death scene from Black Beauty, she couldn't manage to cry unless something physically hurt. She still easily howled for a grazed knee or banged elbow, but really creative crying, the sort where sad tears trickled down a perfectly still and beautiful face, this was beyond her. Perhaps if she could produce these instant magic tears, then Simon would just happen to come looking for his lighter, and find her, and comfort her . . .

'What on earth are you doing?' Tamsin's strident voice startled the pony, and his head bounced up, knocking Suzy off-balance.

'Bluebell! You stupid animal!' she yelled at him as she stumbled against the tree, grazing her arm. Tears did threaten then, just when she didn't want them.

'Thump him. They have to learn,' Tamsin advised from a safe distance, leaning against the paddock fence.

'No, he didn't mean it. You frightened him,' Suzy said, recovering quickly and stroking the pony calm again. His eyes were wary of Tamsin, who wore discomfiting fuchsia pink. 'He's probably worried someone might want him to go out for a ride. He thinks it's too hot, and he doesn't want to run about or carry anyone.'

'He's a bit small for carrying anyone over six,' Tamsin said scornfully. 'How do you know what he's thinking anyway? *Do* they think?'

'Bluebell does,' Suzy told her defiantly, continuing gently with her brushing. She felt as if Tamsin was insulting a favourite teddy bear, laughing at love for an outgrown toy. He was so comfortingly soft to lean on when she felt miserable, the least she could do was defend him.

121

Tamsin idly adjusted her bra strap, a habit that Suzy had more than once bravely told her was really annoying. The black elastic pinged against her chubby pink shoulder and she said, 'Ouch that hurt. This thing is getting really *tight*.' Suzy went on brushing, too miserable to rise to the showing off. 'You should have stayed over with me last night,' Tamsin started saying, getting on with the point of her visit, 'Shane got *really* friendly.' She perched on top of the fence to get a good view of Suzy's reactions.

'Oh yeah? So what happened?' Suzy asked.

'Well, Dopey Darren was going off home with Loopy Lisa, and said to Shane "Are you coming?" and I looked at Shane and he looked at me and said "No not yet." '

'And? What then?'

'Oh he had some more drinks and I asked him if he fancied a midnight swim, but he said he couldn't, he hadn't brought his stuff, so I said he could borrow Simon's, but really I thought we could just skinny-dip – Mum and Dad had gone indoors to start on the gin, and then he said no thanks again and went home. I think he took a couple of bottles of champagne with him, but don't tell Dad.'

'Is that *it*?' Suzy put the brush away in her grooming kit and wiped her hands down her T-shirt. 'Nothing else? No snogging in your changing hut?'

Tamsin looked a bit disconsolate. 'Well no, not yet.' She grinned, recovering. 'That'll be next time. When we go camping on the island.'

'They don't like other dogs,' Julia greeted Heather before she'd even stepped out of the Renault. The two black labradors bounded around the car, sizing up Delia's shaggy terrier like a pair of swaggering teenage boys spoiling for a fight.

'I'll put him on a lead and tie him to your fence under

the tree then,' Heather said, fearful for her car seats as much as for the dog suffocating in the heat. She climbed out and hauled the nervous Jasper after her. It was clear that because she was actually paying for Heather's presence that day, Julia was going to be slow to treat her to the usual courtesies of friendship. It was the price of getting your hands dirty, Heather thought, knowing that if she was being employed to choose wallpaper (though not to hang it) or to advise on a revamped wardrobe (though not to sew up a hem) both she and Jasper would be immediately offered a cooling drink.

Julia was carrying a trug and was dressed for the kind of ladylike gardening that she preferred: deadheading the marguerites, collecting sprigs of mint for sauce, in a faded print frock which Heather knew Kate would kill for if she'd spotted it at the Scouts' jumble sale. 'They won't need much attention will they?' Julia asked anxiously, as Heather lugged the plants out of the back of the car.

'Practically none at all,' Heather reassured her. 'Like anything in a pot, water and feeding are obviously important, but other than that,' and she paused, eyeing the trug full of dead petals and feeling irony creeping on, 'these won't even need dead-heading. Now where are the pots and the compost?'

'I had the garden centre boy take them straight through to the courtyard,' Julia said, leading Heather through her kitchen to a pair of French doors at the side of the house. Beyond was a small sheltered terrace, walled-in and cool, and furnished with five large terracotta pots and several plastic sacks of ericaceous compost.

'Oh good, they sent the right stuff,' Heather said. 'Nigel did explain they wouldn't grow in the chalky earth?'

'Oh yes. But I wanted them here by the kitchen,' Julia said rather dreamily, 'where I can see them and think of Italy.'

'Italy?' Heather started splitting open the first bag of compost, unavoidably picturing Julia engaged in sex that was too debauched simply to require thinking of England.

'Lake Maggiore. Charles and I used to go in the spring to see the camellias on Isola Bella. It's amazing how much you miss them.'

'Camellias?'

'No, husbands. Cup of tea?' Julia, at last remembering her manners, dashed around the kitchen filling the kettle and assembling crockery. 'He's been dead four years now and there are still little things I can't quite do, like give his old spectacles to the Oxfam shop. They're always asking for them for short-sighted Africans. I keep them in a drawer by his side of the bed.'

Heather managed, just, not to ask if she meant myopic Africans. 'I imagine that must happen to everyone,' she told her. 'I'm sure there'd be loads of things of Tom's that I couldn't bear to get rid of if he suddenly died.' Heather stopped pouring compost into the third pot and thought for a moment. What *would* she find impossible to part with? Most of Tom's personal bits and pieces disappeared with him on such a regular basis that if the police came round and asked her to identify him from only his luggage (assuming some awful mishap where his body was distressingly unseeable) she'd probably be quite shamefully unsure of what was his. Even his watches changed frequently, as he picked up irresistible bargains in the world's best duty-free markets.

'You do too much tidying up after they've gone,' Julia was saying, bringing tea out to Heather. 'You arrange it so you can manage alone and then find you've overestimated what they actually *did*, because you know mostly when they get older they just sit about in a chair, trying to look important, with a large newspaper. When you've realized that then you have to find things to keep yourself busy.'

'Like the Parish Council. You do a lot for that.'

Julia smiled. 'It was my way of getting back into being social. People are very kind at first, they invite you everywhere and after a while, when you can face it, you invite them back. But really you are much preferred if you are half a couple.' She laughed. 'The English are embarrassed about the solitary ones, in case they need something emotional that partners are supposed to give each other hidden away in privacy. Now I'm part of a committee instead of half of a pair, I've regained more or less a safe position.'

Heather dug and planted and thought about how Julia tended to call for jumble or donations at drinks time. Loneliness, she should have realized. Another time she would try not to see her as a nuisance. 'What about marrying again?' she asked.

'Impertinence!' Julia said with a grin. 'And how many men in their sixties or thereabouts do you imagine are left freely available for more than ten minutes in this county? Or any county come to that?'

'There's that writer staying with Margot,' Heather suggested disingenuously, turning her reddening face down and concentrating on heeling in the third of the plants.

'Oh him. I've heard about him. Doesn't look at anything over twenty. That's the trouble with men,' Julia said in disgust, crashing her tea-cup into the sink. '*One* of the troubles, I should say. Now come out to the back and look at my garden.'

Heather could see what Julia had meant earlier about leaving herself too little to do. Her garden was planted and planned strictly for minimal maintenance, with well-controlled shrubs and large clumps of old-fashioned, sweet-smelling roses that needed little pruning. Where earth showed, a mulch of pulverised bark smothered any possible weeds which saved both time and Julia's ageing knees.

'There's not that much to do, you see. I used to have a boy for mowing, but then I bought one of those hover things so at least there's that,' Julia said with a slight sigh.

'Vegetables?' Heather suggested, looking at a rather sparse west-facing bed that cried out for bean poles and cabbages.

'Dogs,' Julia explained, glancing back to where the pair of labradors lolled on the terrace, ensuring Jasper didn't dare make free with their territory.

Heather tidied the little patio, tied pale green name tags to the plants, collected her tools and Jasper, and prepared to leave Julia to think of how to fill the rest of the day.

'I chose those plants very carefully you know. Things that meant something,' Julia told her as Heather loaded her car. 'That one called "Charles Michael", that was his name of course, so lucky to find a camellia called that. And "Coppelia", we were very fond of the ballet.'

'What about "Donation"?' Heather asked as she closed the boot. 'Was that because of doing charity work?'

Julia chuckled. 'Only in a manner of speaking. It was my little joke, Charles would have appreciated it. When he died it was very sudden, lots of bits of him were still in working order, so rather than waste them, someone out there has got a kidney, and the corneas went too. Donation, you see.'

As Tom loaded his bag into the car boot, hung his jacket from the rail over the back seat and settled himself in the car, he felt home life slipping away and work life taking over. The outside shell of home-Tom, the man who lolled about drinking beer in the afternoons, made comfortable love to a warm woman and generally pottered about in an unthinking way, taking for granted

126

an easy family life, was being sloughed off like a snakeskin as he started the car's engine. Work-Tom took over. His clean pink hands on the steering wheel looked as antiseptic as those of a scrubbed-up surgeon just about to perform an appendectomy. He was already thinking ahead to the other life, weeks of conditioned air instead of fresh summer garden smells, dull flavourless mineral water instead of fragrant heady wine, but there could also be the rough sexual thrill of a wiry man's body to compensate for the lack of Heather. Hughie might or might not be on the crew this time. Half of him hoped he wouldn't be, but only the half that was frightened of aircraft and still wishing he didn't have to leave Oxfordshire. The other half of him, the bit that thought kerosene on the wind was a better perfume than Chanel No 5, was already mentally in a Singapore Sheraton pretending that he was engaged in nothing more devious than a spot of assisted wanking.

Heather rushed home, superstitiously eager not to let Tom leave home for work without saying goodbye to her. It was all that talking with Julia about dead husbands. The automatic gates were opening just as she arrived, and Tom was about to pull out into the road. 'Wait, don't go yet!' she called out of the window to him as he waved casually, showing no signs of stopping. Heather gave the horn an urgent blast and she pulled up on the grass verge by the gate, blocking Tom's exit. As he got out of the car Heather noticed that he didn't appear too thrilled to be stopped. He looked grouchy and defensive, as if he expected her to be about to ask if he'd remembered something mundane, such as had he put the dustbins out or paid the electricity bill.

'I just wanted to say goodbye properly,' she told him as she wrapped her arms round his surprised body, and wondered if it was the fact that she smelled of warm compost and sweat that made him seem reluctant to touch her. He was so clean and crisp, as if both he and his uniform shirt had been triple starched together. 'You will be careful up there in the sky won't you?' she said by way of a *bon voyage* blessing.

'Course I will. Always am, not that much can go wrong.'

'Don't say that!' Heather laughed and held up her crossed fingers. Over his shoulder she could see a large car slowing as it came out of the centre of the village towards the riverside houses. It was the cherry red Mercedes. She clutched Tom tighter to her and felt him positively twitch with surprise.

He put an awkward arm round her carefully as if afraid of causing creases. 'Hey, it's OK, I'll miss you too,' he was muttering into Heather's hair as Iain, with a passenger, drew level, slowed almost to a halt and grinned mischievously at her. She uncrossed her fingers behind Tom's back and rearranged them into a rude V-sign. Leery bastard, she thought as he swished past as slowly as a kerb crawler before turning the huge car into Margot's gateway.

Chapter Nine

'You know a secret that I don't know,' Margot's voice sang accusingly down the phone to Heather like a child taunting in a playground.

'What kind of secret?' Heather inquired carefully. It could be anything; it could be that Margot suddenly wanted to be told how to grow tomatoes that didn't split their skins while they were still green, or to tell her about a diet guaranteed to lose ten pounds in a week without giving up gin.

'I'll come round and we'll talk about it. Down by the river with a drink where no-one can hear us.' Margot's exaggerated whisper sounded gleeful, and Heather's spirits dropped. Margot was capable of great excitement about both diets and plants, but not to any extent that required tiptoeing to the river's edge to discuss them privately.

From her chair on the terrace, Delia could see Suzy and Tamsin swimming like lithe porpoises in the pool. When she was young, swimmers had breast-stroked steadily up and down and up and down a pool, purely for the exercise, or had rushed in and out of the sea at Eastbourne, gasping at the chill before bravely plunging into the waves for a bracing good-for-you swim. Water had been too cold for playing in then. The two girls lazed, and wallowed in the warm water, luxuriating, twisting, floating and diving like seals under and about wherever they fancied. Delia regretted suddenly that she had never opted to be one of those busy, determinedly athletic old people, the ones she saw from her flat going out after the bus-pass hour in pastel tracksuits and unsuitable tennis shoes that bounced like whitewall tyres, to take part in OAP step'n'stretch classes. She'd always thought they looked so ridiculously, well, American, was the only word that came instantly to mind. They reminded her of Florida, of the old people who banded together to enjoy their Golden Years in hearty packs. What, she thought as she watched the two girls effortlessly flexing their endless strength, was so golden about crinkled skin, muscles that took till lunchtime to regain a full range of movement after a night's sleep, and an ever-growing list of pleasurable things that one was sure wouldn't be done again this side of the next life? *I'll buy a swimsuit*, she resolved, *and cross one thing off that list.*

Margot wasted no time, Heather thought, as she watched her stride up the drive. For a bulky woman she could certainly get around fast when she chose, and she reminded Heather of a floral carnival float breaking the speed limit on its way to the parade. Her mass of strawy hair was flying around as she walked, and her scarlet silk skirt splashed with yellow and white daisies streamed out behind her, filled with air like a racing yacht's spinnaker as she bustled across the gravel path.

'Glad I caught you,' Margot said breathlessly as sheer enthusiastic momentum carried her past Heather and on into the kitchen.

Heather thought these words were ominous. At *what* had she caught her? She feigned bewilderment and busied herself with the intricate preparation of a couple of strong spritzers. 'What's the great mystery, Margot?' Then flinging down the lemon she had been slicing, she gasped dramatically, hand to throat, and teased 'Oh no, you haven't found out about me and Russell and the trip to Rome have you?'

'What? Oh don't be silly,' Margot scolded, not even

pausing for a second to allow for doubt. 'Whoever in their right mind would want to go to Rome with my husband? He'd spend all his time pricing up Ferraris. No, no. What I want to know is what it is you've not been telling me and, please, don't pretend there's nothing going on,' she ordered, wagging her gold-painted fingernail at Heather. 'I know there's some big mystery, and I can't *wait* to hear it.'

'Let's go down to the river. We'll feed the ducks,' Heather murmured as she gained time by rifling through the bread bin.

The two women strolled down the garden, Margot giving an excited little skip every now and then and grinning in a keyed-up fashion that Heather thought almost charmingly childlike. It gave her a few moments to think about what to tell her, but that, of course, depended on what Margot already knew. She must know something, after all. She was positively keyed up with the burden of guessed-at gossip.

'So what's got you all inquisitive then? What am I supposed to have done?' she asked as they settled themselves on the bench looking out over to farmland across the water.

'You're very naughty, you know that?' Margot said. 'You knew him all along, didn't you, and you let me rattle on about Iain MacRae and him being a Sir and all that, and you knew him all the time.'

'Not all the time. Not for a very long time, actually,' Heather corrected her, and took a long sip of the cool drink. 'But why do you think so anyway? Has he said something?' It occurred to her she should have known better than to trust him.

'I was in his car. I saw you give him quite a nasty deliberate v-sign, pretty spiteful for you, you're not usually like that. And I know it couldn't have been meant for me because we haven't had words. Not yet anyway. We will if you don't tell me anything,' she giggled. 'So I reckoned, and with a sod of a husband like Russell you get to be quite a detective, I reckoned that meant you knew Iain well enough to dislike him. But of course when I asked him, he did that awful thing of just tapping his nose and saying "Aha, wouldn't you like to know." I *hate* it when people do that, don't you?'

'Yes I do,' Heather agreed. 'They always look so pleased with themselves. I can just imagine Iain.'

'Ah, so I was right, you *do* know him,' Margot leapt in quickly. 'How well and where from?'

'He didn't tell you then?'

'He said I should ask you. He said it was no secret as far as he was concerned and that it was entirely up to you.' Margot had calmed down now and was placidly lighting a cigarette, confident that she could settle back and wait for a truthful reply. 'It was a terrible thing to say, you know, guaranteed to make me far more curious than if he'd told some suitable lie. So you can blame him.'

'Oh I will, I will.' Heather herself was thinking about a suitable lie. He could hardly be an old childhood friend, Iain was so obviously a perfectly sanded-down, smooth-cornered ex-public school type. If it wasn't that lust was more or less classless, their paths would hardly have crossed out in suburban Staines. Someone she'd met on a holiday? That wouldn't merit a lasting up-yours loathing. 'He's my ex-husband,' she said simply, smiling her honesty directly into Margot's astonished eyes.

'He isn't!' Margot exclaimed. 'I don't believe you!'

'OK, that's fine. You asked, I told you.' Perhaps she should have said that to Tom when he'd asked, and if he'd reacted in the same way then at least he couldn't complain later that she'd been lying. She'd found it a useful trick, when young and still living at home and trekking daily to the college, simply to tell her mother the dreadful truth about what she was up to. It saved

132

having to remember what lies she'd told to cover her tracks and which might need to be recalled on the inevitable cross-examination. When Heather arrived home sleepily on a Sunday morning from a party the night before, her mother would concentrate her inquisitive gaze on the washing up or something interesting in the fridge and ask things like, 'And did all the boys stay the night too? I'm sure Wendy's house only has three bedrooms.'

Heather would yawn and stretch and languidly answer, 'Oh we all just slept together, some on the floor, some on the beds. Just like an orgy, you know?'

'Now don't be silly,' Delia would say, tutting. 'Wendy's not the type to allow that sort of thing.' Wendy *was* the type, though. It was just that Delia wasn't the type to believe it.

And now here was Margot, sitting under Heather's willow, admiring the feathery-fronded astilbes and niggling for a more credible answer. 'No, really. How *do* you know him?'

Heather frowned. This wasn't supposed to happen. Margot was supposed to laugh and then politely give up. She got up and threw chunks of bread to a pair of cruising mallards trailing three half-grown ducklings, the remains of their fox-ravaged family. 'Actually it's true. I told you about it on the way to speech day. It was Iain that I married and I haven't seen him since the day he put me on the train in Edinburgh and sent me back to my mother. Must have been, ooh, all of three months later. And before you ask, I haven't *wanted* to see him, either.'

Margot became unusually pensive. 'What does Tom think of him suddenly turning up here?' she asked.

Heather fidgeted with her glass and picked out a piece of ice to melt over her hot fingers. 'Tom doesn't actually know,' she confessed. 'I sort of didn't quite manage to tell him last night, and today was a bit of a rush and now he's gone off to work.'

'You didn't *tell* him? Your mother must have seen him at the party, what did she think?'

Heather felt very shifty confessing to Margot, 'Well she doesn't actually know either. I'd rather she didn't. All that stuff was over years ago. Years and years ago. It was just a few months out of a lifetime, that's all.'

It didn't feel like 'that's all' the next morning, when Heather was getting ready for the lunch with Iain. It annoyed her enormously that she seemed to be caring quite a lot about what she wore. Neither dowdy nor dressy, but something effortlessly stylish in between was the impression she was aiming for, as she stared blankly into her wardrobe and pulled out a few possibles. He's already taking up too much of my thoughts, she complained to herself as she tried on a sandy linen shirt over a cream body and a long, side-buttoned toffee-coloured skirt. After putting on make-up and then crossly scrubbing most of it off again to ensure that she looked a lot less than eager, she escaped quickly into her car. On the way out she promised Delia, who had a left-out face on, that she wasn't missing a treat, just a boring business lunch at which the relative properties of cow manure versus horse were likely to be the most fascinating topics of conversation. It's not far from the truth, she thought, as she drove through the village, Iain will probably talk a lot of crap.

Kate, on her reluctant way to the kennels, had to wait on the pavement while the scarlet Mercedes glided out through Margot and Russell's massive iron gates. Iain's hand came up and waved a regal greeting to her, but Kate couldn't fool herself that his eyes were on anything but the road. His absence was a disappointment – it left nothing to lighten the tedium of walking two moody basset hounds and a Pekingese with a bladder problem. 'With all that fur, it's hard to tell when he's actually lifting his leg, so be patient with him,' Margot warned her as she searched through the shaggy pelt to find somewhere to fix the lead. Kate hung around on the edge of the orchard long enough for the three dogs to become thoroughly tangled while she watched some of the film crew attaching cables as fat as fire hoses to something in a lorry. Brian, his jeans drooping to expose road-digger's bum-cleavage, was shouting something about a 'jenny'.

'A generator, to you and me,' Margot explained, proud to show off the new knowledge she was acquiring. 'Nothing's happening yet, nothing worth watching. No actors or anything,' she told her as she patiently helped Kate to sort out the leads.

Kate wandered across the recreation ground towards the woods, hoping she wouldn't come across Simon. She hadn't seen him since the party. Hadn't seen him, she reminded herself, since he'd sneaked into the garden and wandered around in the dark like a lovesick swain. *Gutless idiot*, she said to herself, tugging at the lumbering basset hounds, didn't even have the nerve to throw stones at her window. The worst he could have got was a sleepy 'Fuck off' from her; surely he should have had the nerve to risk that. Darren wouldn't have been so pathetic. If he'd gone into the garden in the middle of the night, she was sure he wouldn't have expected to go home without what he and his mates called 'a result'.

The car park at the restaurant by the river was almost full, for which Heather was thoroughly grateful. She would have hated to find that she and Iain were a lone couple, with too many waiters being over-solicitous, and stilted efforts at conversation echoing coldly in an empty room. The Mercedes was already there, having travelled the same route as her own Renault, probably only minutes before. The fact that they had travelled separately from the same place gave the meeting an unwelcome atmosphere of the clandestine.

Heather parked nervously between a Volvo and a Mini, too close to the next car to open her door properly, so she had to struggle out from between the two cars feeling hot and crumpled and undignified. Linen was a bad choice unless you were prepared to stay immobile and upright, she thought, as she so frequently did. The fabric always reminded her of lamb's tongue lettuce – neither could be bettered for their capacity to become unappetisingly limp, almost as you watched, as if the effort of staying uncrumpled was frankly too demanding, and they gave up the ghost quite gratefully after just a few triumphantly crisp moments. As she locked her car door and slid herself sideways between the front wings of the Renault and the Mini, she realized that her hands and legs were trembling and that a few minutes in the Ladies would be useful for deep-breathing her way back into some sort of reasonable composure before facing Iain.

But inside the restaurant, just as her eyes were adjusting from sunlight to gloom so that she could see which was the right door, both her hands were grabbed and Iain kissed her on each cheek with a loud 'Heather, darling you look marvellous!' I don't, she thought glumly, tension and her inept parking making her feel clammy all over, so that's lie number one. She resolved to count them during lunch.

'What would you like to drink?' he went on, leading her by the hand through to the bar, as if he was still taking charge of a teenager.

'Just mineral water please,' she told him primly, fighting a childlike urge to wriggle her hand out of his, as if he were an embarrassing aunt leading her across a road. 'And I'll be back in a minute.' At least now he had to let go.

136

In the cool sanctuary of the Ladies, Heather seethed with a small bout of anger. She wrestled with the poppers of her body inside the cubicle and wondered why such a trivial thing as a pair of social kisses should make her so cross. It was his air of assuming, she decided, as if the fact that she'd agreed to meet him for lunch meant that she was *pleased* to meet him for lunch, completely thrilled, and delighted, as if she'd been waiting twenty-five years for nothing else. As the noise from the flushing loo died down, Heather could hear a pair of women outside the cubicle discussing their respective lunch dates.

'Well, if I have the lobster he'll think that's a come-on, and it'll be an afternoon of the hot stuff. *Too* hot in this weather,' one of the two was saying with a giggle. There was a small silence, for the application of lipstick, Heather saw, as she emerged from the cubicle and took her place alongside them to wash her hands. They reminded her of Margot, blowsy and round-bodied, luxuriating in the large amount of space occupied by their presence, with even their hair teased out and up into extra fullness. One of them, a blonde with long shiny pink talons for nails, was wearing a dress printed with brazen scarlet roses, as if to draw attention to her own plump, seasonal ripeness.

'What about steak then, Maureen?' the other woman said.

'It's not really a steak sort of day is it? And anyway I like it rare and you know what they're like when they see blood,' was Maureen's considered reply. The two women gazed at their reflections thoughtfully, Maureen pursing up her lips into kiss-shape and rubbing delicately at a plummy smudge of colour.

Heather checked in the mirror that her nervous ham-fistedness hadn't resulted in her skirt being tucked into her knickers and opened the door, looking back at the two women.

'Why don't you have Dover sole?' she suggested with a grin as she left them to return reluctantly to Iain. 'No-one could possibly get excited about that.' She would much rather stay in the loo with these two, discussing the sexually arousing, or otherwise, characteristics of food.

'I've organized a table for us by the window over-looking the river,' he told her as he handed her a glass misty with ice-chill.

He looked terrifically pleased with himself, Heather thought, as if he'd just fixed an upgrade from tripper-class to Concorde. She wished she hadn't been so cautious, that her glass contained something less feeble than fizzy water – it looked as if it promised so much, all those excited bubbles, the hunks of ice, bright as diamonds, and the pretty lemon, as if the drink positively deserved decoration. She took a sip as she followed Iain to their table and felt the cool, relieving trickle making its way to her stomach. She sat down and looked out over the towpath at the squawking ducks, wishing she could think of something to say, something pithy, witty, something that would sum up once and for all why she felt twenty-five years worth of anger bubbling gently inside her alongside the fizzy water. True, the anger had simmered till the taste was so very nearly gone, but Iain's return seemed to have respiced it.

'Sorry,' Iain said suddenly, watching her staring blankly at the view, 'I should have realized that over-looking the Thames is hardly a novelty to you. We should have run off to London, parking at separate stations of course, and had a secret rendezvous at the Caprice or the Ritz.' He was grinning at her like a thrilled child.

'It's all just a bit of fun to you isn't it?' Heather said, accusingly, her glass slamming down on the table harder than she expected and splashing beaded water all over her hand. The women who had been in the Ladies were at the next table with their respective partners, looking across at her with frank and friendly curiosity.

Iain raised his hands defensively. 'Hey, well it *is* fun, isn't it? You must admit it's one hell of a coincidence, me turning up here and finding you.' His expression changed to puppy-like pleading. 'I mean, it was such a long time ago, we're all grown-up now, aren't we?'

'*One* of us was grown up *then*,' she retorted. 'Or was supposed to be.'

'Yes, well, *mea culpa*,' he conceded. 'I was a disgraceful cad and I apologize,' he said with mock humility.

How can a man the far side of middle age manage to look so boyishly contrite? Heather wondered. For the first time she looked at him properly, and studied his face. It was deeply lined and harshly textured from wind and weather, but the fine bone structure hadn't been quilted by ageing fat. His eyes were still richly blue and unclouded. Well, mid-fifties isn't so old, she thought, not these days. There were men of Iain's age collecting their children at the village infants' school gate. It used to be the age of your grandparents, of people with sticks and briar pipes and strange-shaped brushes for cleaning false teeth with powder. She smelled, suddenly, the gritty, Germolene-pink paste that Uncle Harold had mixed in the bathroom when she was a child.

Iain was smiling at her, watching her watching him, his own teeth as even and clean as a crocodile's. The sort of man who carries Clorets in his pocket, next to the condoms, just in case it turns out to be a lucky day, she thought suddenly. He picked up the menu. 'What shall we eat? Tell me what is the most delicious here.'

'Everything here is delicious.' She smiled across at Maureen and her friend who were still eavesdropping from the next table, and winked at them. 'I think I'll have Dover sole,' she said, raising her voice slightly.

The two women, to the confusion of their portly companions, giggled. 'Wicked waste,' the thinner one hissed from behind her hand across to Heather, glancing with wanton appreciation at Iain. While Iain concentrated on the menu, Heather took another look at him. He *was* still attractive, she conceded reluctantly, and then hastily amended her thoughts – attractive if you were looking for a rakish old bastard who wouldn't have been out of place as an eighteenth century no-good bounder. Ruthless seducer of young virgins and housemaids, that would have been Iain's *forte.* She could just see him in velvet and brocade making free with the kind of girl who blushed and shrieked 'Oh la Sir!' as he rummaged under her petticoats and changed her protests to squeals of delight. As she mused quietly to herself, the waiter suddenly appeared, bearing an extra-large ice bucket, carrying it flamboyantly over the heads of other diners like a joyous footballer with the FA cup. And no wonder, Heather thought, as he settled it into a stand next to their table and she watched him cheerfully struggling with the cork on a bottle of vintage Bollinger.

'I know you only wanted water, but I thought, as this feels so much of a special occasion, I could perhaps tempt you with this,' Iain said to her. 'You haven't actually gone teetotal, have you?' he then asked anxiously, as the waiter eased the cork out with a delicate and expensive pop.

'No I haven't,' she said, 'and actually I'd love some. But not too much of it.' He'd been good at champagne, she recalled, as she savoured the dangerously seductive bubbles. He'd had a knack of producing a bottle just at the right moment. The first time she'd gone to bed with him, there'd been a bottle first to quench her final doubts and hesitations as he gently freed her from her school uniform.

Here in the restaurant, while she dreamily sipped at her drink, she could quite clearly hear her friend Barbara's voice in the dank school changing room after games. 'Why are you having a shower? We never have showers, Leach the Les might come and get you!' It was true, nobody liked using the showers, with their inadequate curtains, lingering smell of hockey-sweat and the ever-lurking danger of the roving-eyed games mistress. The water had run rusty brown at first, she could remember vividly, the pipes flaking away inside from lack of use. 'You're going somewhere after school,' Barbara had accused, her loud voice attracting a curious group of onlookers as Heather, with guilty embarrassment, dried herself and put on a pair of brand new non-regulation shiny nylon frilled knickers specially for Iain to discover later beneath her uniform pleated skirt. 'Tomorrow you've got to tell. Don't forget,' Barbara had ordered as she'd rushed off to catch the train to Fulham. Telling was compulsory. As they'd lost their virginity, each girl had reported the deed to the others, fulfilling a solemn playground promise made back in the second year, when such an event had still been something to dread in the far-away future, something that each of them had assumed would probably take place on a terrifying marriage bed with a man who had just promised them all his worldly goods. How different reality had been: Barbara, on her sixteenth birthday, had eagerly donated her virginity to a spotty bass guitarist who could hardly believe his luck in the back of a Ford Transit van parked by the Thames near Eel Pie Island.

'One Dover sole.' Heather was jolted back to the present by the waiter.

Iain was watching her with amusement from across his salmon. 'You were miles away,' he commented. 'I hardly dared interrupt your thoughts.'

Heather smiled, 'I was *years* away, actually,' she admitted.

'Was I there?' he asked putting on an expression of mock trepidation.

She laughed. 'I'm afraid so.'

Iain leaned closer, half whispering, and brushed his hand against hers as she picked up her glass again. 'Do you remember that first time, with the champagne . . .'

Heather blushed and put the glass down quickly as if she'd just recalled an old and lingering allergy. She looked down at her food, quickly assembling vegetables on to her plate to avoid Iain watching her remember how he'd trickled the bubbles down between her breasts as she'd trembled with delicious anticipation on his bed. He'd licked slowly at the wine, down across her tight flat stomach, further on down to places she'd wondered if people maybe weren't legally even *allowed* to lick. Barbara hadn't reported anything like this, she'd thought at the time, *none* of the others had. She hadn't been able to use any of the words they'd included: 'Hurt quite a lot' 'All over a bit quickly' 'Probably better with more practice'. The six friends who'd so far admitted going all the way had left her with a blurred impression of a fast, fumbled, uncomfortable near-rape with an embarrassing midway interlude for the difficult (possibly even abandoned) application of a condom. She'd been very lucky, she realized. Perhaps she'd thought she'd never be that lucky again.

'So what have you been doing since – well since?' Iain asked.

'Marrying, gardening and children,' Heather told him. 'What about you?'

He looked slightly surprised, as if she should know, as if he thought she'd have followed his illustrious career with interest and maybe an occasional tweak of wistful regret. 'Writing, still, obviously,' he replied. 'This and that. Film scripts and so on.' Heather was enjoying the sole and didn't comment. 'Seen any of them?' he prompted.

142

'Any what? Films of yours? No, well I wouldn't know, I might have. Name some.'

'*Beyond Treason*, *Dead Lucky*, that kind of thing?'

Heather smiled at him vaguely. She'd seen the books, of course, his kind of sales figures merited prominent shop displays on every release. 'No, sorry Iain, not my kind of movie. I like mine more subtle. I'm more a Merchant Ivory type.'

'Obviously we're not compatible then.'

'Were we ever? The whole thing was always ridiculous, doomed to failure,' she told him, helping herself to more champagne.

The waiter was clearing plates. Maureen on the next table was ordering a *crème brûlée* and Heather wondered on her behalf what sweet and sticky intimacies that would or would not lead to later in the afternoon.

Iain lit a cigarette, still the same brand of French ones she had found so exotic at sixteen. 'I thought we were,' he told her softly. 'It was you who wanted to go home to Mother.'

Heather felt hot and quickly gulped some more of her drink. 'What else could I do? It was that or be murdered by that foul old nanny of yours. Her and her bloody knitting needle.' Heather was starting to feel tearful. She remembered Mrs Kirby sitting in the old kitchen chair in the half light, rocking rhythmically on the flagstones as she knitted something complicated in a Fairisle pattern for her precious Iain. At the end of a row, she'd waved the free needle towards Heather and whispered, 'Any wee problem you might be having, you come to me.' Then she'd leaned across and tapped the back of Heather's fingers with the cold steel needle, 'I can help ye.'

Iain reached across the table for her hand and she snatched it back. 'Come on Heather, she only meant to be helpful. Did you *really* want to start having babies at sixteen? You were hardly more than a child yourself.'

'Didn't stop you hauling me out of school and

143

marrying me, did it?' Her voice was rising. Maureen's rosy frock was leaning across towards their table.

'Nanny was quite experienced, you know, she wouldn't have hurt you,' Iain drawled casually, as if he was talking about removing a splinter.

'Oh, well that's terrific. How many other little abortions had she performed on the ancestral dining table? Or did they take place below stairs in the servants' hall where she thought little sluts like me really belonged?' Heather realized quite suddenly that she had got drunk. Too drunk to drive home, anyway. There would now be the complications of organizing a taxi.

'Would you like pudding?' Iain asked as the waiter approached.

'No. Actually I'd rather just go home if you don't mind. This really wasn't a good idea at all. I only wanted to come to tell you that my family know nothing about you, and that's because you are not the slightest bit relevant to the life I have now. I'd like it to stay that way.'

Iain smiled, conceding defeat with a graceful gesture of his long hands. 'I'm sorry. I just thought it would be amusing to see each other again.'

'You always thought everything would be "amusing". Some things weren't,' she replied flatly. He'd depressed her. The champagne had depressed her. She would have a headache by supper time and have a sleepless night. Sulkily, she decided it was all his fault.

'I'll drive you back to Friarsford,' he said as he signed the credit card slip. 'If you're worried about who sees you, we can pretend your car broke down.'

Heather felt too gloomy to argue and slid, unprotesting, into the creamy leather passenger seat of the Mercedes. Only as she was tiptoeing across the crunchy gravel, hoping to get to the safety of her bedroom and her comforting old gardening clothes before Delia cross-examined her, did she realize that Iain had never thought to ask what became of his baby.

Chapter Ten

Heather quickly shoved all her clothes into the laundry basket and then took them out again, deciding to take them downstairs immediately and give them priority in the washing machine so that she could eliminate the smell of the restaurant, the Gitanes, Iain. Her limbs felt heavy from lunchtime alcohol. She hurried into her swimsuit and then down the stairs to dive into the soothing pool.

Delia, who had been dozing with a detective novel under the walnut tree, was startled by the splash. 'How was your lunch, dear?' she asked as Heather surfaced. 'I didn't hear your car.'

'Er, no, it got a bit overheated. I'll have to collect it in the morning,' she told her, preparing to hide the lie by swimming under water for a couple of lengths. Why hadn't she simply said she'd drunk too much and to drive home was quite beyond her? What could have been simpler or truer? She seemed to be compelled to complicate things as much as possible. It was like knitting a scarf with five different colours at once and, after keeping each strand carefully separate till it was a couple of yards long, suddenly abandoning it for a kitten to play with. She felt pent-up energy churning about uncomfortably inside her, an unreleasable tension, rather too reminiscent of sexual frustration. Perhaps she was already missing Tom more than usual, or perhaps it was true that some women don't reach a peak of sexual desire until they are in their forties. Rather unfair of old Ma Nature if that *was* true, she thought. Most likely it was a combination of sunshine and champagne, she decided as she surfaced and swam on her back, gazing at the arc of blue sky above her. Water cleared from her ears and she floated, letting the sounds of the household start to invade her consciousness. From the paddock she could hear Tamsin and Suzy squabbling over whose turn it was to ride Bluebell. Tamsin had a beautiful leggy Palomino pony of her own, liveried and cared for in immaculate comfort and at huge expense at the village stables beyond the recreation ground. 'Lazy little sod would rather plod round your paddock on Suzy's pony than walk across the rec and tack up her own. It'll get all fat and lumpy, like your Bluebell,' Margot had complained to Heather, only weeks after the pretty pony had been acquired, complete with a full range of equine accessories, and its novelty had worn off. Margot and Russell, first-generation pony-owners, preferred to maintain its board and lodging safely away from their own premises, taken care of by Fenella Kenning, the sort of outdoor woman who owned seventeen pairs of jodhpurs and one out-of-date dusty evening frock, whereas Margot preferred to have seventeen glittering dresses and one never-worn, unrealistically small pair of jodhpurs.

'Have you got any plans for the rest of the day?' Delia asked Heather as she clambered out of the pool.

Heather considered vigorous activities that would help dissipate the bulge of stifled energy that she could still feel. It was worse than chronic constipation, heavy and slightly nauseating, lurking in the part of her stomach where butterflies sometimes feathered anxiously. Double-digging a new potato bed would probably help. 'I'll have to do some hoeing round the lettuces,' she decided, 'and the basil needs potting on. Then, if you like, we could go for a walk up along the High Street and have a look at the shops?'

'Yes I'd like that,' Delia said, then added, 'is there anywhere that sells swimsuits?'

*   *   *

You didn't get into cars with strange men, Kate knew. It was rule one from childhood. Or rule two, anyway, if you counted taking sweets from strangers as the one that came first, simply because you were likely to be younger when you were told it. The man with the Mercedes, the writer called Iain, was slowing down alongside her as she walked back towards home. Was this kerb-crawling? Kate wondered. Was he going to offer her money? That would be something worth telling Annabelle if she ever again deigned to phone. She would refuse, of course she would. She was paid well for walking the disgusting dogs, *really* well, simply because lovely rich Margot, who only read the kind of newspapers that reported on restaurants and royal gossip, was completely unaware that many people actually did all kinds of work for less than £5.00 per hour. But you didn't get to be rich and famous walking dogs. Iain was, after all, a man who had Movie-Power. If he couldn't make her a star, he certainly knew someone who could. The car pulled up a few strides ahead of her and, disappointingly, Brian of the baggy jeans was in the passenger seat. The window slid down and Iain leaned across as she approached.

'Kate. How lovely to see you.' She smiled broadly. He pronounced her name as if she was a box of silky hand-made chocolates. She wished he'd say it again, just like that, with a slight growl of pleasure. He grinned at her and she suddenly realized he *wanted* something. Her smile congealed, she was far more used to being the one who did the wanting. 'Could you do me the most awfully huge favour?' he asked. Brian, and the hot smell of hard manual work was wedged unattractively between her and Iain. 'I need your mother's car keys. She's had to leave her Renault at the place where we . . . she had lunch with someone, and I thought it would be

147

neighbourly to go and fetch it for her,' he finished with another persuasive smile.

He had nice eyes, Kate thought, for someone of practically grandfather age. 'OK,' she said simply, skipping off quickly.

A quick beep on the Mercedes horn called her back. 'And don't bother to tell her, OK? We'll just surprise her.'

Kate ran into the house, raided her mother's handbag for the keys and ambled slowly back down the drive to where the car waited, knowing that she was being watched and not wanting to look too childishly eager. Self-consciously, she felt herself loping with exaggerated elegance, which was difficult in flip-flops, as if she was strolling along a Paris catwalk. She hoped a favourable comparison with Claudia Schiffer was being made. Brian had now been relegated to the back seat, she noticed.

'Coming with us, for the ride?' Iain invited, patting the cream leather seat next to him. Kate jumped in, stretching out her legs to show off their tanned length, then gathering them back in again in case any possible part in this film involved being a very *young* teenager, vampire's victim or whatever, something like Suzy's age, which of course someone who was *really* Suzy's age would be far too juvenile and stupid to play. The drive took about fifteen minutes, during which Iain turned up the air conditioning till Kate's bare skin tingled icily. She didn't want to complain, he'd obviously done it to obliterate the whiff of Brian, who she thought smelled like the lion cage at the zoo.

'I take it you're friendly with Margot's boy, Simon?' Iain said as they swept past fields of rape.

Kate frowned. How 'friendly' was Iain implying? Surely he could tell Simon was a bit on the young side, for her? 'Well I know him, obviously. But we don't have the same social circles,' she said grandly. She glanced

148

sideways and caught Iain's mouth curved into a highly amused grin. He was teasing her, and she minded. 'He's at boarding school, so he's years behind,' she explained, making things somehow worse and feeling silly.

'Oh? I went to boarding school, so I suppose I should know what you mean,' he told her.

She simply thought he was mad; his schooldays must have been at about the time when children were still writing with chalk on little slate boards and calling all the teachers 'Sir'. Iain was a Sir, she reminded herself, thinking how he might have looked quite Lancelot-ish when he was young.

At the restaurant, to Kate's surprise, Iain handed Heather's keys to Brian and left him to drive the Renault back to Friarsford, keeping Kate and the Mercedes to himself. She'd assumed she and Iain would be in her mother's car, with Brian taking the Mercedes.

'Don't worry about the insurance,' he told her, misinterpreting her confused expression, 'Brian's covered for anything.'

'I'm not worried,' she told him, having given no thought to anything as adult and boring as insurance. He switched off the air conditioning and pressed buttons to open the windows wide.

'Real fresh country air, much better isn't it?' he asked her as they pulled out of the car park.

'Better than Brian,' she giggled. 'What's he been doing?'

'Working very hard. It's hot, he's busy. It's only body and heat,' he admonished her.

She wriggled slightly, it was the way he said 'body and heat', quietly and insistently, making them sound vaguely sexual. Nothing sexual about the smell of Brian, she thought, slightly shocked that she had thought of someone of Iain's age in connection with sex. That was for young, lively people with a lot to find out,

149

not for the old who should have found it all out and given it up long ago.

'OK, let's take the scenic route back. Not that there's anything round that *isn't* scenic,' Iain said appreciatively, pulling out of the car park and turning in the wrong direction. Kate felt a moment of alarm, but Iain was grinning at her as if they were out on a secret naughty jaunt. Surely he was really just a bit too old to be dangerous in the rape-and-murder sense? She had some vague idea that the really dangerous ones were actually fairly youngish, fit, body-builders who looked as if they could probably find women for sex through the usual social channels if they could only be bothered.

'You look like you're skiving off school,' she told him.

'Thank you, my dear,' he said. 'That makes an old man feel young. As, of course, does the company of such a pretty young girl.' Kate smiled cynically, well aware that this was a well-polished piece of gallantry. 'Perhaps we could have tea somewhere, if you'd like to,' he suggested.

'Yes please, I would,' she told him, sliding her feet out of the flip-flops and gathering them up on the seat in front of her. Being 'out for tea' was something she associated with her grandmother, an old person's idea of a treat. She thought of the restaurant at the top of Selfridges and the individual silvery teapots with too-hot handles. She wrapped her arms round her knees and gazed contentedly out of the window ahead of her, at the summer glories of the English countryside. Everything was at a peak of ripeness, she noticed. The barley ears were fat and shining. The trees were as intensely green as they were going to get for that year, just waiting, reluctant to spill over into the desiccation of autumn. The wild flowers craned out over the ditches, arching eagerly over each other, competing for passing insects and pollination as if aware that time was running out, and extra effort was needed for this last chance to reproduce.

'You have very grubby little feet,' Iain commented with amusement, as they sped through Streatley and across the river into Goring.

Kate wriggled her toes and inspected them. They were filthy, caked with mud and bits of dry grass. 'Well it's a sign of hard work, just like Brian and his smell. I've been walking Margot's dog-lodgers,' she told him pertly. 'A girl has to earn a living, you know.'

He laughed. 'Haven't you found yourself a lovely rich boyfriend to wine and dine you?'

Kate snorted with delight. ' "Wine and dine"? People like me don't wine and dine, we go clubbing, see bands, have parties. Well sometimes, anyway. Not much happens in a place like this. It's dreadful being a teenager in the country. I can't wait to learn to drive.' She looked sideways covertly, watching to see if Iain gave her the expected sympathy glance. He did, but still seemed to be laughing at her, which was annoying. 'I need a proper job for the summer really, nothing ordinary of course.'

'Course not,' he agreed.

She slid her feet back down to the floor and crossed her legs. 'I'm quite good at acting. I mean if they needed—'

'This place looks OK, don't you think?' Ian said, interrupting and infuriating her as he pulled off the road in front of a small café half-submerged beneath a jumble of honeysuckle. 'It says "Cream Teas". Would you like that?' Iain asked Kate, taking her hand and leading her through a small wooden gate into a shady orchard dotted with benches and tables.

Kate wondered about the hand that was holding hers. *Was* it being fatherly, or even grandfatherly? It was certainly a hand that was taking charge of her as if she was so very much younger than she was. He wasn't

151

quite old enough for grandparent status, or somehow proper enough for a godparent either, she decided, looking at the back of his head as they crossed the bouncy grass. He had too much hair, quite thick and long and streaky, like an old rock star who still expected to have just one more hit; and he wore black chinos, with a cream T-shirt and black linen jacket, like something out of GAP's window. He was more like one of those men who have a series of families – if *she* was his daughter she would probably already have been an aunt from the day she was born. There would be sure to be various older brothers and sisters, some who were long-ago grown-up with jobs as doctors or lawyers, with smart offices and secretaries of their own. The sprinkling of customers looked up from their scones as they made their way to a table under an apple tree.

'Those women over there are staring at you,' she pointed out to Iain as they sat down. 'The fat ones scoffing cakes. Look like they're on a day off from Weight Watchers.'

'Spiteful little girl,' Iain laughed at her, then glanced round and gave the women a half smile, acknowledging their interest. They blushed and smirked like teenagers.

Kate curled her lip with scorn. 'God, they're like a bunch of Sharons in McDonalds ogling some bloke,' she said. 'Gross.'

'What's "gross"? The fact that they're not in the first flush of youth, or the fact that I'm not?' he asked her bluntly.

Kate felt embarrassed and squirmed a bit on the bench. She was facing the sun and it burned on her cheeks, adding to her uncomfortable blush. Opposite her, Iain's clear blue eyes were looking directly and steadily into her face, waiting for her reply as if he really, truly wanted to know. 'Oh, neither, you know,

152

it's just, just an observation,' she floundered, biting her lip. 'Sorry, I didn't mean—'

'Didn't mean what?' he pursued determinedly. 'That we Aged Adults are all completely past it by the age of thirty? Ought to shut up shop with the first wrinkle?' He was laughing at her again and she smiled with relief. It wouldn't do to get on the wrong side of him, and besides he was nice. He went on, looking intently into her head. 'Katie, honestly, I know it's something you don't want to hear, but the sexual urge doesn't fade away like old-age eyesight. Most of us don't actually need the equivalent of reading glasses in order to get it up after the age of fifty.'

Kate hid in her hair, giggling with excruciating shame as all around her she could see interested heads turning in their direction. She felt like a small child hearing her father say 'fuck' in front of the vicar. Iain had spoken out loudly and clearly and emphatically, like a teacher dictating in two write-this-down-and-learn-it sentences the central dilemma of Othello.

'Sorry,' he apologized gently, reaching across the table and pushing her hair back from her embarrassed face. 'Didn't mean to sound off at you like that.'

'It's OK,' she said, wiping away a laughter tear from her eye. 'It was funny, really.'

'Funny?' He looked at her with a mock-hurt expression. 'Funny? That was my very soul speaking, child. Hey look, here's the waitress with your nursery tea.'

Kate watched as the waitress, a plump and pink young girl who was, she guessed, helping out her mother in the holidays, stepped carefully across the grass towards them, carrying a huge and obviously heavy tray. Kate, shocking herself, cast a quick spell of pure nastiness, willing her to trip on a grassy hummock and drop the lot, just to see how far tea for two plus

153

scones, jam and cream could spread. She imagined it like an infant's painting, great sickly splodges of strawberry, streaks of thick gooey cream, sharp-edged chunks of floral crockery, like a nursery-school collage. She said nothing to Iain about this secret vision as the girl laboriously shifted the contents of the tray on to their table.

'Lucky she didn't drop these,' Kate murmured through a blissful mouthful of scone, thickly heaped with clotted cream and jam.

'Yes, isn't it,' Iain agreed, in a tone of sly irony that told her he'd clearly read her wicked thoughts.

Later, in the car, as they sped back to Friarsford, Kate wondered if she had been missed at home. She imagined her mother was probably doing something mysterious in the greenhouse, or sitting in her little shed-office working out how much she could charge someone for telling them where their lupins would look best. (Or more likely, she thought, advising them if it was currently OK to *have* lupins.) As they cruised along the village High Street, she could see Darren Gibson leaning against the window of the hi-fi shop, trying to look cool. But *does* he? she wondered suddenly. She had never questioned it before. The fact that he was the coolest boy in the village had automatically meant that he was something special – now it occurred to her that perhaps it meant he was merely the sub-standard best of a thoroughly sad bunch. She certainly couldn't imagine having tea in an orchard and giggling about sex with him.

The last time Delia had bought a swimsuit, Lycra hadn't yet been invented. The blue-and-white striped fabric seemed extraordinarily lightweight, too insubstantial to be holding in her baggy stomach as pleasingly as it did. Her last swimsuit ('costume' they called them then) had held her in place by some kind of boned rubbery scaffolding, which smelled of old mushrooms if allowed to stay wet for too long. She stood uncertainly by the edge of the pool, wishing Heather would go and play with plants in her greenhouse, and clutched her pink cotton dressing-gown round her body. 'Haven't you got to do something with the basil?' she asked her, as Heather settled herself comfortably into a padded chair with a mug of tea.

'Did it before we went shopping, don't you remember? And besides, I ought to be here while you swim, just in case.'

'I don't see why, I'm not a child.' Delia pouted at her. She dipped a tentative toe in the water from the top step, very carefully, so as not to overbalance.

'It's nothing to do with being a child. I don't really like anyone to swim alone. Even Olympic breast-stroke champions can bang their head on the diving board and knock themselves out,' Heather pointed out reasonably.

'I don't think the diving board is likely to be involved,' Delia muttered. The water really was warm. She'd been worried that, in her new enthusiasm, she had overlooked the possibility that when Suzy and Tamsin dived in and came up grinning, using words like 'bliss' and 'boiling', they might simply be grateful that there was no ice on the surface to plunge through. They had young, warm bones. She slipped the dressing-gown off her shoulders and walked slowly but determinedly down the steps.

Heather couldn't remember the last time she'd seen so much of her mother's body. She knew Delia would prefer her not to be seeing it at all. Even as a small child, she could remember her mother always locking the bathroom door, and ordering her firmly to 'wait there' on the far side of shop changing room curtains, which were never quite wide enough. Heather vividly remembered the fussy twitching of the curtains to exclude gaps, and the exasperated tutting as a tug one way left a spying eye-width of a chink on the other. In the chic little High Street boutique where they'd bought the swimsuit that afternoon, Delia had declined to try it on, saying firmly that it looked all right, if it was a size 14 it would be sure to fit, with a small warning glare implying that if it didn't, it was through no fault of her own body.

Delia was making progress down the steps, splashing water over her arms to get herself used to the temperature. 'You could boil an egg in here,' she commented to Heather. 'It must cost a fortune to heat this.'

'The solar's been working overtime. I think the thermostat's a bit wonky,' Heather said. 'Usually it's about 78 degrees, and actually I don't think it's much more than 82 or so.' She watched as Delia's age-crinkled legs disappeared into the pool. She was touched to see that the front of her calves had a faded honey-combed pattern, mottled from sitting too near the gas fire in her flat during winter. She remembered how her legs had been almost burned scarlet each winter, when money had been too much in short supply to heat more than one room, in their boxy thin-walled house. Small deprivations at the time had been scoffed at, as if a preference for comfort was a sign of moral deficiency. Heather's friend Barbara had possessed an electric blanket on her bed, which Heather had greatly envied. 'They're dangerous things. And they're not at all good for you,' Delia had sniffed, showing she had more in common with Iain and his family than she would ever have guessed.

Delia was now cautiously making her stately way across the pool, a gentle breast-stroke with her head held carefully clear of the water, well within her depth.

'Goodness, Grandma's swimming!' Kate flopped down in the chair next to Heather.

'We are allowed to, you know!' Delia called out to her

from the water. 'Just because I'm old doesn't mean I've forgotten everything I've ever learned.'

'Sorry! Didn't mean to be rude, just that I've never seen you do it before. You're pretty good at it!' Kate called back, grinning at her. She looked at Heather and smiled. 'Second time today I've been told off for being ageist,' she confessed, biting her lip and feigning humility.

'Oh?' Heather said with interest, 'And who was the other one?'

Kate was gazing into the far distance by now, looking as if she was being easily distracted by the ducks. 'What? Oh, no-one particular, just this bloke I got talking to.'

'When you were out with the dogs?'

Kate got up and wandered along the side of the pool, filleting a geranium leaf as she walked. 'Yeah, sort of. Don't worry, I don't talk to the dangerous sorts of strange men, Mum.'

With parental hyper-instinct, Heather felt she was not getting the whole truth, but put it down to Iain-induced paranoia. Why on earth should Kate report every conversation she ever had? And, contrary to sound mother-advice, if you never talked to strangers, you never met anyone interesting.

'Your car's back, by the way,' Kate called from her perch on the end of the diving board.

Delia, who was now bravely tackling a full length of the pool, grabbed the end of the board. 'Who brought it?' she asked Kate, as if she knew (also instinctively) that there was some mystery here that was not going to be satisfactorily unravelled by her daughter.

Kate spoke loudly enough to include Heather. 'Brian, the one from Margot's who does electrical stuff. Don't ask me how he got here in it though, I couldn't tell you,' she said, shrugging her shoulders in a don't-care, not-interested teenage sort of way.

Heather was not deceived. *OK I won't ask you*, she thought, *not this time.*

Hughie's approach to flying was like that of an overgrown plane-spotter, Tom thought. He found every aspect of the plane fascinating. While passengers dozed or doodled, or stared unseeingly at the film, he hung around in the cockpit asking about this dial and that lever till Tom's co-pilot started making despairing faces at him. 'I'll bring some tea,' Hughie offered. Tom was happy with that. If Hughie was doing the serving, he knew he wouldn't be on the wrong end of the First Class purser's grudges. He knew what happened to passengers and crew who crossed her, and others. He'd heard them all giggling over drinks in the Singapore hotel about passengers who had dared to click their fingers demanding service. 'Only wiped the tea bags round the toilet bowl first, didn't I?' one of them had been saying. They'd all shrieked with vengeful laughter, like a coven of witches disguised behind the make-up, sunbed tan and nail polish. Faced with a collection of the women in a hotel bar, assembling ready for a nightclub sortie, he'd find himself sidling nervously past, as if terrified of being grabbed and debagged. No wonder he preferred the company of the boys, he reasoned to himself.

'One sugar?' Hughie asked softly.

'Please,' Tom replied. Hughie busied himself with the tray and the tea, looking cosily and contentedly domestic. Tom sighed. He had never expected that he would be in this awkward position. He'd always assumed it was only men who had affairs with their secretaries who had to do the dreadful scene where they gently explained that it was only a bit of mutual fun, surely they couldn't really have been expected to leave their wives. There was something far too adolescent and *girly* about all this painful drama – only one step away from eyeing up diamond-and-sapphire clusters in Singapore's duty-free. However could he have foreseen that Hughie was going to be the type who read the Habitat catalogue in bed, biro in hand, drawing circles round the code numbers of his favourite sofas?

Chapter Eleven

The weather changed over the next few days, for which
Suzy sent grateful thanks to God. It was colder, cloudy
and with rain skittering down in ten-minute bursts.
Tamsin's plans for camping on the island had become
very complicated, and Suzy was beginning to panic at
the scale of the adventure. All she had wanted was to
play Swallows and Amazons but without the sails –
rowing about in her little boat between the island and
the railway bridge, having picnics and laughing at the
boozy holiday-makers trying to deal with their hire-
cruisers. Then the real fun would be putting up Tam's
tent, cooking supper over a fire (sausages, it had to be
sausages) and sleeping out beside the duck nests and
the roosting swans. There didn't seem to be anything in
the plans that would worry even the most protective
parent, and she didn't expect any opposition from her
own mother.

Tamsin, however, was using the escapade for a
chance to practise a major piece of deception. 'I'm
going to tell Shane that we're going,' she told Suzy
excitedly up in the tree house, 'and then he'll come. I'll
get him to bring a friend for you,' she added with
terrifying kindness.

'What will we do with them, though? Will they stay all
night? Where will they sleep?'

'We can take a tent each,' Tamsin said, as if it was
quite obvious as a solution.

'Oh I see, we'll sleep in one and they can have the
others,' Suzy said and then immediately wished she
hadn't, for, judging by the look of complete scorn on

Tamsin's face, she had admitted a shameful amount of naïveté. Surely they weren't going to sleep with boys? Not at their age? Her class weren't even scheduled for the lesson in putting the condom on the plastic willy till after next Christmas.

'Tamsin, you're only just thirteen!' Suzy protested, horrified. 'We can't!'

'Oh we won't *do* anything, it'll just be a giggle, and for practice for when we're older. You could call it a dry run.' She giggled into her hand as if she'd made a dirty joke.

Suzy wasn't sure if she had or not and so resorted to trying to look superior. 'Suppose the parents find out?'

'Oh we'll tell them the boys just turned up, nothing to do with us.' Tamsin put on a big-eyed innocent look, as if she was practising that in advance as well.

'And how would you explain us taking a tent *each*?' Get out of that, Suzy thought, as Tamsin frowned and pondered carefully, inspecting her hair for split ends to help her concentration. A few slow moments passed and Suzy began to hope Tamsin would abandon the whole crazy plan. If she didn't, she'd just have to tell her she wasn't coming and that was the end of it, she didn't care how shaming it would be. No way did she want to spend a spooky night on the island with Shane and his terrifying huge mates. They'd drink lager and fling themselves about and make belchy noises to impress each other, like they did to annoy the mothers by the swings on the rec. She wished quite suddenly she'd joined the Sea Scouts instead, then she could do all this fun stuff on the river without having to try to get Tamsin to remember she was still a child. She could have been doing proper sailing, or gig-racing, or going to a proper camp with songs and games. One day, not too far ahead, Suzy predicted, Tamsin would be the star of the village bus shelter, her reputation scrawled up in letters even bigger than the ones about Lisa Gibson.

'I know!' Tamsin dropped the hank of hair and scattered picked-off ends down on to the orchard grass. 'I've got it, we'll get Simon to come too. Then Mum will think the tent is his. You wouldn't mind about sharing with him, would you?' Tamsin asked with a knowing grin, adding with insulting truth, 'And you'd be quite safe, after all it's your sister he fancies, isn't it? Everyone knows that.'

Suzy peered down from the treehouse and out across the orchard to the back of the house. The film crew had organized the whole façade to be covered in scaffolding, from which was being draped huge black cloths. Kate was there, talking to Brian but looking around her all the time as if Brian was really the last person she wanted to be with, but couldn't find anyone else who was better. At least Simon wasn't with her, not just at that moment. Probably, she thought, he was lurking behind a tree gazing at her from a safe distance. Somehow it didn't even cross Suzy's mind that Kate's darting eyes were searching for *him*.

Uncle Edward was clearly deteriorating. Heather drove her mother to the clinic and sat with her in his room, listening to the old man's uneven breathing as he dozed. Sometimes it seemed to stop, and Heather would hold her breath too, and wait. Then he would sigh suddenly through the silence and his shallow breath would resume. She was unbearably moved by, of all things, his hair, which a diligent nurse had carefully combed flat across his beige head. The hair, what there was of it, went the wrong way – Edward's parting was on the left, not the right – and Heather thought he looked as if he had been arranged for his coffin by an unobservant but well-meaning undertaker.

Delia seemed to take comfortable satisfaction from his steady downhill progress. 'I thought he was looking quite a lot worse today,' she told Heather as they sat at the bar overlooking the river in the Black Swan in Friarsford, ordering a ploughman's lunch along with ham and chips for Suzy and Kate who were joining them.

'Did you?' Heather commented. 'I honestly couldn't see any difference. He just looks as if he's already dead to me.'

Delia sipped her lager, made a face about the bubbles and stared around the bar. Like most old English pubs, it had decor more suited to winter, with its low beams, smoky yellow walls, treacly paintwork and cosy, scarlet-patterned carpet. Its brass knick-knacks, baskets of pine cones and vast log fire really only came into their own in the ever-lengthening Christmas season. In August the fireplace was neglected and dusty, as if no-one quite knew how to fill the space suitably, and the only real concession to summer was a vase of spiky and rigid gladioli perched awkwardly on the bar. In good weather, customers were expected to be outside, admiring the scenery. Today the lighting was gloomy to match the weather outside, and a few aged locals sulked in corners because the saloon bar was full of burly film crew bitching about the professional shortcomings of absent colleagues. Heather listened in and felt glad, as she so often did, that she was self-employed, with no office in-fighting or petty corporate jealousies to join in with.

'Of course he could go on like that for weeks,' Delia was saying about Edward.

Heather almost choked on her white wine at the thought that her mother might still be a house guest well into the autumn. Weeks more of tiptoeing round, pretending she wasn't conscious of being observed. Weeks more of Iain, sod him, living just yards away, ever likely to run into Delia at a village cricket match, the church fête or at a drinks party. The pub door opened and Kate and Suzy dashed in, accompanied by a cold damp blast of air and . . . Iain. Heather looked across at him in sudden panic, and he smiled at her over the top of Kate's wind-blown hair before heading tactfully for the other bar. He had a smile like a pirate, she thought, all badness behind the glamour. Suzy was pushing her way towards them, her freckled nose wrinkling from being on a level with too many armpits. Kate, Heather noticed, had disappeared, then she caught a quick glimpse of her, the mirror over the fireplace picking up her and Iain, heads close together in the other bar. Iain was still doing his pirate-smile, and Kate was talking fast at him. Then she saw him laugh, put his finger to his lips in a 'ssh' gesture, and gently push the girl back towards the saloon. He's been telling her, Heather assumed angrily. He's told her what our stupid secret is, and he's told her to keep it secret too.

'Here she is,' Delia announced as Kate slid on to the bench next to her grandmother. 'You nearly missed your lunch,' she admonished as the barman arrived with his overloaded tray.

'No I didn't. I *never* miss food,' Kate replied with a broad smile.

She looked suspiciously flushed and excited, Heather noticed. 'You look happy. What have you been doing this morning?' she asked in an innocently conversational way. Through the mirror she could see Iain sitting alone at the other bar, reading a newspaper and sipping Scotch and soda.

'Trying to break into films. That man staying at Margot's says he thinks he can get me into a crowd scene really soon. Isn't that *brilliant*?'

She was bursting with it, Heather could see. There was clearly nothing else at all in her head but the possibility of fame. She felt faint with relief, and relaxed enough to start eating her lunch.

'Working as an extra, you mean?' Delia was asking.

Kate put on a grand look. 'We call it "Support Artist", not "extra",' she explained.

'Oh "we" is it?' Suzy chipped in with envious mockery. 'D'you think they could find room for me and Tamsin?'

'Not a chance. The scene is supposed to be a cocktail party. There definitely wouldn't be any children.'

'Not unless they're hiding under the piano,' Suzy commented. 'I keep seeing films on TV where kids are hiding under the piano while grown-ups do things.'

'What sort of things?' Delia asked.

Suzy started a slow blush which told Heather and Kate exactly what sort of things.

'Oh those sort!' Delia snapped. 'You shouldn't be watching those sort of films,' she added, looking sharply at Heather.

'Mother, she's nearly fourteen, for heaven's sake.'

'All the more reason,' Delia stated obtusely, concentrating on her cheese and pickle.

In the mirror, Iain was wolfing down a sandwich. How easy it should be, Heather suddenly thought, simply to say to them all, 'Hey look in the other bar, there's a bloke I married,' as if he was no more significant than a chap who'd once done a pretty good job of rethatching the house. A bit late now.

While Delia rested that afternoon, Heather put on her fleecy-lined Musto jacket and her gardening boots, and took Jasper for a walk across the recreation ground to the woods and up the steep hill beyond. She had lettuces to thin out and there was a sudden ripe glut of tomatoes that needed picking from the greenhouse, but she wanted to get out and breathe the sharp, wilder air close to the big trees. Rain drops trickled on to the path from the overhanging chestnut trees, bringing with them a tangy scent which reminded her of bath oil. The sun was beginning to break through the oozing clouds, and the air was becoming steamy as the soaking ground blotted up its warmth.

'Hallo! Heather!' Julia Merriman, accompanied by her black labradors strode across the damp grass to meet Heather as she started climbing the hill.

'Hi Julia! How are the camellias settling in?'

'Perfectly well, they've each got a few new pale leaves already,' she said.

Heather smiled, satisfied that she'd got it right, though it would have been a pretty poor gardener who hadn't. Julia was bustling along with her dogs like a woman with an over-full diary, but Heather remembered how she had seemed, on her own premises, sadly under-occupied. Perhaps her own mother felt like that, filling the long days in Putney. Here at least Delia felt needed, even if it was only to tend a dying man and to scurry around getting cross about the state of Heather's kitchen.

'You could under-plant the camellias with tiny white cyclamen for the autumn,' she suggested to Julia, 'and then maybe sow something hardy and annual for when they've finished flowering, like mignonette or Virginia stocks.'

'Something to smell good you mean?' Julia mulled over the suggestions. 'Yes, that would be lovely, right by the kitchen.'

'Mix in night-scented stock seeds when you plant the others, then you'll get evening perfume wafting through into the house,' Heather told her.

Julia smiled broadly. 'Do you know, I haven't grown things from seed since I was a child? Mustard and cress and broad beans on blotting paper up the sides of jars. Charles used to do a few lettuces, which he then hid under cloches away from the dogs, but I've always been a plant buyer, not a seed sower.' Heather felt pleased:

166

Julia was looking quite excitedly inspired. 'We've still got an old propagator in the greenhouse,' she said, 'I could use that.'

The two women trudged to the top of the hill and turned to look back at the view. 'I never get tired of all this,' Julia said, gazing out over the village, the gentle curve of the river and across to the wide grassy flood meadows towards the hills beyond. 'Charles and I used to come up here on Sundays, before Evensong, in summer, with Fiona in her pushchair. I wonder if she ever thinks of this view, over there in Brisbane?'

'Probably,' Heather reassured her. 'It's probably one of those memories that gives her the odd twinge about missing England.' Julia had a lonely, faraway look. Heather crossed her fingers that Kate or Suzy wouldn't choose to live half a world away from her and Tom. It seemed to be what all men did, enchanting daughters far away from their homes. Her own mother must have felt, all those years ago, that Iain's ancestral castle was almost as far from Staines as Australia – in those days it took as long to get there by train as it now would for Julia to fly to visit her daughter. 'Do you still go to Evensong? I'm sure my mother would like to join you while she's here.'

'No, actually I go to Family Communion,' Julia confessed as if it was a wicked secret. 'They do proper hymns, Ancient and Modern and all that, but in addition, there's a lot of jollity and coffee and a biscuit afterwards and a chance to chat. I like that. Sometimes I make gingerbread men.'

'I'll tell my mother, then. She's fond of gingerbread,' Heather said, laughing.

Julia looked serious. 'I don't know what she's used to, churchwise,' she said warningly, 'but there's a certain amount of, well, chumminess. Signs of peace and all-join-in and such.'

The two women started the downhill trek, catching

up with Jasper, who, panting on his short legs, was still on his way to the top. As the path turned towards the village, they could see flurried activity centred on Margot and Russell's house. A small crane was hauling something that could have been lighting up close to the top of the scaffolding, and figures, tiny from up on the hill, criss-crossed the garden busily.

'Has anyone actually seen any actors or anything yet?' Julia asked, following Heather's gaze.

'Kate has, she says it's all going on inside the house. That's what the black-out stuff is for. They have cameras out on the scaffolding platforms filming in through the windows.'

'Can't think why they didn't do it all in a studio, if they're having to go to all that trouble,' Julia sniffed.

'Mystery to me too, but Kate's fascinated,' Heather said. Down below, Margot's automatic gates were opening and the cherry Mercedes glided like a toy down the drive, past the garden cottage and towards the road, indicated right and headed fast out of the village along the Oxford road. Good, thought Heather, now it's safe to go and see Margot.

'You've been avoiding me,' Margot accused Heather, waving the gin bottle at her. 'You knew I'd want to know how lunch with your ex went. I've been dying to know.'

Heather grimaced. '*Please* don't call him my "ex", Margot!' she said laughing. 'I don't like to think of Iain as "my" anything!'

'Sorry,' Margot said with exaggerated humility. 'Can I tempt you to a drink? I'm just going to have a teeny refill.'

'Tea would be nice,' Heather suggested, wondering if Margot usually made a start on the aperitifs before five in the afternoon. Margot made a face but went to switch the kettle on. Jasper paced around, his claws clicking on the beechwood floor, and he sniffed the air suspiciously, trembling gently as if aware that Margot carried the scent of every huge dog she was currently boarding. To humans, the kitchen simply smelled of its fresh sky-blue paint and new wood.

Margot bustled about opening and shutting the sleek maple cupboards, rummaging clumsily. 'Can't find a thing yet,' she grumbled, finally locating a box of Earl Grey tea bags. 'These do?' she asked, unwrapping the pack anyway and shoving them firmly into a blue glass jar.

'It's all terrifically pretty, Margot,' Heather complimented her, looking around the room. She sat on the window seat cushion, which was covered with blue, white and yellow flowered fabric piped with navy. 'I wouldn't mind living here myself.'

Margot grinned at her. 'Yes you would. It looks cute, but you'd miss the space. There's nowhere to be *separate*. Russell and I are falling over each other, which makes him think I'm always watching him. And you know how much space teenagers seem to need: Simon just seems to be all feet. I feel like bloody Marie Antoinette playing in that Wendy House thing she used to have.'

'Petit Trianon.'

'That's the one. I'm going to advertise for a nice couple to come and look after the rectory and they can live here. It would be lovely for two.' She stopped and splashed gin generously into a glass, adding tonic from a family-sized bottle in the fridge. She chucked in a couple of ice cubes, sending splashes over the granite work-top, which she mopped at with her finger and then licked. 'I'm sick of all those bloody au pairs. I'm not having any more of them,' she said, taking a gulp of the drink. 'Russell took more than a bit of a fancy to the last one. Did I tell you about that?'

She had, at length, Heather remembered, wondering if Margot's brain was starting to be clouded by alcohol. 'You did mention it, but it was ages ago,' she remarked gently.

'Not that bloody long or I'd have forgiven him by now. Little Swiss slut, topping up her earnings,' Margot said after another large swig of her gin. Heather got up and went to deal with the boiling kettle, finding a mug on the draining board. Margot was settling cosily into a cushioned cane chair and had forgotten about the tea. 'There's nothing particularly fancy about foreign, I keep telling him,' she was continuing. 'They're such stupid things, men: can't quite believe that *down there*,' she giggled and pointed towards her thighs, grazing her hand on the edge of the table as she did, 'we're all *exactly* the same. He's out late *again* tonight – says he's got a meeting. Huh.' Then she asked, rubbing her sore hand, 'D'you ever worry about your Tom, always out there in foreign parts, if you'll excuse the expression?'

Heather looked out through the window, through the trees and shrubs towards Margot's treasured rectory, which at the moment looked as if Christo had decided to have a go at turning it into one of his wrapped art-works. The roses climbing the walls underneath would suffocate, she thought. So would she and Tom if they didn't feel at least partly free. 'I don't think about it,' she told Margot, fairly honestly. 'I think it's my own arrogance really – I sort of imagine he doesn't exist when he's not here with us.' Margot was looking puzzled. 'He probably feels the same about me,' Heather added quickly. 'You could drive yourself mad imagining the worst all the time. Really, you can't even imagine accurately what kind of wallpaper is in someone else's hotel room, let alone exactly what they get up to in there, who they talk to, whatever. Pointless to indulge in that kind of torture.'

'Easy to say,' Margot said glumly, topping up her glass from the gin bottle. 'Easy enough to bloody say.'

'Hi Margot! Oh hello Heather. Is it drinks time? Shall I help myself?' Iain was suddenly strolling round the kitchen as if he owned the place. Heather noticed that he seemed more capable of finding his way around the cupboards than Margot was. Trust him to have made himself completely at home, she thought nastily. He quickly concocted another gin for Margot and assembled two vodka and tonics, one of which he put on the table in front of Heather, whisking away the remains of her tea at the same time.

'I really ought to be going actually,' Heather said, cursing herself for sounding so prim.

'Oh please don't, not yet,' Iain said, with his smile of ultimate charm, putting an insistent hand on top of hers to keep her in place. 'I just wanted to tell you how sweet I think your daughter is. So like you at that age.'

'Lovely girl,' Margot agreed, nodding over-emphatically.

Heather decided to invite her to come home with her for dinner, then she couldn't spend the evening getting even drunker and imagining Russell draped over one of his classy motors, persuading a gullible client how accommodating the back seats were.

'Good with the dogs, Kate. That's something else – Russell hates dogs.' Margot's whole face was puckering, collapsing like a balloon that's been too-long treasured after a child's party. Iain glanced across at Heather with a between-us look of anxiety. 'He says I should have given up that kind of work. Says it's beneath him to have a dog-shampooer for a wife.' Margot's round face was decidedly crumpled now and big, calm tears overflowed and trickled evenly down her cheeks. She clutched her drink tightly, as if afraid Heather might take it off her. 'And I don't want to be Margot any more,' she wailed, 'I want to be Maggie again, like I used to be.'

'Maggie?' Iain mouthed towards Heather. 'Who's "Maggie"?'

'I'M MAGGIE!' Margot roared angrily, jabbing herself hard in the chest.

Iain leaned back against the window, moving slightly closer to Heather.

'Margot is really a Margaret,' Heather explained quietly. 'Russell's always called her Margot, it's just sort of stuck.'

'Posher, that's why,' Margot growled. 'God I'm tired.' She yawned, her mouth wide and pink and uncovered, like a sleepy child.

She had a gold filling in one of her back teeth, Heather noticed. That was probably post-Russell too. 'Why don't you come home with me and have supper with my lot?' she asked, leaning forward and gently taking Margot's hand.

'I think I'll just have a little lie down actually,' Margot replied, wiping inefficiently at her leaky eyes with the back of her hand.

'Come on upstairs, then. And I'll phone later and see how you are.'

'Not ill,' Margot mumbled as she hauled herself out of the chair. 'If I get any fatter that chair will come with me when I stand up. Nearly does now,' she said, with a sad little laugh.

Iain made a start on clearing up the glasses while Heather manoeuvred Margot towards the stairs. Her bedroom was painted pink and white, with frothy white blinds at the windows. Everything was new and bright and clean, like the kitchen, with a wall-full of hand-made cherry-wood cupboards that still smelt slightly sawdusty. The glazed cupboard doors were lined with floral fabric, and Heather could hardly begin to guess at the final bill Margot must have run up at 'Inside Story'. She must have bought miles and miles of stuff for this little house, she thought, it's a real work of love and

172

bank balance. She settled Margot on the huge brass bed and went to unfasten the the blind cords.

'Mistake, those blinds. I should've had proper curtains. Those just remind Russell of tennis players' knickers,' Margot said, smiling damply. 'Russell hates pink, too, says it's like sleeping in a tart's boudoir,' she went on. 'Hates pink, hates dogs, hates me,' she said, lying back on the pillows and closing her eyes.

'Are you comfy?' Heather asked softly. 'Feel all right?'

Margot grinned, eyes still closed. 'I haven't got the whirling pit feeling, so I'll be OK. And Heather?' her eyes flashed open and she looked anxious. 'Don't, you know, don't—'

'Tell?' Heather said quietly. 'No, of course I won't tell. See you soon.'

Iain was still waiting in the kitchen, pacing about with his drink like a father excluded from the labour ward, but he had, she noticed, washed the glasses, found the right cupboard for the gin and left no trace of Margot's lonely binge. If Russell came home now, she could probably get away with claiming a migraine. Jasper was whining impatiently at the back door and scratching at the new paint. Heather clipped his lead on and took him outside, where he peed generously against a pot of expensively topiaried bay.

'Poor Margot. Is she often like this?' Iain asked quietly with a wary look up towards the windows above.

Heather didn't feel like explaining away her friend to him. He'd be gone soon, the sooner the better, she thought. Perversely, she found herself blaming him. If he and his crew weren't making the film, Margot would still be in the rectory, where she and Russell could put enough yards of carpet between them to keep them both happy. Russell could entertain his business friends, play with his model soldiers, show off his symbols of success and compliment Margot on how wonderfully she did the organizing. He seemed to need that constant feeling of being pleased with himself. And if he didn't have it, he looked for someone else to feel pleased with him instead.

Heather was walking towards the gate and to home, and Iain was still with her. 'Do you remember when I took you to Tramp and you got really drunk and fell out of the taxi?' he asked as they crunched down the drive.

'I remember being sick on your snake-skin cowboy boots just outside Harrods,' she said, laughing. It was a relief to think about the silly and fun side of being drunk rather than the maudlin-Margot aspect. She remembered the episode with the op-art duvet, too, of course, but somehow didn't want to start talking about beds with Iain – too many unsuitable sexual connotations there. 'Margot's all right really, you know, but she doesn't seem to have any confidence in herself at the moment,' she told him. 'And Russell really can be a bit of a pain. She's kept her own business going all this time, just because she loves the dogs. He met her when he took his aunt's Old English sheepdog to be trimmed at the place where she worked – he kept bringing it in so often just to see her, the poor dog became practically bald. "Hair of the Dog", she said the salon was called.'

'That's probably what she'll be needing by tomorrow morning,' Iain said. They stopped to open the gate and he turned to look at her properly. 'You know, I'm really terribly sorry about the other day, lunch and that.' Heather waited, while he chose words that seemed to be difficult to find. 'I didn't mean to be flippant about when you were pregnant. I did try to contact you after you left Scotland, but your mother said you'd gone away to France and wouldn't be back.'

Heather said, 'I did go, but not for more than a couple of weeks.'

'Did you ... did you have an abortion? I rather assumed you did,' he asked.

'No,' she replied. 'No, it just died by itself. On the

174

train home.' Heather could feel her lip trembling and told herself impatiently not to cry, not twenty-five years too late, not for something that she'd convinced herself had been no more than a collection of unviable cells.

'I'm so sorry Heather,' he said, and he wasn't saying it from a distance, but with his arms round her, nuzzling into her hair, his mouth close to her ear where she could feel his warm breath. What she really minded most was that she found she liked it, very much.

Chapter Twelve

Simon sat on the middle section of the see-saw, one foot on the ground trying to keep it balanced. He took his tobacco tin out of his pocket and started the artistically satisfying process of constructing a cigarette.

'Think you're hard, do you, skinning up out here in public?' Darren Gibson plonked himself onto one end of the see-saw so that Simon was almost catapulted off on to the bark chippings beneath. He just about managed to keep his balance, his hold on the tin and his dignity. He felt his usual reflex twinge of fear which veered dangerously towards laughter when he noticed that Darren was wearing his white baseball cap perched so fashionably high on top of his hair that he looked like he was wearing an extra, false head.

'Wearing that hat for a bet, are you?' Simon taunted, unable to resist taking the risk. Even Darren wasn't likely to beat him up, with no audience other than two bored young mothers sunning themselves on the bench and a gaggle of toddlers squabbling on the roundabout.

'What?' Darren's hand went up vaguely in the direction of the cap and he shoved it down hard so that it bent the top of his left ear. Simon smirked and quietly lit his neatly rolled cigarette. 'What you got in it then, Lebanese?' Super-cool Darren was clearly impressed.

'Golden Virginia,' Simon replied nonchalantly, inhaling deeply. He watched Darren have another little think and savoured the rare moment of superiority while he could.

'Oh. Right. Thought it was a spliff.'

'Wish it was,' Simon admitted, at last making his bid

for acceptance. 'Haven't had any since school. I'm not going back, got thrown out,' he said as casually as he could, eager not to look as if he was showing off.

Darren grinned. 'That should impress that girl you fancy.'

Simon felt an uncomfortable boyish blush creep up his neck. 'Which girl?'

'That Kate. Likes a bit of rough, that one. Likes me.' Darren sat upright, the green and purple dragon on his T-shirt swelled out proudly. Simon decided he loathed him. 'I could have her any time, just like that,' Darren bragged, snapping his fingers

Simon's own fingers were trembling now and the cigarette paper was starting to feel soggy. 'Why don't you have her then, if it's that easy?' he managed to ask.

'*Too* fuckin' easy, that's why. And she's not my type. She's skinny and she's posh.' He spat on to the bark. 'You wanna come out with me and my mates some time, find yourself some nice little slag that's not so picky.'

'Thanks a lot,' Simon grunted, feeling insulted yet somehow pleased. It felt good, halfway to being included.

'D'you drive?' Darren suddenly asked.

Simon didn't like to confess he wouldn't be seventeen till October. 'Yeah, why?'

'No reason,' Darren said, watching his own foot trying to kick a stone out of the bark chips. 'Just a thought.' He stood up and yawned. 'See you,' he said, and strode off in the direction of the neat row of council houses.

Simon rolled another cigarette, less elegantly this time, so flakes fell out on to his jeans as he smoked. He could drive a car, he hadn't lied about that, but he was too young to have a licence. Russell, car-mad and with a fantasy that involved his son becoming another laurel-garlanded British world champion Formula-one driver,

177

had given him off-road lessons since he was about ten and could just about reach the pedals. Simon had also once gloomily but obligingly raced with other young teenagers in a special event at Brands Hatch, miserably aware that this was the blissful fulfilment of all the other competitors' wildest dreams, whereas he would have preferred to be playing tennis. Perhaps Darren wanted advice about buying a car from Russell, he thought, then dismissed it as wholly impossible, unless Darren had had a major secret win on the National Lottery.

Heather felt as if she was suddenly living on the wrong planet. There didn't seem to be enough oxygen in the air, and she was doing a lot of deep inhaling followed by lengthy sighs. It had been going on for days now and she was starting to wonder if she was making herself ill with hyperventilation and lack of proper sleep. She felt as keyed up as if she was about to take a major examination, and the ground was spongy beneath her, as if she was walking just a millimetre or two above it, and not quite having the usual amount of firm contact. In the sultry-aired privacy of the greenhouse, she gave herself up to what she was pretending wasn't on her mind and thought about Iain and warm, delicious contact with his body. Only a small hug, she reminded herself, and one she hadn't wanted, *definitely* hadn't wanted, so it was all his fault, really. Only it wasn't a small hug, she recalled, as she shakily felt the green peppers to see if they were ready to pick. A hug was what she might give Margot, to make her feel better – a small, top-of-the-body squeeze of friendly affection, nothing complicated. Iain had been expressing more than a bit of amiable cheering up. You didn't do cheering up with your whole length of body. You didn't *press*. She thought about the smell of him, how it had seemed, even this many years on, snugly, smugly,

178

sexily familiar – hints of Floris and clean skin. She didn't even like him – the last thing she wanted him to do was touch her, really, honestly. But when the phone in the shed rang she jumped and dashed to answer it, conscious that her blood pressure was racing up. She said hello and could hear her voice echoing back at her, the irritating delay on the line telling her instantly and with shocking disappointment that she was probably about to talk to Tom.

'This is Hughie. I expect Tom has told you all about me,' said a hesitant voice.

'Well, no he hasn't actually, should he have done?' Heather asked politely, wondering if she was about to be punished for feeling lust towards Iain by the news that Tom had fallen victim to something dangerous and tropical. Weren't there poisonous spiders in Australia?

'Oh,' the voice said, then 'Oh' again while Heather wondered if the echo was getting worse, or if the news was going to be even more awful than she could immediately imagine; it came over as 'Oh-oh-oh-oh', like a keened lament.

'We've become very close. I was sure he'd have told you by now,' Hughie went on.

Heather, hearing everything as if in an empty Albert Hall, was having trouble making out his meaning. 'Close to what?' she heard herself saying, absurdly thinking close to dying, close to crashing the plane, close to a man-eating tiger. Close to each other was eventually the only one left. For a disorientated moment she couldn't quite remember where Tom had flown off to. She pictured distant Mongolian sands, with Tom costumed in a Lawrence of Arabia outfit and saying something along the famous lines of 'Have that boy washed and brought to my tent.' She wasn't sure if it was the shock of Hughie's bombshell or the idea of Tom in desert regalia that made her want to giggle.

'Are you still there?' the anxious voice was asking. He

sounded, she thought, like an assistant in a menswear shop, dealing inadequately with a customer's enquiry. She could just tell he would be twittery and hopeless and incapable of finding, say, the green polo shirt in size 42 that the customer was sure he'd tried on and wished he'd bought the day before.

'Yes I'm still here, why are you calling me? Is Tom all right?' There was a hissy quiet on the line.

'I just wanted to say, you know, sorry for any trouble. We didn't mean it to happen.' He was almost whining now, almost tearful. Perhaps he'd realized, she thought, that he hadn't been important enough for Tom to tell her about after all, poor boy. He sounded so like a child – 'we didn't mean it' – like a cowardly schoolboy caught and confronted after a vicious bout of name-calling.

Heather switched the phone off and sat down in her battered old cane chair outside the tool shed, trying to sort out her reactions. She had a peculiar sense of being slightly underwhelmed by Hughie's revelation, as if the disclosure was only a superficial shock instead of being a lightning bolt that bordered on electrocution. Perhaps it wasn't, deep down, as great a surprise as it might have been, given Tom's wariness of full-bodied women. But numbly unstunned as she was, it still took one hell of an imaginative leap to go from knowing Tom tended to back nervously away from excess cleavage to picturing him indulging in boys-only shower-play. She tried to visualise the scene that might now be going on down at the other end of the phone line. Hughie, she imagined, would go straight back to Tom and accuse him of not loving him enough to tell his wife he was leaving her. Tom would start making plans to disentangle himself from Hughie and there would be another deluded casualty of romance weeping in the back of the plane all the way back to Heathrow along with the usual quota of broken-hearted stewardesses. She went back into the greenhouse to pick tomatoes and caught herself sighing again, this time from something nearer to despair that Fate, or whatever it was, couldn't allow her just a *small* amount of adulterous lust without whamming straight in with some punishing complication. If Tom had overseas adventures, and she'd never been so foolishly complacent enough to assume he didn't, they should not intrude into home life, not even over long distance telephone calls. Suppose he really *did* retire soon, she thought, and then got bored and, following on from the discarded Hughie, started looking for boyish playmates locally? There was nothing better than scandal for linking a rather fractured community. The church organ fund would benefit at least, she thought, due to increased attendance at gossipy bring-and-buys. She imagined the two of them eventually separating and the rumours going round the village about 'another man', one each, his and hers, like newly-weds matching bath towels.

'Are you in there? It's only me with a peace offering.' Margot, bright-eyed and leading a swaggering Dalmatian dog, came into the greenhouse. 'What do you think?' she asked, 'Isn't he pretty? I was so tempted to put on my black and white spotty dress to match him. We'd look like something out of My Fair Lady,' she said, patting the dog's head.

'He's absolutely lovely but you haven't brought him for me have you?' Heather asked, horrified. Julia's Labradors could tear up a newly planted flower bed in ten minutes flat and they were an elderly, fairly sleepy pair. This young, bounding thing would have the whole garden in shreds in seconds. He was already eying the tomatoes, his tongue hanging out over sharp tiger-teeth as if working out where to bite through the stems to cause maximum speed of destruction.

'No, no, don't be daft. I've got you a teeny crate of Champers, it's up in your kitchen – got Brian to carry it round for me. I'm sorry I was such a drunken old slut.

181

You and Iain were terrifically kind to me.'

'You and Iain' Heather thought, 'Me and Iain' grouped together, linked. She closed her eyes for a moment and imagined she could smell him again, strong as hyacinths but decidedly not as sweet.

'Are you OK? I am forgiven aren't I?' Margot asked anxiously.

Heather grinned at her. 'Yes of course you are. It could be any of us. We all get these miserable moments, just sadly we're usually on our own, which makes them even worse.' She picked a couple more tomatoes, put them into her trug and led Margot and the dog towards the house.

'I can't imagine you having miserable moments, not drunken ones anyway.' Margot commented, 'You seem to have everything too well organised.'

'I do have them, though, Margot, of course I do. Wouldn't be human otherwise.' Heather just managed to stop herself sighing again so as not to provoke an outburst of worried, confidence-inviting concern from Margot. If only Tom *had* been having a fling with a full-bodied woman, this would be the moment for her and Margot to embark on a 'Guess what the sod's done *now*' empathy session covering the comfortably familiar all-men-are-bastards territory. For this one, Margot would probably be able to offer little more than lots of drink and an embarrassed lack of comprehension.

Early that evening, while Kate and Suzy were bickering over the washing up and Delia was examining the bookshelves, looking for something to read that had plenty of violence but no sex in it, the phone rang again. Heather was in her bedroom, searching the back of her wardrobe for the ancient battered school geography folder in which she'd kept small mementoes of her teenage years. A couple of faded black-and-white photos of her wedding to Iain should be among them. There hadn't been any official photos of course, but one of the witnesses, a girl on her lunch break from the nearby petrol station, had lent them her Instamatic containing most of a reel of film.

'Heather?' Iain asked softly as if, she thought, he was just about to tell her a delicious secret. 'I thought you might like to come round to the rectory. They're filming a scene on the river as soon as it's properly dark, which might be fun to watch.'

'You know my mother's still staying here? I really don't want her to know that you are who you are, if you see what I mean.' She looked round warily, as if her bedroom walls really could have ears.

Iain laughed at her. 'You could sneak out . . . I won't say like the old days because I know you'll get mad at me, but do come. Margot's hoping you will – and please, do bring Kate, I know she'd be interested.'

Heather abandoned the wardrobe search and went immediately to have a shower, overdosing heavily on the perfumed soap. She put on clean jeans and a cream cotton sweater, hoping she would almost, but not quite, look as if she'd been wearing it all day. She brushed her teeth till her gums ached, washed her hair quickly and fluffed it out with the hair dryer, all the time telling herself not to be so silly, so juvenile, so disgracefully, cravenly infatuated.

As she wandered casually into the sitting-room, Delia immediately asked, 'Going out? At this time? Some-where nice?' probably almost knocked senseless by the wafts of Diorella.

'No, no, just thought I might stroll round to Margot's. She says they're filming a river scene, and it might be amusing to watch for a minute or two.' She was, she realized, picking at the fringe on a cushion, unravelling it and wrapping the threads round her fingers with nerves. Ridiculous, a voice of common sense (which sounded like Delia's) told her from inside her own head. 'I won't be long,' she said, 'probably won't be that much fun really,' she added, shrugging and attempting to look as if nothing could be more boring.

'Can I come?' Suzy ever alert to the possibility of a spot of Simon-gazing, piped up from her usual TV watching position on the floor.

'And me?' Kate said, from the lazy depths of an armchair.

'Well, yes if you like,' she told them. 'You won't mind being on your own for a bit will you Mother? We'll be back very soon, I'm sure, and it is getting a bit chilly—'

'Well . . .' Don't you dare want to come with us, Heather's less sensible inner voice was demanding. 'Better be someone here in case the clinic phones,' she suggested, hating herself. Delia was frowning, calculating, but her slippered feet were tucked comfortably under her body and as she was settled with the book on the sofa, she showed no signs of unfolding herself to come with them. 'I'll take the mobile phone in case you need to contact me,' Heather went on, heading determinedly for the door. 'Come on then girls, don't want to miss it do we?'

From the road, Margot's garden was lit up like an airport and outside the cricket pavilion, across the road close to the playground, groups of after-match drinkers were staring at the bright spotlight on top of the crane that could be seen slowly winching itself high, clear of the trees down by the river. As Heather, Kate and Suzy made their way towards the rectory, they could hear small rumbles of disapproval from across the road.

'They always *complain*,' Kate grumbled. 'Don't they have any sense of fun?'

'People don't like anything that's different,' Suzy agreed.

Heather thought they were right. 'I expect they'll all

be happily queuing to see the movie when it comes out. Or getting the video and saying to all their friends "Look that's the lane by the church" and that sort of thing.'

The village seemed like a cage very suddenly, full of hostile people who were too wary of excitement, who thought that *different* equalled *threatening*. The watchers looked just like disapproving observers, looking out for signs of trouble at the edge of an illicit pop festival. She told herself it was her own peculiar mood, a feeling that she was on the edge of being overwhelmingly thrilled. Her jeans, as she strode up Margot's drive, were just a bit uncomfortably tight, chaffing rather pleasurably and reminding her that the overwhelming thrill was nothing but a purely transient sexual one. God, if he just so much as touched me, she suddenly thought, biting her lip at the idea and feeling glad that it was now dark enough for a blush not to show.

Iain wasn't in the small crowd by the river, Heather realized, as she peered through the half-dark and the shadows cast by the circles of spotlight that picked out groups of activity. Good thing, she tried to make herself think, but she then felt cross with him for not being there when he'd promised Kate he'd talk her through what was going on. Just one more example of his unreliability.

'Everyone looks so . . . so *busy*,' Kate commented, watching all the faces full of earnest concentration, the chewing of pencil-ends, the consulting of notes and clipboards, the adjustment of cameras, the crane, the lighting.

'Perhaps they'll give *us* something to do,' Suzy said, nervous in case they did just that.

'What've *you* come for?' Tamsin, embarrassed to be caught swanning about in a crushed velvet dress and jailbait make-up, demanded of Suzy.

185

'Iain asked us,' Suzy replied nonchalantly, looking the absurdly glamorous Tamsin up and down with an expression that told Heather and Kate that she was trying not to laugh. 'Why are you all dressed up? Did you think they'd let *you* be in it?' Suzy giggled, unable to stop herself.

Tamsin looked haughty and glanced at Kate. 'Well I don't see why not,' she told Suzy. 'After all, I mean if Kate thinks *she* can get a part . . .'

Kate glared furiously at Tamsin and flounced off in the direction of the action and the river. The two younger girls followed at a safe distance and, left alone, Heather shivered and folded her arms across her body, shoving her hands up her sweater sleeves for warmth.

'You need a little drinky to keep you warm.' Margot appeared at her side, clutching a jug of steaming mulled wine and a couple of mugs. 'Everyone will think it's coffee,' she whispered with a giggle. 'Only giving it to the chosen few.'

'You'd make a party out of anything, Margot,' Heather told her admiringly, gratefully accepting the warm, spicy drink. 'If the Grim Reaper came calling, you'd invite him in and open the Bollinger.'

'Got to have someone to drink with,' Margot told her. 'Russell's not here – again. And anyway, what's wrong with being nice to Death – there's always that chance that Death just might be nice to me.'

'Eternal paradise and harps and all that?' Heather asked.

Margot snorted. 'Not bloody likely, just a decent spot not too uncomfortably close to the fires of hell, I should think. Come down to the river and let's see what they're all doing.'

Margot's river frontage was two hundred feet of stone steps and ornate balustrading, with chained gaps for access to Russell's Slipper launch and Simon's dinghy. Now it had been transformed into what looked like a small dock, with a canal barge which an over-eager stylist had decked out with more flowers and decorative enamel knick-knacks than any serious bargee would ever have found room for. Beyond it was moored a small Edwardian pleasure cruiser with a striped canopy, and a tray of drinks set out on a white ironwork table. Fierce spotlights exposed a crazing of dry lines on the decking, just as cruelly as the lines of age showed on women of a certain age in harshly lit rooms. Iain still wasn't anywhere to be seen and Heather felt uncomfortably conscious that she, Margot and their children were distinctly excess to requirements. She thought that any moment they would be asked to move along, as if they were gawping passers-by, ghoulishly hovering around at the scene of a gory murder.

'Oh look, just like a real movie,' Margot suddenly said, nudging Heather's arm and pointing towards the crane. The director, or so she assumed, was climbing onto a small platform and being hoisted up above the crowd. He wore, to Margot's great delight, a leather jacket, black baseball cap, was smoking a baby cigar and carried a megaphone.

'Did you know they still actually used those?' she asked Heather. 'I thought they'd have gone out with Laurel and Hardy.'

'No, I thought something more of a phone type of thing would be what they used, wouldn't you think? All hi-tech and terrifically cool. Of course they've probably got that as well. He probably likes the megaphone thing because it's *big*,' Heather said with a giggle. 'You know what men are like . . .'

'What *are* men like?' Iain suddenly appeared at her side and smiled at the two women.

'*Men* are always adding *length*,' Margot informed him cheekily. 'One way or another they're always at it – flashy cars, guns, truncheons, whatever.'

Iain laughed and put his hands up defensively. 'Not me, I promise. Never felt the need.'

Heather feigned intense interest in the flurry of action as a man encased in a diving suit climbed heavily into a dinghy with a couple of technicians. She couldn't look at Iain, couldn't risk him giving her a conspiratorial wink that Margot just couldn't miss.

Kate crept up and stood next to her, with Simon a few loyal paces away. 'What are they doing? Is someone going to jump in?' she asked.

'That's the plan,' Iain told her, leaning close to her and pointing towards the boat which was motoring upstream towards the island. 'It's supposed to be a chase sequence, which it won't at all resemble till it's all edited together. In fact, right now it'll look pretty slow. I'll give you a running commentary,' he promised her.

'Lights! Run sound! Cue smoke!' the director yelled from his lofty podium.

'Heavens, they really say it!' Heather whispered to Margot. The small boat chugged slowly back towards them, with Brian sitting up in the bows wafting a smoke machine across the water.

'Supposed to be river mist,' Heather heard Iain explain in a whisper to Kate. She waited for Kate to make one of her accustomed teenage-rudeness replies along the lines of 'Well believe it or not I can see that for myself,' but instead she just nodded and smiled. Good grief, thought Heather, please don't let her be turning into one of those women who play dumb to let men think everything they say is just so clever. Then she wondered if she was thinking this because it was Iain, or if it would be the same if Kate had been listening as avidly to Simon.

The man in the wetsuit stood up and prepared to jump into the river, just as a distant roaring sound was heard overhead. Heather smothered a giggle as the director shouted 'Cut!'

'Is that supposed to be part of the sound effects?' Kate commented to Iain. 'If so it's not very, well, effective.'

'No, it's Concorde running late out of Heathrow,' Heather told her, 'You should know, you've been hearing it for years.'

Kate gave her a sharp look. 'OK, OK, don't stress,' she said.

'Respect for your mother,' Iain said to Kate with a teasing smile and a wagging finger. Again, Heather waited for the scowl and the suggestion that he at least naff off and mind his own, but instead the girl's face was lit by a broad and captivating smile.

'Sorry, Mommy dearest,' she purred, linking her arm through Heather's as if trying to create a cute on-show tableau of family harmony.

Simon, at a discreet distance under the trees, was watching Kate and feeling angry and chewed up inside. She was practically bloody kittenish with that leery old man – could hardly stop smiling at the old goat. He'd never seen so much of her orthodontically-perfect teeth. They, and her bright hair, shone so ridiculously in the dark, he was surprised the director of the film hadn't ordered her off the set for messing up the light-readings. Darren was right, he should either settle for something a lot less challenging in the way of women, or make more of an effort to get her interested in him. He'd secretly read several of Tam's copies of *Just Seventeen*, and knew that was what feisty Nick Fisher on the problem page would have advised him to do (if, of course, he was the sort of bloke who wrote in – it amazed him that so many did . . .). So he'd do the effort bit first; the other was like giving up altogether, and he wasn't about to do that without a fight. What kind of effort, though? That was the problem, one that even N. Fisher would find hard to solve. Perhaps Darren would have an idea, seeing as he seemed to be pretty clued-up about everything else.

Heather couldn't believe the attention to detail that went into the filming. She and Margot sipped their mulled wine and watched the dinghy make five more runs with its smoke machine and the diver jump over the side just twice. He was to swim under the water towards the two moored boats, with just his flippers occasionally visible for the cameras. The first time he swam too deep and arrived at the boats with the director shouting that he might as well have been a bloody trout, could he please manage a *soupçon* of visibility.

'Is he usually so rude?' Heather whispered to Iain.

'Yes, absolutely all the time. Especially when something like this takes hours when it could be done in minutes if things went right.'

The next time the dinghy sputtered down the river with its dripping diver, the engine died out. 'Cut!' was yelled furiously from above on the crane.

'I think someone's been sitting on the fuel line, don't you?' Kate commented to Heather, pointing to Brian awkwardly manoeuvring himself around in the boat.

Heather had stopped concentrating, beginning to think it would be rather nice to go home and get warm. Feeling ridiculously keyed-up about Iain had made her unusually shivery in the clear and dewy night, and the grass beneath her thin canvas shoes was uncomfortably damp. She'd wait for a suitable gap in the action and then leave, she decided. This time, as if in celestial compliance with her wishes, the smoke trailed from the dinghy just as it should, the diver swam with his flippers aloft like an exuberant sealion, and just as he reached the Edwardian boat Heather's mobile phone trilled out bright and loud through the silence.

'Cut! Fucking cut!' yelled the director, flinging his baseball cap down across the boats and into the river. He and everyone else in the garden turned to look as Heather hastily and with enormous embarrassment fished her phone out of her pocket.

'Better come over here out of the way,' Iain said, propelling her across the garden towards the deserted terrace while she fumbled with the aerial. All she could think of was that his hand was pressing firmly into her back as she walked, making it hard even to think of what she was supposed to say to greet whoever was calling.

'Heather? Are you there?' her mother's anxious voice squawked down the phone. Heather, as if she could be seen, pushed Iain's hand away and she turned to face the house so she didn't have to look at him.

'What's wrong, are you OK?' she managed to ask.

'No, well yes, I am, but Edward isn't. The clinic phoned and he's now got Cheyne-Stokes breathing and isn't likely to last the night.'

Chain smokes? Heather, her mind not really on the call, tried to sort out what Delia was talking about. Her mother liked medical terminology – bones were always 'fractured' never just broken, people she knew got a 'carcinoma' not plain old cancer, although anything remotely gynaecological was referred to as You Know, accompanied by a meaningful downward glance.

'My extremely old Uncle Edward is dying. I'll have to go. Where are Kate and Suzy?' Heather, feeling rushed and flustered, said to Iain at last. He made a move towards her, with the excuse of being comforting, but she moved faster and walked past him back towards the crowd.

'Why don't you go on ahead and take your mother to the hospital, and I'll find them and explain to them what's happened,' Iain suggested. 'And will they be all right at home on their own, or shall I ask Margot to put them up?'

She hesitated, thinking how competent he was being, how helpful and decisive, and how very many years too late. 'They'll be fine at the house, if you could just tell them. Thanks,' she said.

'No problem,' he said softly, leaning across and kissing her gently on the electric area at the edge of her mouth. 'Take care driving, won't you?'

Chapter Thirteen

Kate knew the phone call had been bad news the moment she saw Iain lean across and kiss her mother. The old uncle must be dead, she assumed and Iain was being the first person to have to express a bit of sympathy. He really was a terrifically kind man, she thought as she watched him coming over alone towards her. She wondered, curiously, if he would kiss her, too, in sympathy, and how it would feel, having an elderly mouth in contact with her face. After all, it wasn't as if he was family. As Iain approached, he collected Suzy on the way and led her by her reluctant hand to where Kate was waiting to be told what was happening. While she waited in the dark, walking a little way up the lawn and separating herself from the rest of the gathering, she wondered how she should compose her face to react to the death of someone she neither knew nor particularly cared about. She wanted, she realized, to make Iain *want* to comfort her, put his arms round her and pull her against his large body. She hadn't even been properly kissed since Annabelle's birthday party, and she decided that if she was trying to make such a much older man fancy her, she must be getting sexually desperate.

'Sorry about your uncle,' Iain said in a voice that was cheerfully normal, and he put his arm round Kate's shoulders, disappointingly as if she was a fellow chap in a rugby team. 'He seems to be on his way out. Your mother's had to leave. Now will you two be all right at home on your own?' he asked, looking intently at Kate. 'Or would you rather stay with Margot?'

'I am nearly seventeen!' Kate blurted out with automatic scorn.

'And I'm not a baby,' Suzy added, smiling, though, to emphasize that she did intend to be passably polite, even if Kate couldn't manage it.

'Fine, I was just asking,' Iain said with a grin, moving his arm away from Kate.

'Sorry,' Kate mumbled, wishing he would put his arm back and that she could snuggle cosily against him. Perhaps it was her dad she was missing, she thought, confused, though he'd never been all that much of a *touching* sort of father. He was affectionate enough in a distant sort of way, just hallo and goodbye kissing, and she'd always been thankful that their family wasn't like Annabelle's. *They* had frequent awful things called 'bug-hugs', where they all gathered in a circle and put their arms round each other, making cooey noises and assuring each other loudly how much they were adored. She knew this because they'd once done it in front of *her,* when Annabelle's youngest brother had had a major telephone row with his best friend. She'd felt left out, she remembered, and she'd thought them very impolite to brandish their mutual smug love like that in front of her. It was her first suspicion that the nuclear family might not be altogether a wholly good thing. Too excluding and pleased with itself.

'Could we go home *now*, do you think?' Suzy asked Kate. 'I'm a bit bored really.'

'OK,' Kate told her, 'I don't suppose anything exciting will happen now, anyway.'

'I'll walk you back, you can at least let me do that,' Iain insisted.

'Where are you going, aren't you staying?' Tamsin, a huge blue mohair sweater now dousing the effect of her short slinky dress, challenged Suzy.

Suzy looked determinedly solemn. 'Someone is dying,' she announced importantly, watching Tamsin carefully, but without much hope for any sign of genuine sympathy.

'What, that old uncle you've never even met?' Tamsin demanded, 'Why does that mean you've got to go home?'

'Actually,' Suzy stated bravely, 'I'm going because I'm bored stiff, if you want the truth, though I don't suppose you do.'

Tamsin's mouth fell open in surprise. 'Oh. Oh well see you sometime. You will come camping with me though, won't you?' she asked anxiously.

'I might, it depends,' Suzy told her loftily. 'I'll phone you.'

'About time you stood up to her,' Kate said admiringly as the three of them walked down the drive towards the road. 'She runs rings round you.'

'Not any more, by the sound of it,' Iain commented, watching Suzy stride on ahead with a newly confident bounce in her step. Kate turned to smile agreement at him and stumbled over a large stone. 'Careful,' he said, grabbing her hand to steady her. All the way along the road back to their own house, Kate waited for him to let go. It was only when they reached her gate and he still hadn't that she realized she'd wasted all the time she could have enjoyed the feeling of his warm, firm hand, waiting for that feeling to end. What an idiot, she thought to herself. What a complete idiot.

The nurse assured them that Edward was completely unconscious, though Heather noticed she was still careful not to talk about him in his room as if he wasn't yet there at all. Outside the room she'd explained to them about his breathing. Of course Cheyne-Stokes had been nothing to do with chain-smoking, it was just an unfortunate near-eponym.

'He takes one long breath, then nothing for a while, so you might think he's gone, and then there are short shallow breaths and the whole thing starts again,' the nurse warned them with a big, jovial, inappropriate grin before they went in to start the grim vigil. 'I just had to mention it, otherwise you'd be forever pressing the buzzer to tell someone he's passed on.'

Delia was looking pale and was wearing her pink straw comfort-hat. Heather sat down on the opposite side of the bed and thought about asking her mother why on earth they were actually there, but the question sounded too bizarrely existential when asked across so nearly dead a man. Surely they could have simply been telephoned when he'd actually gone, especially if he had no idea they were in the room with him. And, poor man, if he *was* aware they were there, he could hardly fail to know he was about to meet his maker – why else would two distant relatives be summoned to his side in the middle of the night, other than to watch for his departure into the everlasting darkness? It was probably all to do with Administration, Heather concluded, as she curled her feet under her in the soft chair and tried to get comfortable. Perhaps if they could get his death over with, certified and tidied away in the night, the clinic could have another profitable patient occupying the room by midday tomorrow. It would disrupt their timetable if they had to leave Edward tidily laid out for a late-morning Family Viewing. What a cynic I'm becoming, she thought, her own long sigh coinciding noisily with one of old Uncle Edward's.

As she sat waiting in the half-dark, she thought about Iain. She put her finger to the edge of her mouth where he had so lightly and thoughtlessly kissed her. She stroked the edge of her lip, absent-mindedly trying to revive the sparky feeling. He had, quite literally, touched a nerve.

'Do you think . . .' Delia cleared her throat and continued in a loud whisper, 'do you think I should hold his hand?'

'I don't know. Perhaps if you feel like it,' Heather whispered back. It occurred to her that not only she, but also her mother, might never have seen anyone dead before, though surely she had seen her own husband, paid those dutiful last respects? Perhaps Delia was frightened, she was certainly looking pale and nervous. They both looked at Edward's hands, which lay as dry and brittle as winter twigs on the white sheet. Every few moments his crab-claw fingers fluttered slightly, as if the trembling was to remind them there was still a tiny trace of life flickering feebly inside him and that it wasn't yet time to pull the sheet over his face. Maybe the twittering hands didn't want to be held, didn't want to have their last free movements stilled by well-meaning confinement.

Heather tried not to doze off. It was so silent, apart from the hoarse, irregular breathing of the old man, that she was sure she could hear a clock ticking out in the corridor. Unless that was Edward's slowly thudding heart, she suddenly thought, jerking herself back from the edge of sleep. 'Shall I fetch us some tea?' she whispered across to her mother.

'Please,' Delia said. 'But don't be long,' she added fearfully.

Heather wandered, almost on tiptoe, along the brightly lit corridor, past the ticking clock (a relief there actually *was* one) to where the night-nurse sat at her desk and concentrated on some intricate pink knitting.

'Tea?' she said, over the chattering needles. 'I'll get it for you, no trouble – you go on back.'

'No, I'll wait if you don't mind. It's nicer to be out of there, to be honest,' Heather told her, pleased to be with someone who could almost certainly be relied on not to be in the next world with her next breath. While she waited for the tea, Heather looked at the framed paintings on the wall. No two were remotely alike, and she wondered if they'd been done by patients undergoing occupational therapy, or those grateful to have been successfully discharged. Perhaps, she decided, they'd been ordered in bulk from the local art circle, set a project on 'local landscapes – a personal interpretation'. She was looking closely at a very pretty and colourful one depicting an intricate naïve scene of Oxford market when the nurse came bustling back, carrying a tray.

'You go on ahead, I'll carry this. Don't want you keeling over with the stress of it all,' she told Heather.

'Do people usually keel over then?' Heather asked, as she trailed behind the nurse back along the corridor.

Delia was at the open door waiting for them. 'I think he's gone,' she said in a quavery voice. 'He just growled and stopped, and now I think he's not there any more.'

Heather squeezed her arm and walked past her into the room, half expecting the bed to be empty and the window open, as if the Grim Reaper had been in and claimed the old man's body along with his soul. The curtains drifted feebly in the breeze, and that was the only movement in the room. Edward looked exactly the same, but somehow empty. Whatever it was, life force, soul, whatever, Heather could see had vanished. She imagined him now in committee with St Peter and his keys, St Michael and his clipboard, and with God at the head of a long and important table.

'I didn't do anything, he just went off. I didn't even quite catch the moment,' Delia was saying, flustered as if someone was about to accuse her of suffocating the old man the moment she'd got him alone.

'Would you like the tea now?' the nurse asked and Heather thanked God in his celestial boardroom for England's silly rituals.

It was quite flattering to be sought out by Darren. The film crew were an obvious draw, but Darren didn't seem to be showing any interest in the action by the river. Simon had been on the point of losing interest himself, giving up and going back into the cottage to brood sullenly over Tamsin's Megadrive. Anything to take his mind off Kate and the way she hardly even *looked* at him any more. At least they used to be friends, now they didn't seem to be even that. She looked *through* him, not at him; could hardly even be bothered to say hello. Darren came swaggering up the rectory drive as if he owned the place, followed at a respectful distance by his brother Shane and a couple of large and shambling friends. Simon had a fleeting moment of wondering if they'd come to beat him up, but they all looked excited about something and he assumed it was connected with drugs. They might, he thought, have something to sell him that would cheer him up.

'Remember you said you could drive?' Darren said, separating himself a little from the others who hung around under the apple trees smoking and scuffing at the ground in the dark. They should watch out for dog shit, Simon thought, quickly realizing it would be uncool to say anything so motherish.

'Yeah. I remember,' Simon confirmed, sensing with slowly growing dread that something was about to be required of him. 'What about it?'

'We need a driver. Simple,' Darren said with a shrug and a broad grin.

'Now?'

'Yep, now. Right now. Well in your own time, the next couple of hours or so,' he added generously. 'For a little job. Nothing difficult.'

'Illegal?' Simon asked, horribly sure it was a stupid question.

'Not very, not for the driver anyway. No worries,' Darren said, offering him a cigarette.

Simon wanted the cigarette, but didn't want the crime

that went with it so he refused. 'No, I don't want to get involved in anything, you know . . .'

Darren glanced at his shuffling group of friends. One of them had climbed a few branches and was investigating the treehouse.

'My little sister's den,' Simon called to him. 'Be careful up there.'

'He won't fall, not Bugsy,' Darren reassured him, misunderstanding his concern.

Simon had no doubt that Bugsy, who was five feet five and built four-square like a pallet of bricks, would be safe enough – he was more concerned for the treehouse.

'I just wanted to help you out,' Darren was saying persuasively to Simon, having led him out of earshot and towards the deserted front of the cloth-swathed rectory. 'That girl, Kate, I just saw her going home. That old man was with her, the one that's staying here, and he was strolling along holding her hand.'

Simon groaned. 'Bastard, jerk,' he murmured.

'Exactly,' Darren agreed. 'And when I say holding her hand, I don't mean like some little kid that needs taking across the road. She obviously likes things – men – that are a bit different, if you know what I mean. She needs to see *you* that way, not some *old* sod. She thinks you're just ordinary. You want to show her you're not.'

Simon considered for a moment. 'I'll have that fag now if that's OK.'

'Fine,' Darren said, grinning across to the others, 'and then you just come with us and we'll show you what we need you to do.'

It was a pity she'd gone home, Simon thought, it would have been good if she'd seen him, ambling along comfortably next to Darren with his hands tucked into his jeans. He felt a bit embarrassed about the gloves – all he'd got was padded stuff for skiing, packed away somewhere in a tea-chest in the rectory attic, and Darren had said to be sure to bring *thin* ones, so he wouldn't get clumsy. Also, he'd said they'd stay on better. 'You know, like johnnies' he'd said with a nudge and a smirk. The pink rubbery Marigolds, purloined from the cupboard underneath the Garden Cottage sink, had a mixed aroma of Jif and J-cloth that was so strong it reached his offended nostrils all the way from his inside pocket. This made it impossible to pretend, as he would have quite liked to, that he was out with the SAS on a clandestine moonlight rescue mission. Like trained soldiers, the group of boys was moving fast and surprisingly quietly. Simon had never seen Darren and his mates when they weren't taking up maximum space and acting up with maximum volume. Now it was as if they'd been turned into street foxes, slinking along silently and with purpose. He still hadn't much of a clue what they were all up to, but he felt quite heady with importance. Whatever it was they wanted to do, they obviously couldn't do it without *him*. Eventually, at the far end of the small modern development at the back of the High Street, Darren came to a halt against a wall, out of the range of the street lamp.

'Look, Neighbourhood sodding Watch,' Shane sniggered, pointing up at a poster clipped to the lamp post.

'Gives it an edge,' Darren said, grinning evilly. Simon felt nervous, suddenly wondering if it was all a ploy and he was actually about to be beaten up for being just too posh. But they could have done that as they passed the rec, could have dragged him beyond the swings, given him a thumping (or worse) and left him for dead behind the cricket pavilion.

'This one,' Darren was saying, pointing across to where a green VW Polo was parked on a slope in front of its garage. The gardens were all open at the front, with no fences or gates for thieves to have to contend with, but providing nowhere but a few tatty laurels to hide behind as a result. Simon stared at the car, trying to put together the awfulness of what he was slowly realizing he was about to do.

'It's one we prepared earlier,' Darren explained with another wolfish grin, putting a firm hand on Simon's shoulder to help him not to have a sudden change of mind. 'It's already open, Bugsy just needs one second for hot-wiring, then we're all off, OK? Any questions?'

'Off to where?' Simon's voice came out more squeakily than he expected.

'It's only round the corner, Harbutt's Hi-Fi. You don't even have to look where you're going, we'll tell you what to do. You just listen and do it.'

The words 'do it' were accompanied by a punch on the shoulder that was not to be argued with. Simon, thinking about Kate in the way that drowning men are supposed to think about their mothers, would rather die (and at that moment this seemed like a real option) than not do as Darren asked. He didn't, he reminded himself, even have to break into the car, all that was done for him, although he wouldn't swear that the police would appreciate the difference. He crossed the road behind Darren, terrified that bedroom lights would go on along Meadowside and that furious junior executives would stream out in Paisley pyjamas, armed with umbrellas and lawn rakes. Some fast fumbling went on under the Polo's steering column and then Simon, in the shaming Marigold gloves, climbed in to the driving seat and immediately set off much too fast, skidding out of the cul-de-sac into the main road.

'Hey, I thought you could drive,' Shane complained scornfully.

'Leave it, he's just nervous,' Darren, in the front passenger seat retorted quickly.

Simon was glad he wasn't expected to speak, terrified that at any moment he would hear his own voice blurting out a confession of just exactly how limited his behind-the-wheel experience really was.

'Stop!' Darren ordered suddenly and Simon stood on the brake pedal, forgetting about the clutch and stalling the engine.

'Wanker!' Bugsy yelled in a panic. 'Now I'll have to get it started again!'

'Sorry,' Simon murmured.

While Bugsy restarted the car, Simon tried to imagine what was going to happen next. He assumed he would wait in the car, engine running, while the others dashed round the corner and speedily did their out-of-hours shopping, probably via a broken window.

'OK drive. Just past the shop and then reverse it, quick as you can,' Darren ordered.

'Reverse it to where?' Simon asked, mystified.

'Through the fucking window, cretin,' Bugsy said.

Simon grinned through the mirror at him, pretending he could see a joke.

'That's right. Through the window – you drive it hard, backwards. We pick up everything we can and then we all piss off. Thirty seconds, max,' Darren said proudly.

The sound of so much glass breaking all over and round the car in the still dark night was really very thrilling, Simon had to admit. It stopped him feeling quite so sick, anyway. He concentrated on keeping the car from stalling again while the others frantically hurled in as much stock as they could gather. It reminded him of a supermarket trolley-dash he'd once seen on an early morning TV show, competition winners, greedily snatching at anything in their path, all dignity gone. When they'd finished, and thrown themselves breathlessly back into the car, he pulled the severely dented car away from the shattered shop-front with a roar that wouldn't disgrace Damon Hill and as they raced out of the village on to the Didcot road, Simon wondered if he was the only one with an erection.

'Not bad,' Darren told Simon.

'Yeah, ace,' Shane echoed. 'Wanna CD Walkman?' he asked, handing over a package from the back seat.

'Got one already,' Simon replied, wishing immediately that he hadn't.

'Oh yeah, I nearly forgot. You don't *need* to do this do you, rich boy?' Shane sneered. 'Mummy buys you everything you want. I bet you've even got a TV and video in your room.'

Simon, who had, denied it. 'Don't be stupid. OK I'll have it, thanks. Actually I could do with another CD player,' he said. 'Where shall I put the car?'

'Take it back to the owners if you like. Then they can check out the damage in the morning,' Darren said loading a pile of loose CDs, the CD Walkman and a clock radio into Simon's lap. 'Otherwise you can drop us off behind the rec.'

Kate heard the crash just as she was getting ready for bed. She'd been quite enjoying having the house to herself. She didn't count Jasper who was snoring on a rug in the kitchen, or Suzy who had collapsed into bed with yet another Arthur Ransome book and was likely to fall asleep with her light on and her teeth unbrushed. Not my responsibility, Kate thought as she smoothed Body Shop oatmeal cleanser across the bridge of her nose where spots might just dare to consider appearing. She liked the efficient little cosmetic rituals that involved sweet-smelling pots of gloopy stuff. She didn't really care whether they worked or not, she was just happy to be part of the grown-up sisterhood, linked worldwide by the daily application of magic potions. She switched off the bathroom light and, outside in the night the crash happened right then, as if she'd triggered it. She stood still on the landing, listening carefully in case any tremendous noises were going to

203

follow the first one. She'd heard glass, and imagined it strewn all over the road. Along with the glass, only a millisecond later, her imagination had added large chunks of car, lots of blood and the twisted limbs of her mother and grandmother.

'What's happening?' Suzy emerged from her room and asked Kate.

Kate, scared-frozen with her hand on her bedroom door-knob, looked at her crossly. 'How should I know? Do you think I'm psychic?' Then she felt mean, it was hardly Suzy's fault she'd interrupted a horrific stream of imaginings. 'Sorry. I mean it was probably just a car backfiring or something. Go on back to bed, Suze. I expect we'll find out in the morning if it's anything else.'

Suzy was too tired to argue, and tottered straight back to bed quite willing to find anything Kate said, as resident grown-up, conveniently comforting.

Kate, though, couldn't comfort herself. She was too scared, and too undressed now, to go out into the road and find out exactly what had happened. Outside was now eerily silent, and her mind went on doing its worst – her mother and Delia were now lying and dying unattended, while the indifferent village slept and ignored them. Perhaps the car had gone off the road into a ditch, the corner just before the church was pretty sharp, and maybe no-one would see them down there. Her heart was beating hard inside her, and she pulled her old towelling dressing-gown tight round herself and crept downstairs, wondering what to do. Her mother, she remembered, had her phone with her, so she went into the kitchen where Suzy would not be able to hear her and worry and dialled the number. A cool voice told her that the number she was calling was temporarily switched off. Did that mean, awful thought, that it was lying in pieces in the ditch under the car? Under her mother?

Kate opened the front door warily, hoping it wouldn't creak and disturb Suzy. She could tell her she was letting Jasper out for his late-night pee. It was too much, the responsibility of being the house adult suddenly – why was her father so many thousands of miles away? Her ears strained for the expected sounds of ambulance and police sirens. Surely someone should be there by now. All she could hear were the normal sounds of the few passing cars outside, someone driving much too fast was shrieking their tyres round the church corner, and someone else was revving up a motor bike. Kate came back in and went back to the phone, deciding that the thing to do was to phone Margot. Her fingers were shaky as they dialled the rectory number, and only when Iain answered did she remember that Margot would be fast asleep in the Garden Cottage and not in her own palatial home.

'I heard a crash, and I'm scared it might be Mum coming home and missing the corner,' she told him, on the basis that one older person would do as well as another.

'I'll be right round, don't worry. I'll check out what's been happening on my way,' he told her.

She felt instantly reassured, in the same childlike way that Suzy had been. Suddenly she knew it wasn't her mother, just because she was about to find out what the damage really was. She knew she felt better when she realized she was in front of the hall mirror, brushing her hair and smudging the last trace of the oatmeal cleanser away from the side of her face.

'Everything's fine, well almost. It was a bunch of yobs ram-raiding the hi-fi shop,' Iain reported only minutes later. 'The police have just arrived. No sign of the villains, of course. They'll be long gone.' He grinned at her, watching her face relax into a hugely relieved smile.

'I am sorry to drag you out,' she said, 'it's just that

Mum's not answering her phone, and she might be driving all upset or something, and not be concentrating, and I sort of imagined . . .' Kate felt she was starting to crumble and her voice was giving way.

Iain had his arms round her, gathering her in and softly rocking all the worry out of her. His mouth gently brushed against her hairline as he soothed her, until she realized that she wasn't feeling exactly soothed at all, but was a long way from calm, in a completely pleasurable way.

Abruptly, as car headlights lit the drive, Iain pulled away and Kate was left startled. 'I'd better disappear,' he said quickly, kissing his index finger and putting it to her lips. 'Sleep well,' he added, with a strange, lopsided grin.

He's teasing, she thought, feeling her face fall into a glare as he made for the kitchen and the back door. She could hear the car doors slamming outside and went to open the front door for Heather, just as Iain changed his mind, returned and, with his hand warm on the back of her head, planted a less than gentle kiss on her mouth.

'Happy dreams,' he ordered for her and fled through the back door.

Kate waited at the front door, hoping her mother would assume she was trembling from the cold night air. They looked exhausted, and Delia was clutching a handkerchief so Kate knew the papery old man had died. She waited patiently to be told, but her mother had a suspicious and wary look about her, grasped Kate's arm firmly and pulled her into the kitchen. 'OK, tell me. Who did I just see leaving by the back door?'

Chapter Fourteen

At least Kate hadn't been devious enough to lie, that was something, Heather thought the next morning as she drove out of the village to take Delia shopping in Oxford for Edward's funeral.

'It was only Iain,' Kate had explained, reluctantly and stroppily. 'I heard this awful crash, like a bad car accident and I got worried.'

'Why ever didn't you ring Margot?' Heather had asked over breakfast, wishing she didn't sound like an amateur courtroom cross-examiner.

There was an immediate huff of exasperation from Kate. 'I *did.* But I forgot where she was and rang the rectory.' It was all a very typical adolescent muddle. Kate, sleep-dishevelled and slopping around in her T-shirt-nightdress, was giving her mother the 'what on earth did you expect, I'm only a teenager' look across the toast crumbs on the kitchen table.

Heather could hardly blame her, could hardly accuse her of being up to something, something she didn't quite, herself, want to put into words. She could hear her own mother's voice, echoing in her head from long ago, commenting on neighbours' misfortunes. 'The apple doesn't fall far from the tree,' had been one of her favourites, although when Heather had come back from running off with Iain, this had changed to mutterings about some unfortunate families being blighted with black sheep.

'*I* don't know why he wanted to go out the back way,' Kate had answered to the question that hadn't, actually, been asked. 'Perhaps he didn't want to scare you or something. Or intrude on your grief.'

Kate was now being sarcastically bolshy, and Heather prudently decided not to pursue the subject, not to give any clue that what Iain was up to might actually matter in the slightest to her. Because it didn't, of course it didn't.

'Do you think pine or oak, or do they do beech or maple?' Delia was saying as they sped up the dual carriageway.

'What? Oh for a coffin,' Heather replied, dreamily imagining ranges of chic kitchen units. 'I don't know, does it matter?'

'I want to do the right thing for him.'

'They're only going to burn it,' Heather said unthinkingly. 'And whatever you get it's probably only chipboard with a bit of veneer.' She didn't want to be making this trip. Selfishly, she minded the sudden urgency of making disposal arrangements for Edward, when he himself had been relatively so leisurely about the dying process. She'd promised Nigel she'd call in and see him about a customer of his who wanted to pay someone rather a lot to tell him what to do about deep shade. She was desperate to be busy – avoidance therapy, she assumed, so that she wouldn't have to think about either Tom or Iain.

Delia sniffed and scrabbled in her bag for another of her lacy hankies. 'You've turned into a hard woman, Heather. Your poor uncle is lying dead—'

'Oh I'm sorry,' Heather said, feeling guilty remorse. 'It's just that once you're dead all the vultures come down and take their pick. I'm talking about the undertaking business, all wanting to sell you fancy brass-look plastic handles and pastel, frilled polyester linings. I just think it's a tacky trade, that's all.'

'You're lucky you haven't had much contact with it,' Delia said darkly, as if warning Heather of awful prospects to come. 'I dread to think what you'll do with me when it's my turn. Shove me in a cardboard box and bury me under your compost heap, I shouldn't wonder.'

'Actually,' Heather said, smiling, 'I think that's a wonderful idea. Ecologically sound – at least, I think it is.' It depended what you died of, she supposed. Simple old-age heart-failure would be all right, perhaps, but who would want a cirrhosed liver or tumorous bowel lurking and leaking into the humus?

Delia sat and sniffed, and thought about the shortness of life and the awful insensitivity of the young – they had no idea how tragically short even the longest life was. It seemed like only days ago when she'd been preparing dainty salmon and cucumber sandwiches (cut corner to corner, no crusts) for Edward and Harold's visits. She'd had a powder-blue two-piece trimmed with navy binding that Edward had much admired; men *appreciated* women who went to a bit of trouble in those days. Even now, she would rather be shopping for a hat than for a coffin, and wondered if Heather would think her hypocritically frivolous if she managed to combine the two purchases.

'We could pop into Debenhams for coffee or lunch if you like,' Delia suggested as they parked in St Giles. 'Or *I* could. You could just go home if you'd prefer. I can get a bus. Probably.'

Heather made an effort and didn't sigh in resignation – she was tempted to comment that there was a whiff of smouldering martyr. Nigel would have to wait. Old uncles didn't die on a daily basis, and she was being irritably selfish entirely because of bloody Iain. It felt good blaming him, a small step back to a much more convenient, much more comfortable indifference towards him. Perhaps the worst was over, she thought, after all, he wouldn't be around for much longer; he'd drift off back to London or Scotland, or wherever he was currently living, and stay out of her life and stop disturbing her for at least, she hoped, another twenty-five years.

They bought a rather cheap pine coffin. Heather thought it was a lot of money for something that in just over a week would be set fire to, but Delia thought it was just as well that bodies didn't go to the eternal flames with a price tag on the coffin handle, so that relatives and friends could comment on how stingy the purchaser had been. In the awful peach-walled silence of the undertaker's office, where even breathing was muffled by heavy and depressing maroon velvet curtains, Heather asked about the difference between oak and pine.

'About a hundred and fifty quid,' the salesman, lacking a suitable amount of unctuousness, had replied.

'He wouldn't have wanted me to be wasteful,' Delia whispered to Heather while the man went to get a brochure on 'fittings'. 'And he did say something about leaving his money to a children's charity, the NSPCC I expect, so that'll mean more for them won't it?'

'I'm sure it'll be fine,' Heather reassured her.

Heather drove past Oxford gaol on the way to register Edward's death, and parked behind a ribbon-swathed white Rolls-Royce that obviously awaited a bride and groom.

'You'd think, wouldn't you . . .' Delia sniffed, as she and Heather got caught up on the steps with the wedding party, and an impatient photographer waved them, with their respectfully dark clothes and solemn faces, out of the way of the noisy, jubilant celebrants. Crossly, and with exaggerated fuss, Delia brushed confetti off her jacket sleeve and felt no need to finish her sentence. Heather, behind her mother's disapproving back, smiled at the bride and silently wished the radiant couple a lot more luck than she had had with Iain, and perhaps just a little more than she'd had with Tom.

Back in Friarsford, Simon got up late and swaggered into the kitchen, still feeling enormously pleased with himself. Not such a wimp, huh, he smiled to himself in the little shell-bordered mirror, where he saw reflected no habitually useless schoolboy but a fully initiated getaway driver. He wondered if he'd feel the same when he actually managed to have sex for the first time or if, once you'd *had* that feeling, whatever it was about, it was never quite the same again.

'What're you grinning at?' Tamsin asked looking up from her bowl of Coco Pops.

'My glorious self,' he replied, twisting his head so he could see as much of his face in profile as possible.

'You're nuts,' she replied placidly, then looked up again and eyed him with more speculation. 'Simon?'

'Hmm?' He was now on his way to the coffee jar.

'Simon,' she said again, with a note of pre-persuasion in her voice. 'We, that is, me and Suzy—'

'Suzy and *I*.'

'Suzy and *I* are going to play a game, and it means we're going to sleep a night on the island, you know, just past Suzy's garden. Anyway, we were wondering if you and a friend or someone would like to come with us.' She filled her mouth with Coco Pops and chewed noisily.

Simon pulled a face. He'd long since grown out of even remotely wanting to play games with his little sister. Even when he was little he'd only really done it because his mother had persuaded him he was being *helpful*, occupying Tamsin and keeping her quiet in between au pairs, and during their many afternoons of time off for 'study'.

'Tammy, why on earth would you think I'd want to play at wolf cubs in a tent with you and Suzy?'

Tamsin wrinkled her nose, a sure sign that she was thinking carefully and choosing her words. At last she selected an expression of serious appeal and beamed her large brown eyes at him as he sat down opposite her with his coffee. 'I *know*. I'm sorry to have to ask. It's really, really boring, but Suzy's mum won't let her come unless she's absolutely sure she'll be safe. I mean, not all mothers are like ours, you know.'

Simon thought about the enormous number of bottles that rattled off in the back of the car each week to the recycling bin (green section) behind Waitrose. 'No, I don't suppose they are,' he agreed glumly.

'So she'd let her come if *you're* there. Do you see? And Suzy was *so* looking forward to it. You can bring a friend, maybe, er, let me think . . . Shane Gibson or someone. And we'll have two tents.' She was suddenly busy with her cereal again, not looking at him, waiting for him to think it through.

Simon, with unconscious obedience, thought, slowly. And then he thought some more, rather faster, wondering if he'd been quite as clever as Darren had convinced him that he had. What did he actually have to show for the night's terrifying activities? One lousy CD player and a heap of tapes, most of which he'd already bought, that was what. And 'showing' as such was hardly on the cards in the circumstances. Even if he'd got seventeen CD players and a selection of miniature TVs stashed under his bed, how was Kate ever to know just how daring he'd been? He needed to talk to Darren. And he needed to do something a bit more high profile and public to impress Kate. He was beginning to feel he'd been used. Darren must be crowing, he thought. He'd show him, all of them, and Kate.

'OK Tam, but not just one friend. Perhaps we should

have a bit of a party. What do you think? And what do you think about not mentioning it to anyone?'

Tamsin's eyes gleamed with delight. 'Wow, wicked!'

'Possibly very wicked, quite possibly,' Simon agreed solemnly.

With the intrusion into the village by the film crew being old news, the robbery provided the residents with something else to talk about, which pleased all those connected with the film very much and let them off the hook, at least for a while. Julia Merriman came across a small knot of people clustered outside the Spar while she was on her way home from dog-walking. The shattered window from Harbutt's Hi-fi, two shops along, had all been cleared away, so there weren't even shards of glass to wonder over and complain about, and several of the onlookers had slightly disgruntled expressions, as if the night's crime should have left them with something more to do their onlooking at. One or two of the younger women, refugees from London, were quite excited. Urban crime – high street robberies, muggings and joy-riding – was something that had been on the list of things to be Thankful to Have Got Away From when making that great move to the country. Now some of them were quietly acknowledging just how much they'd missed the vicarious drama of danger, the ever-present exhilarating nee-naw of police cars and ambulances speeding about and being urgent. More than one was secretly delighted. In the long-term plan for escaping back to the city, the fact that there was nowhere, not a single village, that could be guaranteed free of crime, could be a useful lever with a husband who still thought it was only rabbits that were stealing his summer bedding plants and that he could safely leave a camera in his unlocked car's glove compartment.

Julia had her own suspicions about the culprits, and she assumed most of the village would too. She slowed down and eyed the hardboard tacked across Harbutt's window space. She didn't quite like to stop and gossip, not once she heard Mrs Gibson loudly holding forth about how ram-raiders drove miles for a suitable hit, everyone knew *that*, it was hardly likely to be local boys now was it. Darren and Shane, of course, were nowhere to be seen.

Delia was thrilled with her new pink-and-green hat. She kept it, still in its bag, on her lap in the front of the car as Heather drove them back to Friarsford. It had completely made her day, Heather could see, buying something so flowered, veiled and ribboned that could easily outdo in trimmings anything that Nigel's mother, the flamboyant Clarissa, might happen to have shelved in her wardrobe. Delia sat like a rewarded child, thankful that the day of awfulness, of form-filling, coffin-buying, and body-disposal arrangement was over – at least till the actual funeral a week ahead.

The closer they got to Friarsford, the more Heather started thinking about Iain again. His presence made her so very unsettled. She would be glad, she decided, when he left and things could get back to normal again – or as normal as they ever were. Though what was so 'normal' she asked her confused self, about sharing her life with a man who apparently liked, in his off-duty time, to indulge in recreational sex with his work colleagues? Perhaps once safely abroad, away from home-ground conformity, Tom underwent man-to-man sex in much the same way that others might casually pick out a suitable looking chap in a hotel bar for a game of squash. The presence of Iain was reminding Heather that there was more to sex than marital habit. It was pitiful, she thought, as she turned the car into her own driveway, how the slightest touch from an admittedly attractive man could have sent her into this silly state of sexual tension. She wondered how many other women trotted through life's daily chores feeling like this. But then perhaps they didn't need to – perhaps their husbands didn't admire them for the fact that they resembled, bodily, people who only had curves when they demonstrated the emergency inflation of life-jackets. Not for the first time, it occurred to Heather that Tom might have made an effort and phoned; he owed her at least some reassurance that he hadn't risked infecting and possibly killing her. Or perhaps Hughie had been right, after all: he and Tom *were* intending to fly off into the future together and set up a bijou home. They might choose, she thought, somewhere under a flight path where, during Tom's imminent retirement, he could be reminded of his past career by the morning scent of kerosene wafting over the suburbs.

Unusually early a few days later, Kate took a phone call that left her in an ecstatic flutter, whirling from room to room looking for the right shoes, the right hairbrush.

'I'm going to be *in it*, right now, today!' she shrieked to Heather as she dashed through the kitchen.

'In what?' Heather called after her. 'Do you mean in the film?'

'Yes! They're doing a big drinks party scene and I can be a guest. The hero gets shot at and we all have to fall on the floor and look terrified.'

'Whose idea was it about you being in it? Did Margot fix it?'

'No, course not. She'd rather be with her dogs. No, Iain just rang and told me. You could come too, if you like, he said.'

Heather made a face. 'I'd probably be discarded by the director for being too old and wrinkly – I can't face that much humiliation! You go and do it by yourself, I'm sure you'll have a wonderful time. But be careful.'

Kate, who had been halfway up the stairs, stopped and came back down a couple of steps. 'What is there to be careful of?' she asked.

Heather wasn't sure what of, but was sure she had to say it. Just in case. 'Oh you know, anything really.' She laughed lightly at her own lack of articulation. 'Careful of the casting couch, I suppose.'

'Oh Mum!' Kate, laughing scornfully, took the stairs three at a time and disappeared into her room.

When Kate arrived at the rectory, she was more nervous than she'd expected to be. She hovered by the doorway, watching everyone else rushing about as if they all had terribly important jobs and knew exactly what they should be doing. When Brian noticed her and sent her to the right room, all the crowd of actors in it seemed to know each other. She was fascinated that they all 'darlinged' and air-kissed, just like people did on television when they were *acting* at being actors. She started to feel very grand, being ushered along to Make-up, a coach parked at the side of the house under the leafiest trees, presumably to try to cool the stifling effect of all the lightbulbs. The make-up girl, who looked so young Kate suspected she might be doing Work Experience, didn't given her much attention, just briskly brushing her cheeks and eyelids with choking clouds of various powders and frowning at her in the mirror as if she felt it was beneath her considerable dignity to waste her time on 'Support' actors when there were stars to be cosseted. Wardrobe was even more disappointing. She joined a line of chain-smoking chatty women, loudly reminiscing about *Four Weddings* and was eventually handed, after the briefest up-and-down look at her body for size, a slinky black lycra dress with translucent sleeves – a better version of which she had lying scrunched up under her own bed.

It was decided that her own shoes, her favourite black ones with a dolly bar, would 'just about do'. 'Give them a quick rub with your sleeve dear,' she was ordered. All around her she could hear busy gossip that included phrases like 'getting into character', 'God-awful *per diems*' and 'No smoked salmon, can you believe it?' from the gaggle of professionals, but nobody spoke to her.

Where's Iain? she wondered, wishing a friendly face, especially his, would turn up so that she could be taken care of. She also wanted to show this over-confident, gabbling crew that she might not know them but she *did* know people who mattered. Just for once it was an enormous relief to see Simon. She caught sight of him, dressed as a waiter with his hair slicked back, and immediately burst into giggles. The dab-chick was all got up as a flunky, in a dinky white bow tie and trying to put on a face like Stephen Fry playing Jeeves. How, she wondered, could someone so scrupulously clean put up with having such thickly greased hair?

'Jeez, you do look funny,' she told him.

'You don't. You look amazing,' he said before he could stop himself.

Kate felt her face going pink under the powder. She wondered if it showed, as a blush now bloomed on Simon, though perhaps they didn't smother the men quite so much in cosmetics. 'What have you got to do?' she asked. 'Do you have to say anything?'

'Definitely not, they'd never let me. I have to wander round with a tray of drinks and look busy. Shame I've not been cast as another guest, then we could talk to each other.'

'True. Though I could be one of those women who runs off with the butler.'

'Talking of parties . . .' Simon started, seeing an opportunity that might not come again, along with Kate in a good, almost flirty mood, 'there's going to be an outdoor one on the island, probably on Friday, we thought, if it's a really hot night. Would you like to come? Loads of people will be there, I mean even kids, so it's no big deal, but it might be fun. I thought you'd want to be invited. I mean, it's not as if there's much to *do* round here.' He shrugged dismissively as if he didn't care one way or the other, just thought he'd let her know then she wouldn't feel left out.

'Yeah. I'll come,' she told him, watching out of the corner of her eye the cast of extras being assembled for their scene. 'Though on one of the days I've got this funeral to go to. I'll need cheering up after that.'

Driving over to Nigel's nursery that afternoon, Heather's thoughts were concentrated determinedly on plants for shady areas. She drove out of the village behind the council estate and thought of hellebores and polygonatums and tellimas. Martagon lilies could be good, she thought, as long as the client was interested enough to check for lily beetle, otherwise the plants would be a complete waste of time. Her mind ran on to violas and hostas and euphorbias, and possible colour combinations. Delia sat quietly by her side, now feeling slightly concerned that her new hat still wasn't grand enough to rival the glorious lime green straw cartwheel that Clarissa had been wearing at Margot's barbecue. For all its ribbons and roses that she had been so thrilled with, it somehow wasn't *magnificent* compared with the careless flamboyance of Nigel's mother. All her life Delia had aspired to discreet good taste only to discover that there were social circles in which this was simply prissy gentility. It was all to do with class, she concluded, sighing to herself. She was, though, very much looking forward to the promised tour of Clarissa's famous rose garden and some tips on the eradication of black spot. In

Putney she had a small row of hybrid teas out in the small garden at the back of the flat.

'Do you think Clarissa will be able to tell me, without actually seeing them, whether I'm over-pruning? My roses do seem to end up a bit on the scraggy side,' she asked Heather anxiously.

'*I* can tell you that – you *are* over-pruning. But you have also got some varieties that really aren't going to get very big, anyway. Why not intersperse with the odd shrub rose, plus a climber or two along the wall behind them? Then you'd have a wonderful display, much more extensive. And think of the heavenly scent.'

'Hmm, perhaps. I'll see what Clarissa thinks.'

Heather smiled to herself and understood the subtext: her mother couldn't believe that Heather *really* knew about plants, especially roses: that was for her own generation, and best of all it was for *men*, preferably the sort who grew exhibition standard onions and the sort of long, pale, flawless carrots that always made her think of underused penises. It would go well against the grain to acknowledge that Heather actually knew something that Delia didn't. Delia wasn't sure about rambling roses either, Heather recalled from the days when, as a young and self-conscious teenager, she'd been uncomfortably certain that the creepy man next door was always fiddling with his marrows whenever she went out to sunbathe in her bikini. She'd crossly suggested to her mother that trellis and a good thick and thorny climbing rose might keep the man's prying eyes away from her. Delia had said that climbers were untidy things and got out of control. Heather had argued that it was the man next door who needed controlling and Delia had told her not to be so silly, he was perfectly respectable, an executive in Local Government and a member of the Round Table, so he couldn't be spying on her, could he? 'And besides, if you will go making an exhibition of yourself . . .' had closed the conversation on rambling roses.

They'd reached the far side of the village, out beyond the estate and the green, when Heather's phone rang. Delia tutted and muttered something about concentrating on one thing at a time as Heather fumbled with the aerial.

'Don't you ever look in your rear-view mirror?' Iain's voice, jaunty with amusement, purred down the line to her. Heather's right hand twitched on the steering wheel as she glanced into the mirror, trying to look indifferent through her soaring blood pressure. The scarlet Mercedes was following her round a slow bend at a discreet but unnerving distance, and she felt in danger of driving into a ditch.

'Yes Kate, I'll be home for supper, no problem,' she heard herself saying, sure that her nose was growing from telling lies.

Iain laughed softly. 'How about having supper with me? We could go out somewhere, go to London if you like.'

Heather could feel Delia listening hard and wondered if her hearing was still so sharp that she'd be able to make out that this was a man's voice, nothing like Kate's. She jammed the phone hard against her ear, just in case, and thought how out of practice at this sort of thing she was – she should have pretended it was the plumber. It would have been better not to do any pretending at all, but she felt it wouldn't be half as much fun.

'Er . . . no. Well not tonight anyway,' she replied rather squeakily, hoping she wouldn't giggle.

'Another night? There's something I really need to talk to you about,' Iain persisted, clearly enjoying her predicament.

'Maybe, I'm not sure – we'll talk about it later. Oh and be an angel and get the spaghetti out of the freezer for me would you please?' Heather felt quite delighted with her inventiveness, but instantly realized there would be no defrosting pasta sitting on the kitchen worktop when they got back. Delia would notice, no question. Kate would be told off and not know what on earth was the problem, and so the web of falsehoods would weave itself in awful knots.

'Certainly, no problem. I'll be the *perfect* angel,' Iain said, and then rang off.

'Was that Kate? I thought she'd gone off filming,' Delia said with a disapproving sniff.

'Hmm. Yes, just wanted to know, er, if I'd be back later. I expect she wants to borrow money or something. Perhaps she's going out with Annabelle.'

They'd reached the nursery by now. Delia stepped out and looked across the Renault roof at Heather. It was a look of deeply speculative suspicion, one Heather, with her life of more or less tedious respectability, hadn't seen for years. It told her that her mother thought she was Up To No Good, and it made her feel quite sparky inside. About time I had some fun, she thought as she returned her mother's frown with a wide and uncontrollable smile.

She was wrong if she thought she'd heard the last of Iain for that day. Delia was dispatched to Nigel's ancestral home for her rose-garden tour and a cream tea, while Heather went into the unusually spruce coach-house office to meet her new client. 'Nigel, you've tidied up,' she commented as she sat down next to the window and stroked his enormous cat.

'Did it for you. Didn't want this chap to be put off *you* by the appalling state of *me*. I want him to want you to buy *everything* I've got out here.' He waved his arm in the direction of the greenhouses and poly-tunnels beyond the stable yard. 'Then I can sell up and get rid of the whole sodding lot. I quite fancy a gallery next . . .' Nigel was off into dreamland, and Heather glanced out of the window. The cherry Mercedes slid round the corner and pulled up across the yard with Iain's hand waving gently to her out of the window. The car then circled with hardly a sound and drove away, back towards the road. She stifled a giggle. The awful man was following her, surreptitiously chasing her, blatantly amusing himself. How much more fun Iain was as a new secret than as the old one. She was feeling just as she had when he had boldly driven the E-type into the staff car park at school, blocking everyone's exit, and waited for her Latin class to finish on Wednesday lunch-times. Then he'd whisked her to the pub, sometimes cramming a friend or two into the seat with her, her white PVC mac covering her uniform, and her tie stuffed in its pocket.

While Nigel ranted on about the awfulness of trade and the despicable tendency of plants to die on him, she realized that if she got the opportunity she would definitely take the chance of a night of passion with Iain. If Tom was about to leave her, she no longer had anyone who cared whether she did or not. She counted up in her head the number of men she'd slept with in her life. Only five (three of them eager but hopeless boys from college) seemed a minute collection for someone who'd been part of the free-love end of the sixties. Iain wouldn't even add to the total, and besides, surely one's very own ex-husband didn't count?

Chapter Fifteen

Delia really felt she could have done justice to a house like Clarissa's. It was Palladian and golden, with parterres and rose gardens, and plenty of sheltered sunny niches for outdoor tea with cakes she would neither have made herself nor bought in Safeway. You had to have servants, a cook, staff to enable you to rise above the mundane and to glory in the architecture, the vista, the sumptuousness – although what Delia could see of the curtains seemed to be shockingly faded. But there was a certain nobility about the rotting away of grand things, she thought. Polyester/cotton velvet falling to shreds could only look tawdry, ancient silk velvet could not. She could have adapted to this sort of thing very easily, had life's cards been differently dealt. She could have locked the door of the Putney flat and walked away without ever once looking back if she'd had somewhere glorious like this to move on to. Perhaps if Heather had only . . . but that was long ago, and in Scotland, and only the damp and the chill and the loneliness had made any impact on her. What a silly child she'd been, stupidly impulsive and with neither staying power nor sense of history. For now, Delia was content to sit on the upper terrace, looking across the fancy iron balustrade towards Clarissa's magnificent roses, waiting for tea and enjoying the certainty that her new hat from Oxford was, after all her trepidation in the car, *just right*. Clarissa, who was wearing a straw hat so ragged Delia at first thought it was a piece of old sacking, had actually been impressed enough to make just the right admiring comments before disappearing into the house to organize tea. Delia trusted she had done this by pulling on a bell-rope of age-matted *petit point*, as in a historical TV costume drama.

'Sorry to be so long, Julia's just arrived and we thought we should water her dogs first.' Clarissa plonked a large butler's tray down on the dark green wooden table. Delia inspected the crockery with interest, hoping to see some delicately patterned Meissen, but being disappointed to recognize a floral tea-set identical to the one her friend Peggy had bought in the John Lewis sale. Delia thought it entirely appropriate to put the dogs before humans: it was suitably aristocratic.

As tea was being poured, Julia came out carrying a large chocolate cake and accompanied, as always, by her labradors. 'Hello! How lovely to see you! Oh and don't touch the dogs, one of them has been in something disgustingly foxy and he stinks.' She put the cake on the table and waved her arms at the dogs. 'Boys! Get away! Go and roll on some fresh grass!' she commanded.

'Lovely cake,' Delia commented.

'Mmm. These weekly WI sales are marvellous aren't they? I buy all my cakes and jams at them,' Clarissa said with enthusiasm, shattering another of Delia's illusions. So much for the teams of cooks and kitchen maids. It was probably like anyone else's kitchen really, all Magimix and muddle. It probably wasn't even 'below stairs'. 'So is the whole village still in chaos with the film company? Or are they almost finished? I heard a rumour they were going to take over the churchyard and that everyone's furious that all their old Auntie Doris's graves will be vandalized. We're so on the edge of everything out here, I hardly know what goes on,' Clarissa asked Delia.

'We don't see much of them,' she replied, wondering at the same time why there were no cake forks, and if it would be rude to ask for one. The chocolate icing was very gooey, and she hoped there wasn't any caught on her lip-edge.

'Not even that attractive chap staying at Margot's? That writer, Iain whatsisname, Ross?' Julia asked through a mouthful of cake.

'I haven't seen him at all, in fact I'm afraid I don't recall him being mentioned,' Delia confessed apologetically. She felt she was disappointingly under-informed. Both women had a rather beady gleam in their eyes as if he was someone who *should* have been the talk of the village, and that somehow she was supposed to have brought with her a useful amount of gossip.

'Of course Ross is just the name he writes under. You *must* have heard of him, surely, all those gory crime novels?' Clarissa was saying. 'His real name is Iain Ross *MacRae. Sir* Iain, I should say. Owns an awful lot of Scotland.'

Delia suddenly found it impossible to swallow her cake. She had the same feeling she'd had on the train at Reading, short of breath and with her blood pressure going haywire. She immediately had no doubts, none whatever, that Heather had known all along that he was there in the village. She'd been keeping secrets again, of that Delia was suddenly certain. She thought about leopards not changing their spots. Then she thought about the phone call in the car and Heather's silly girlish grin and knew there would not be spaghetti defrosting in the kitchen when they arrived home. She unfastened the top button of her blouse, tangling her fingers awkwardly in the pussy-cat bow ribbons, and tried to regulate her breathing. The tea was making her perspire.

'We used to know his people,' Clarissa was continuing, calmly pouring more tea. 'I should have had him over for drinks of course, dreadfully remiss. Father knew *his* father out in Kenya. Old Sir Cuthbert died out there, I believe. Couldn't stand the frozen north, so he stuck to his plantations and the decadent ex-pat life – all gin and giraffes I imagine.'

'Do you know,' Julia leaned forward towards them both in a confiding manner, 'when Heather came round to bring my camellias, she did make the slight suggestion that he might just *do* for a lonely widow like me!'

'No, oh no he wouldn't do at all.' Delia heard her own voice coming from somewhere. They were looking at her in polite surprise and she looked back blankly, feeling much as she had the last time she went to the dentist and had come out of the anaesthetic murmuring about cushion covers.

'No, you're quite right my dear, I've heard he only likes the young ones. Absolutely typical man! Think they can have anything they want!' Clarissa said with a snorting laugh.

'They usually can,' Delia added grimly.

'Did you have a good look round the roses?' Heather asked her mother as they both climbed into the baking hot car for the homeward journey.

'Yes. Quite lovely,' Delia replied briskly.

Heather waited for her to be more forthcoming. She thought that she'd at least, on this occasion, done the right thing by Delia. It was just her sort of outing, not only a visit to a historic house, but tea with its owner who could quite reasonably be referred to as a friend. She'd been thrilled enough to be joined for tea by an Earl, the previous summer, when on a Townswomen's Guild visit to a famous garden. She'd mentioned it, as if in passing, then quipped, 'Well of course it's probably included in the entry fee,' but there'd been no disguising how delighted she'd been.

'Were there any you took a particular fancy to?'

'Any what?'

'Roses. Did you jot down any of their names? Nigel might have some in stock, we could come back again before you go back to Putney and have a look.' Delia seemed vague and Heather's insides tensed, wondering if her mother was actually ill. Now that the strain of Uncle Edward's care was removed from her, the sudden relaxation, combined with the August heat that had been grilling the car when it was parked, might be enough to bring on a stroke.

'There was a very striking "Masquerade",' Delia said pointedly.

Heather, driving along the narrow road, risked a sideways glance at her. Her mother sat impassively, staring straight ahead through the windscreen. It was a very intense stare into the middle distance, Heather thought, for someone who didn't have to think at all about where she was going.

'Are you all right? Shall I open the sunroof?' Heather asked, reaching up for the handle.

'*I'm* fine. Nothing wrong with *me*,' was the reply which made Heather smile. It was just so exactly like when she was young and she was supposed to guess what she had done wrong, while her mother fumed and brooded and sulked and cultivated an atmosphere that reminded Heather of a severe choking fog. Then, once she'd worked out that it was probably because she'd been an hour or two later home from the college than she'd said she'd be, she would resolutely play a game in which she behaved with complete cheerful normality. She'd bang around the kitchen making cups of tea for them both, make a start on her homework, switch on the TV and chat about how envious she was of Val Singleton presenting *Blue Peter*. It was like staring someone out, waiting for her mother's patience to crack when she would at last blurt out her grievance. I must have grown up at last, she thought now. Life is much too short for these grudge-games.

'OK, so what's wrong?' she asked as they turned on to the main road leading to the village.

'You know,' Delia said.

'No, as a matter of fact I don't,' Heather told her. 'I don't want to play games, and you'll obviously want me to know what it is in the end, so out with it.'

'*He's* here,' Delia said, still looking straight ahead. 'That man you ran off with.'

'Oh you mean Iain,' Heather said, in a more blasé and easy-going manner than she actually felt. There was a small amount of relief, but only a tiny one. She'd been quite savouring the secret. All those gossiping old ladies must have been discussing him over tea. She'd like to have been a fly on the ivy-covered wall when Delia realized who they were talking about. Her mouth twitched dangerously towards a broad smile.

'And you've been seeing him, haven't you?' The interrogation continued, a sharp accusation, ludicrous from one adult to another.

'Hey, does it matter?' Heather protested. 'Though actually I haven't been "seeing" him, as you put it. Not in that way.' She wondered if she should start crossing her fingers on the steering wheel to fend off the results of what might start to be lies. A single magpie flew in front of the car as she slowed down near her own gateway.

'One for sorrow,' Delia remarked, with a note of satisfied prediction.

'They're always single in August,' Heather told her. She parked the car under the pergola and sat, thoughtful for a moment, fiddling with the keys in her hand. 'I never got round to telling the girls I was married before, so they don't know anything about Iain. It might as well stay that way now. I've missed the moment for telling them, and besides, he'll be gone again in a week or so,' she said eventually. 'Actually, he's been very nice to Kate, getting a part in the film for her. She's delighted.'

Delia opened the car door and looked back at

Heather. 'Well she would be, wouldn't she? She's a lot like you were at that age. You should keep an eye on her. A very close eye.'

More warnings, Heather thought, sighing as she climbed out of the car, her mother had obviously missed her true vocation and should be dressing up in shawls and earrings to tell fairground fortunes.

Up in Suzy's room, she and Tamsin were assembling the necessities for a night on the island.

'Shall I take clean knickers for the morning?' Suzy said, half to herself, as she made a heap of possible clothing on the bed.

'No, don't be stupid. We'll just go home, you won't need anything extra to wear at all,' Tamsin insisted impatiently. She was sprawled on the bed reading *Just Seventeen* and flicking off Suzy's clothing as it landed on her.

'A nightie?'

'In a tent? Are you mad? You can sleep in your clothes, though if you're sharing with Simon you'll probably not want to be wearing anything. I shall take perfume of course, something *irresistible*.'

Suzy gave her a quick, intense look. Tamsin was so flippant it was hard to know what she meant and what she didn't. Was she, she wondered, still intending to share her tent with Shane, and if so was she intending that he should remove *her* clothes, all of them even . . . She shuddered slightly and wished she didn't keep thinking ahead about possible awfulness. Suppose Tamsin changed her mind about not really *doing* anything with him? And then did *it* and got pregnant. Could you get pregnant before your periods had actually started? Or suppose she *didn't* change her mind, but he started to feel he'd been conned and then raped her . . . There was something in the bus shelter

229

about a girl called Trace being a prick-teaser – somehow you just knew they hadn't written that because they liked her being one, not like the thing about Lisa. They'd be stuck out there on the island like . . . well, like sitting ducks.

'Can't wait till next Friday,' Tamsin was saying from the chest of drawers where she was gazing into the mirror inspecting a potential spot on her forehead.

'Friday?' Suzy yelled.' I can't go on *Friday*, it's the uncle's funeral.'

'Well it won't take all night as well as the day, will it? Unless you lot are some fancy religion or something?' Tamsin asked via the mirror.

'Well no, it's just . . . I don't think Mum will like it, or at least Gran—'

'It's *got* to be Friday, it's all arranged. I fixed it with Simon and he's agreed to come, so you've got to.' She turned round to give Suzy her full, rather threatening, attention. 'And if you don't . . .'

Suzy gazed straight back at her, refusing to be intimidated. 'And if I don't, then what?'

'Nothing.' Tamsin had a thinking face on, then looked up and beamed at her. 'If you *do* I'll give you the new Blur CD. Simon's got some spares.'

'Spares? Why's he got spares?' Suzy asked, mystified that anyone would want more than one of *anyone's* CD, however brilliant. She'd seen and coveted the new album in Harbutt's Hi-fi only the other day . . .

'Don't ask,' Tamsin replied, turning back to the mirror with an infuriating wink.

'And then we all had to look really *terrified* while the man, the bad guy, came in with a shotgun and threatened to kill us. I had to drop my glass of champagne, but it was OK, it wasn't Margot's carpet. I wonder what they've done with all her stuff?'

Kate had been bubbling over with her day of stardom through the whole of dinner. Delia had given the stir-fried chicken and vegetables a hard and meaningful look, as if food cooked that fast couldn't possibly be all right, but Heather had decided to ignore it. She was too old for all this. Perhaps, she thought, as she added the raspberries to the fruit salad, she should tell her mother all about Tom, the *real* Tom. She could march her into the sitting-room, or even the study to make it seem more serious, and astound her with the probability that at this exact moment, and she checked the kitchen clock as she opened the fridge to get cream, at this moment Tom was as likely as not having his penis nibbled by a comely airline steward. The steward, Hughie, Heather assumed, would look exactly like the sort of neatly suited good-boy types who had got clerking jobs in banks straight from school when she was a teenager.

In Staines High Street, Delia had frequently pointed one out and said something like 'Now *that's* what I call a nice-looking boy,' as if informing Heather what husband-material she could have chosen instead of Iain. Delia had never much approved of Tom – she'd have preferred someone much closer to Heather's own age so that he could be somehow moulded into the perfect, dutiful son-in-law and grow up into agreement about the advantages of spongeable vinyl wallpaper and British-made cars. Tom had come too ready-finished for her liking. He didn't need her ever-ready opinions on mortgages, career-moves, pension schemes or how to make the most of the National Savings scheme. One day, Heather remembered, she had mentioned an airline black-tie event they were going to, and Delia had later telephoned Tom to tell him she'd compiled a list of places where dinner suits could be hired. Tom had told her politely that he'd owned one for years and it was at that point, Heather was certain, that Delia had finally conceded defeat: even she recognized that it was a sign of a fully mature grown-up to have one's own dinner jacket. Unfortunately fully mature grown-ups also arrived with their sexual quirks more or less sorted out too, Heather thought glumly.

'And Iain says they might be going to film a fake wedding and he says if they do I can be a guest . . .' Kate could hear her voice rattling on like a toddler who's just been to the circus. She hoped they wouldn't guess how much she was exaggerating; the day had been filled with too much hanging about, boredom and the dreadful suspicion that she was doing everything wrong. Every time the director had roared 'Cut!' she'd been sure it was her fault. She didn't want to admit that in front of her family – her grandmother would be sure to say 'Nonsense, why ever do you think they'd be looking at *you*?' which was probably just the sort of thing she would have said to Heather years ago. The other actors hadn't exactly been over friendly, and she was pretty sure that when the film came out any possible view of her would be obstructed by a particular plump gingery woman in a feathered hat, who'd elbowed everyone out of the way so she could hog the camera. She never thought she'd be so glad to have Simon around. She'd have preferred to have Iain to talk to, but he'd only arrived just as they were all packing up. She'd pouted and been cross at him for abandoning her to all these people and he'd merely laughed infuriatingly and kissed her on the top of her head like some uncle. Not, she was having to admit to herself, the way she wanted him to kiss her at *all*.

'And Iain says I can meet him and some of the crew in the pub later, so if that's all right . . . ?' Kate started collecting plates together hurriedly, crashing them about rather too much and endangering their wholeness.

'Iain says, Iain says,' Delia twittered mockingly. 'He *has* made an impression on you, hasn't he? Isn't there a nice boy in the village you could be friends with?'

Kate froze and stared at her grandmother, looking, Heather thought, quite stricken, even shocked.

'That's enough Mother, leave her alone.' Heather slammed a dish down on the table, hard enough to crack it. 'Kate, leave the dishes, Gran and I will deal with them. You go and get ready.'

'Thanks Mum,' Kate said softly, leaning across and kissing her swiftly. Heather caught her radiating a glance of pure hatred at her grandmother, who had the grace to look down at the remains of her fruit salad.

'How could you do that? Whatever made you speak to her like that?' Heather demanded the moment Suzy, rightly sensing an atmosphere to be avoided, had gone outside to tend to her pony.

'You're right, I'm sorry. I shouldn't have said anything. I just felt, I don't know, *angry* that she seems to be as much smitten by him as you were at her age,' Delia replied. The two of them were going through the motions of tidying the kitchen, running taps, opening cupboards, moving out of each other's way in a complicated dance so that they wouldn't actually come too close.

'Oh don't be ridiculous. He wasn't even thirty then, now he's well past fifty, for heaven's sake. What on earth do you imagine Kate's going to see in him?'

'Yes I'm sure you're right, it's just that it only seems like yesterday,' Delia sighed deeply.

'Well it wasn't. It was half a lifetime ago, over and done with.' Heather was shaking with rage. 'And it was something that happened to *me*. Not to you. *I* ran off with him, *I* married him, *I* got pregnant and lost *my* baby. It's about time you stopped pretending that it was all done just to spite you, and that you were the person most affected by it.' Heather could feel that she was close to tears. She wished that when Iain had phoned her, car to car, she'd said yes, she'd love to go out to dinner that very night. They could be out somewhere now, laughing over a bottle of something delicious and lazily eating their way through that day's menu-special. They could be in a pub garden, wondering if it was going to get too cold to eat outside, or in a hushed and horribly empty restaurant laughing at the too many hovering waiters.

'I'll be going home straight after the funeral,' Delia was saying with a sniff. 'And don't worry, I won't say anything else to Kate, not if you don't want me to.' She had her wronged face on, Heather recognized.

'You *know* I don't want you to,' Heather said with exasperation, wondering if anything at all had been achieved. It so rarely was between generations, she thought.

Kate went into the pub and hoped Iain would have got there first. She felt so geed up, she wondered if she might have to sit near the door in case she felt sick. It wasn't like anything else she'd done, not like meeting any of the boys she and Annabelle had picked up when they were out clubbing, or at parties. It felt *beyond,* in the same way that leaving school had felt.

'Hello, Star,' Iain greeted her from the bar, drink already in his hand.

Kate assumed he expected her to smile cutely, so she didn't. Her grandmother, formerly so doting, had put her in a contrary mood.

'Oh, too grand to talk to me now are we?' he teased.

She glared, staring at his teeth which, although she felt so cross, were nevertheless fascinating her. They were so big and white and even, not like old people's usual graveyard teeth that seemed to lose brightness like the rest of their bodies, but like teenage polished ones, freshly released from orthodontic hardware. They looked dangerous, in the same way that even stupid Little Red Riding Hood should have sensed, the moment she saw the wolf in the forest. What took the girl so long to catch on? Kate wondered.

'Please don't wind me up,' she said forlornly. I'm not in the mood.'

'Let me get you a drink. White wine and soda? Or does the barman know you're still a *minor?*' He leaned forward to whisper the last word, his breath grazing her ear.

'White wine will be fine,' she told him, finding a smile at last.

'Now tell me what's bugging you. Didn't you have a good day?' he asked, as they sat at a corner table close to the dartboard that only rainy night teenagers ever used.

Kate sipped her wine and then dabbled her fingers in it, playing with the ice and stirring the lemon round. 'I had *quite* a good day. Everyone seemed to know each other except me and Simon.'

'Well at least you had Simon. Don't think I don't arrange these things for a purpose,' Iain said.

'Yeah, but *Simon*,' she said, pulling a face. 'He's nice and that, but you know, I've told you before. Too young.'

'And I'm too old,' he said, as a statement, not a question.

'No,' she replied. 'I think age is a weird thing. Some people you can't imagine ever being young. Like my grandmother.' Kate stopped and sighed gently. 'Do you know my grandmother told me off tonight for talking about you?' She gave Iain a fierce look, as if searching in his face for a possible reason for Delia's hostility.

He looked down at his drink and swirled it round the glass. 'Well perhaps it depends what you were saying,' he told her.

'Not much,' she shrugged. 'Not enough to fuss about. I expect it's because you're *old*,' she giggled. 'Mum got angry with her. When I left I think they were having a row.'

'Didn't you creep up and listen?' he taunted.

She elbowed him hard in the ribs. 'Certainly not. That's the sort of thing Suzy might do.'

'Oh you mean *you're* too old for that sort of thing?'

'Oh well, yeah I suppose so. But you know what I mean about age, don't you? I mean, take Tamsin, Simon's little sister. She can't *wait* to be about twenty-seven. It's her mental age, and probably always will be. She's desperate to dress up in clingy lycra frocks and red high heels and have a corkscrew perm with a slide through the back of it that looks like a dagger. She'll probably work in a travel agents and absolutely *love* it. She'll always be the same, a version of the same thing even when she's seventy.' Kate hesitated and then added shyly, 'And then there's people like you.'

'Go on.' Iain was looking at her more seriously than she'd seen before. He idly stroked her hand with his finger, which she watched. The last boy who'd held her hand, she suddenly remembered, had had ground-in grey nails. She'd known, deep down, that it was probably from playing rugby or something, but some-how she had thought instead about surreptitious nose-picking and felt slightly sick. Apart from Simon who took it too far, you couldn't really trust them to be clean. You had thoughts about where their unwashed hands had been, whether they'd decided that yesterday's, no, the day *before's* socks were just about all right. Iain's nails were short, square and perfectly clean. She didn't have to have those teenage suspicions about him. She wondered what it looked like to other people, this man, this man of *his* age playing with her fingers in a way that would tell anyone watching that he certainly wasn't her dad, or her grandad even. Up at the bar there were loud laughing people, balding men with big blowsy women whose flesh overhung the bar stools. One of them was wearing a low-cut pink T-shirt, leaning forward and showing cleavage like a crêpey canyon. Kate couldn't imagine her own sheeny-sheer skin ever looking like that.

'I think that with people like you it's not really anything to do with how many years you've had,' she said to him, 'it's probably about not getting stuck, and about letting new thoughts have space in your head.'

Iain was smiling sadly at her. 'It isn't as easy as that, you know. Some new thoughts, well, one day you'll find they can be quite a problem.'

Chapter Sixteen

Heather lay awake worrying, and blamed her mother for it. Kate hadn't come home yet and it was well past pub closing time. She imagined her daughter in various scenarios, the most likely, she decided, being that she'd gone back to the rectory with Simon and Iain and a rowdy collection of technicians, where they would be working their way through a crate or six of lagers, and skinny-dipping in Margot's pool. Other, less crowded, more unnerving scenes also made their way into her head, ones in which Iain and Kate were alone. She placed them in various locations – in Russell's boat chugging in the dark up the river; up in Tamsin's treehouse discussing the state of the world; in Simon's bedroom where Simon currently wasn't. Here her mind tried to select something else. She turned over in bed and tried to dismiss the thoughts as being quite ludicrous. It was all Delia's fault, perverse old woman even *thinking* about it, *warning* about it. How could she? It was almost as if she was willing the worst, whatever that was, to happen.

Downstairs the front door was slammed with Kate's usual carelessness. Jasper barked dutifully but without enthusiasm, so she knew Kate had come home alone. She pulled on her dressing-gown and tiptoed down the stairs making Kate, whom she found gazing hungrily into the fridge, leap with fright.

'Why are you creeping around like that Mum?' she demanded, grabbing a lump of ancient cheese from a plate at the back of the fridge.

'I'm not,' Heather told her, walking over to switch on

238

the kettle as if all she'd come down for was a cup of tea. 'I'm thirsty and I'm wearing no shoes, that's all.'

'Hmm,' Kate mumbled, through a mouthful of cheese. She perched on the edge of the kitchen table and inspected her mother, waiting for questions.

'Nice evening?' Heather enquired.

'Not bad. Just the pub, you know.'

'Anyone there?'

'Not many. Bloke from "Inside Story" rabbiting on about how his cat shredded his seagrass carpet or something. Some people talking about the robbery at the hi-fi shop. The whole village thinks Shane Gibson did it, which isn't fair. I mean, they don't know, do they, and it's just because he did something *before*. If this was the old mid-west they'd probably hang him from a tree on the rec.' Kate finished the cheese and jumped down from the table.

She's waffling, Heather thought, and then felt angry with herself. She was truffling out deviousness just like her mother did, and she wasn't being either straight with Kate or fair. 'All that cheese, you'll have nightmares,' Heather commented as she poured boiling water into the mug.

'Not me. I'm going to have *wonderful* dreams. G'night,' Kate said, whisking out of the room and taking the stairs three at a time.

Heather drank the tea and then continued to lie awake, this time blaming the caffeine. She gave up at about 2 am and started leafing through *Gardeners' World* magazine, trying to get terrifically interested in the various forms of euphorbias available. She thought about making notes towards planning the new client's shady garden, but couldn't make her hand reach out for a pencil and notebook. She did, though, make her hand reach out for the phone the second it rang.

'Heather? Hi it's me. How are things?'

'Tom? "Things" are fine. Apart from Uncle Edward

dying, but that wasn't unexpected. Things with you aren't so fine, though, I gather,' she said, wondering if this was the moment at which she'd be told she was about to become a lone parent. Surely he wouldn't, not over the phone, not after all these years. Just let him dare.

'Aren't they? Oh.' Silence followed, which Heather refused to help him with.

'Oh you mean Hughie,' Tom continued eventually. 'Well he's got things all wrong, the silly sod. That's all I can say. I'm really sorry. He shouldn't have phoned you. I did tell him.'

'Things' again, Heather thought, nothing specific. She sighed wearily.

'I'll be back next Thursday night,' he said, recovering some of his usual cheerfulness.

Heather laughed softly. 'Well that's good, just in time for the funeral.' Jetlag was not going to be an excuse for getting out of it, she decided, replacing the receiver. If Tom wanted to come home and be remorseful, he would have to do a bit of joining in. She couldn't recall the last time they'd both chosen colours from a paint-chart, or gone together to a parents' night. Perhaps she should encourage him to do more of it, she thought as she switched off the light; perhaps he felt, perhaps he'd felt for years, that he was too much a visitor in his own home. No wonder he had found it so easy, when working, to behave as if he hadn't really got one.

'I've made a decision,' Margot said, watching Heather hoeing the herbs. 'I'm going to tell Russell I'm leaving him, and then check into a health farm.'

'Do they still call them "farms"?' Heather said, straightening up and rubbing her aching back. 'It makes it sound as if you're to be fattened up for slaughter, not thinned down and sent home looking gorgeous.'

'True. But it's the only way I'll stop drinking and get myself put back together. I feel like a car that's got a good-enough engine, but needs its rust dealt with. And perhaps then Russell might spend more time with me and not be forever running off to "conferences" with "secretaries".' Margot's lip wobbled and Heather led her to the bench from which they could see the placid cows on the opposite river bank, stolidly munching grass and being enviably free of cares and pressures.

'I think he likes you now, deep down. He'd be devastated if you really left him.' Heather briefly thought about Tom: he'd be devastated if *she* left *him*, too.

'They'll be going next week, all those people, so we can move back into the house. I think I'll let Russell do all the organizing, *then* he'll see what it's like.' Margot dabbed at her eyes with a tissue. 'Some woman called Delphine keeps phoning. At first I thought, well what kind of a name is that? It sounds like a brand of lavatory paper. Then I thought, it's a *young* sort of a name, that's what. Now we haven't got an au pair, he's up to the usual with someone else's. He told me this morning he's got a big trade dinner in Coventry next week, staying over of course. Pull the other one I told him – couldn't stop myself, it was last night's gin talking.'

'Couldn't you two do some proper talking? Or see someone from Relate or something? Going off is a bit drastic,' Heather said, biting her lip and wondering if, having said this, she could actually ask Margot the favour she had been planning to.

'Later. First I'm going to make myself feel good, then I can deal with him from a stronger position. You know, I could never be unfaithful to *him*,' Margot confessed, twirling her crumpled tissue.

'Couldn't you?' Heather said, making Margot look directly at her.

'No,' Margot insisted. 'It would be just the worst thing. Don't you think?'

'Er, not necessarily. There *must* be worse things,' Heather said evasively. She wondered how Margot would react if she told her about Tom and Hughie. She partly wanted to tell her, but couldn't. If Hughie had been another woman, she could have run round to the Garden Cottage at drinks time and wailed, 'Guess what the bastard's done *now*,' and been able to count on sympathy and comfort and a tactful forgetfulness when the episode and upset were over. But Tom with another man was somehow what Kate would call 'beyond'. Once told, it would be like cut skin where a silvery trace of pale scar could be always just seen. And then there was Iain. She looked round the garden rather furtively, half expecting her mother's beady eyes to be peering through the ceanothus by the wall.

'Margot I need to tell you something, just for a kind of insurance. I hope you won't mind.'

'Go ahead. Don't tell me *you're* up to something?'

Heather laughed nervously. 'No I don't think so. Unless you count going out for dinner with my ex-husband. Pretty innocent stuff really. It's just my mother, you know. She always thinks the worst. She now knows who Iain is, thanks to the village old-girl mafia, and she's hopping mad I didn't mention it before. As if that would have improved things.'

'So where and when are you going out?'

'Wednesday. The Manoir au Quatr' Saisons, and I've told them all I'm seeing a client miles away. I wish I hadn't.' Heather sighed, wondering if lying had been such a good idea. She could have just brazened it out and tried to ignore Delia's pointed looks, sniffs and huge hints of disapproval which would eventually have had the girls asking questions. 'Thing is,' she went on, 'when you tell a whopper like that, so that no-one knows where you really are, it's like saying, "Come on lightning, strike the chimneys and burn the house down", or willing the car brakes to fail on the M40. That's why I'm telling you, so at least *someone* will know just where I am, in case of emergencies.'

'Especially if you don't come home at all because Iain has strangled you in a fit of jealous passion because he realizes he should have hung on to you.' Margot laughed but Heather didn't.

'I think I'll cancel—' she said.

'Don't be silly, it's only a meal, what can it hurt? What time are you supposed to be back, so I know when to worry?'

'Ah. Well, er, that's the thing. Don't start to worry till lunch-time the day after.'

Margot's eyes widened and she gulped. 'Oh, like that is it? You *are* up to something!'

Heather stared hard at the river rather than risk seeing Margot being appalled at her Russell-like lack of morals. 'No. Well not yet, probably not at all,' she said with a shrug, stabbing at the ground with the hoe. 'Really it's just in case . . .'

'Well I don't suppose he counts, really,' Margot conceded kindly.

'Just what I've been telling myself,' Heather agreed.

It was what-to-wear time again. Heather felt as dithery as the first time she'd ever gone out with Iain, when she'd known she was in for something a lot more sophisticated that the inept breathless snogging that boys of her own age could just about manage. She remembered then worrying about her body and having a good look at its smooth, sleek lines in the bathroom mirror. Was it *all right*, she'd wondered, as probably all girls did, or would Iain's marauding hands and probing fingers come to an abrupt, alarming halt, confirming the unmentionable certainty that there was something *odd*.

Years on she was looking at it again, this time sure that the mechanical bits and pieces were all much as everyone else's (Margot and her 'We're all the same *down there*' coming into her head). But this time she wondered if her bottom could only be described, *à la* Noel Edmonds as 'crinkly', and if her small breasts, which she'd thought more or less all right, perhaps twenty-five years on would remind Iain of over-stretched empty woollen mittens. She would have to count on age having given him failing eyesight.

Le Manoir and its famously delicious food had been a smooth and irresistible temptation down the phone. 'Have you been there before?' Iain had asked. Heather had, and said so, though, still childishly in pursuit of sophistication, didn't mention she had only been once.

'Did you spend the night there?'

'Yes, actually.'

'Oh.' He'd sounded slightly miffed.

'What is it? Did you think I'd have a truly dull life with anyone other than you? Never go anywhere scintillating?' she teased.

'Did you go with your husband?' he asked.

'Well, yes, why? Who else would I spend the night in a hotel with?'

'Oh, no reason for asking really, just wondered,' was the unsatisfactory reply.

Now, as Heather dried her hair, she was ninety per cent sure what he'd been getting at. Obviously he intended they should stay the night there, though she wished he'd made that absolutely beyond-doubt clear. She stashed spare knickers, toothbrush and moisturiser in a large handbag, too wary to take anything more and risk looking foolishly presumptuous. Surprises were one thing, but she was a grown-up parent with arrange-ments to make, even if the arrangements were just a suitable set of lies to be prepared. She *wanted* to stay there all night, she was quite certain. Tom had been a complete sod and he owed her one, more than one, if anyone was to do any painful counting. She shut the hairdryer away in a drawer and thought of Uncle Edward in his coffin. *That's what we all come to*, she thought sadly, toying with the tarnished brass handle of the drawer – just faded out, and dead and gone as a pæony flower. *At least*, she thought, *the pæony plant gets to revive in time for the next spring, keeps having another go at getting things right, which is more than we do.*

When she left the house at seven, Heather, guilty at being so devious and sly, was only half ready to meet Iain – decorative trimmings would have to be added in the car, just like back in the days when she'd skilfully used the mottled mirror in the swaying train compartment to stick on her individual false eyelashes and dot freckles on to her nose. 'I'm having dinner with the client, and then staying in a little B&B – it's just too far to drive straight back,' she'd told Delia and the girls. 'I'll take the phone in case you really need me, but I'm sure you'll all be all right.'

'Must be a very generous client, taking you out for dinner,' Delia commented.

'It's a very big garden,' Heather replied. 'It'll be a good lot of work for me. These customer relations, planning stages, are the most important you see.'

'You do look nice Mum, hope you have a great time,' Suzy told her.

Heather felt hot, wondering if the sky-blue rough silk suit, even without the heavy silver necklace and earrings that she'd got hidden away for later in her bag, was too give-away dressy for a simple 'business' dinner. She felt a spiky twinge of guilt. It didn't feel right having Suzy wish her a lovely evening, when she was all keyed up for a spot of hectic adultery. At least Kate was still out dog-walking for Margot – that made things slightly easier.

245

As she drove out of the village, she could see her plodding across the rec with a basset hound lumbering along inelegantly at her side. The Gibson brothers lurked among the swings watching her, and Heather wished, for Kate, divine intervention – a heavenly gift-pack of gorgeous and admiring young men that all good and lovely teenage girls deserve. She drove past the pub, checked her rear-view mirror for cars that would recognize hers and, seeing none, turned quickly up the lane past the church towards the golf course car park. The scarlet Mercedes was already there waiting for her, like a spy waiting for a contact in one of Iain's own books. As she parked under the chestnut tree she could see his hand out of the window, tapping rhythmically on the edge of the roof. She tried to imagine what music he was listening to and realized she couldn't even begin to guess. It could be anything – Beethoven or Blur, or the closing music of *The Archers*, for all she knew. All she knew about him, in fact was very, very little, and always had been.

'This is all very clandestine, meeting up here,' she said as she approached the Mercedes.

'Well what would you prefer, this or me swanning up to your front door and escorting you out under the eyes of your entire family?' he said with a grin as he opened the passenger door. 'It's all for your own protection – you're the one who thinks secrets are for keeping.'

Heather's mouth felt dry with nerves. She looked back at her little Renault, abandoned under the trees, as they drove out of the car park. Perhaps she had left it just that bit too close to home. Suppose Julia Merriman took it into her head to have an early nine holes the next morning? Suppose Kate went walking a Great Dane that needed extra leg-stretching miles? Or Suzy and Tamsin braved the fury of the golf club squirearchy and trotted their ponies up this way? By the time she got home in the morning, police from three counties could be out

246

searching for her body, which instead of being horribly mangled in a ditch would be deliciously ravished in a four-poster. *Fingers crossed, anyway*, she thought.

They were early, as Iain had planned. 'I thought you'd like time to look round the garden,' he told her as the car swished over the car park gravel.

Heather smiled and nodded. 'I've only seen it in winter before,' she told him. 'There wasn't much to see then, of course.' A little doubt nibbled inside her as they strolled past the lavender-bordered beds of herbs. They could surely have wandered round the grounds in the morning. Wouldn't that have been just the thing to follow a lazy breakfast? And besides, she was thirsty.

'So where are you this evening?' Iain asked as they approached the lake.

'Gone to see a client about his garden. A nice far-away client,' she added.

'Are they often "far away"?'

'Sometimes as far as Banbury,' she teased. 'You can see how famous I am.'

'What are you going to advise the client?'

'Not to have a box-hedge knot garden,' she said, 'unless he's planning on living to at least a hundred so he can see it at its best.'

They stopped at the edge of the lake and Iain leaned on a tree, looking at her. 'What plants would you advise for me?' he asked.

Heather grinned at him. 'At your great age, I'd say not to count on anything more long term than hardy annuals.'

He laughed, but without conviction, Heather thought, and then took her hand. 'Come on, let's get a drink and look at the menu. You must see the dovecote too. It was voted one of the ten best hotel rooms in Britain.'

The dovecote was a two-storey, circular brick building, a grassy, flower-flanked path away from the main

247

building. A miniature house, like something gorgeous for a big child to play with. *How lovely,* she thought, *ultimate privacy.* Iain ordered champagne and they went through to the hotel drawing-room, where he showed her the inside of the dovecote in the hotel brochure.

'Perfect for honeymoons, I should think,' he said. 'Remember ours?'

'Such as it was,' Heather murmured, looking at the photo of the pink-and-white circular room, the bed drapes suspended by doves that looked, magically, as if they were in flight. She and Iain had spent their wedding night at a hotel in Edinburgh, whose splendour must have started fading into dingy shabbiness at least fifty years before their visit. Their arrival had caused a flurry of outraged disapproval throughout the bleak reception area, the manager to be sent for and their marriage certificate scrutinized for several long minutes in which the breathing of the staff could be heard, filtered through gritted teeth as if terrified that immorality was an air-borne infection like chickenpox. Heather had been giggle-smitten as Iain, presenting a face comically composed into a caricature of sobriety for the manager, had at the same time been fondling her bottom with his hand up the hem of her tiny skirt.

'Goodness, remember that hotel, all faded mahogany and dirty cabbage-rose wallpaper? It all smelt of old age and depression,' he reminisced. 'I wish there'd been somewhere like this to take you. You were much too young for a place like that.'

'*Everyone* was too young for a place like that, even you. Even – let me think, who was really old back then? Churchill was already dead wasn't he? OK, General de Gaulle.'

'Are you sure it's politically correct to be so ageist?' Iain asked her, putting on a mock-hurt expression.

'Probably not. Strange though, the age gap between

us isn't anything much now, is it? I mean, I don't know whether I've caught up or you've stayed youngish or if, when you get past, oh, thirty-five or so, everyone's much the same till they fall seriously foul of the ageing process.'

'You're right,' Iain told her as they walked into the dining-room and attracted no curious attention from other diners. 'Everywhere I went with you back *then*, heads turned, and not just in amazement at your stunning beauty.'

'Especially in pubs,' Heather laughed. 'All those landlords asking if your daughter wanted orange squash.'

'When I used to read about Bill Wyman and Mandy Smith, I always wondered if he felt as nervous as I used to when he tried to get her into nightclubs.'

Heather savoured her lobster ravioli and thought about the things that had been going on in the world since she had started and stopped being married to Iain. When she'd got onto that slow train back to London from Edinburgh there'd been no colour television, no VAT, no food sold at Marks and Spencer, not even, just, decimal currency. Comprehensive schools were an experiment, cocaine was something the dentist anaesthetized teeth with, and ozone didn't come in fragile layers but as something bracing to be inhaled at the seaside. She and Iain had been having separate but parallel lives; reading the same things in probably the same newspapers, experiencing the Gulf and Falkland wars as TV spectator sports, rendering them less shocking than they should have been. Heather sipped her wine and pondered on the impossibility of discussing a quarter of a century of missed exchanges of views. They were little more than strangers really – what would be the point of asking how he'd felt on the death of Elvis or the election of Margaret Thatcher as Prime Minister?

'Kate is really quite talented, of course . . .' Iain was

saying as the plates were cleared away. 'Does she get that from you? I don't recall you being in a school play.'

'I never volunteered,' Heather told him, 'being tallish, there was every chance I'd have to be cast as a boy. You could bet your life that if I got to play Professor Higgins they'd make me kiss Eliza Doolittle – whether the script called for it or not. It was that kind of school.'

'Excitingly perverse,' Iain leered. 'There's something about girls' schools.'

'That's what Kate said, which is one of the reasons why she's left hers. She absolutely hated it and its atmosphere – she said it made the staff just as childish as the pupils.'

'A-levels next, I take it? She seems very bright.' Iain put his hand on hers and looked at her fingers as he stroked them idly. 'She reminds me so much of you at her age.'

Kate's hand isn't age-speckled and dry like mine is now, she thought, quickly banning the thought from her head. Heather laughed lightly. 'Much more common sense, I think. Do you, do you ever miss not having had a family?' She wondered if that had been impertinent, and the spectre of their sad-fated baby hovered fleetingly and vanished. He might have all sorts of reasons for not having one; there might by now be some problem that went beyond his notorious attraction to young and unsuitable women.

'Of course I do. You know, I envy you. You seem to have got it all – husband, good place to live where you know who you are, lovely daughters. I'm still something of a nomad, albeit a successful one career-wise. Things sometimes seem to be working out, but then they just don't. You're still the only one I actually *married*.'

Heather gave him a wry look, wary of his little-boy expression. He didn't need to go for her sympathy-vote to get her into bed. 'Men can breed till the day they die, you've got plenty of time if you need to produce an heir to all that family baggage,' she told him, feeling like a mother comforting a child for the loss of a heartless lover, and not wishing to be doing this at all. She'd been brought out tonight to be wooed, lusted after, guiltlessly seduced; she would have enough emotional mopping-up to do when Tom got home.

Glorious food came and was eaten. 'All this trouble these chefs go to and all we do is *eat* it,' she sighed over the last spoonful of a celestial coffee soufflé. 'There should be some other process of savouring this that's different from the method that's just the same for munching boring old fish and chips.'

'I'm so glad you agreed to come,' Iain suddenly said, leaning forward and giving her an almost fiercely direct look. 'Having met you again like this, it would have been awful not to find we could be friends.'

'So civilized,' she murmured, immediately wishing she wasn't blighted by instinctive sarcasm. She wondered if that was anything to do with why, rather suddenly, there seemed to have been coffee, the bill, the way out and the beginning of the long drive back to the village. She felt a mixture of things: mildly drunk was one of them, but along with that was rejection and dejection, and the pathetic futility of trying to have the kind of adventure that seemed only to be available to those who were too young to need it. If she'd been one of Iain's sweet girlish things, she was certain she'd be still in the hotel and by now down to at least her underwear. 'Romping', a word so treasured by the tabloid press, was obviously an activity reserved solely for those barely out of rompers. She sighed quietly and thought about her unappealing flesh, coarsened by sunshine and wind and lacking youthful 'give', like over-washed elastic. Good-looking rich men of any age had such choices, she thought glumly Surely the whole point of this lavish dinner hadn't been to apologize for

251

the day he'd put her on the train and out of his mind like a used-up disposable razor?

'By tomorrow I'll be thinking of all the things I intended to say to you and didn't,' he was saying as the car swung into the Golf Club car park.

'You could try saying them now,' she replied, suspecting there was nothing *to* say.

'When I think I'll try, I somehow can't find the right words – awful admission for a writer,' he said as he stopped the car next to the Renault under the chestnut tree. 'Sorry, but I just want you not to think badly of me.'

'It shouldn't matter to you what I think, not now,' she told him, opening the car door. 'You should stop thinking everyone thinks about *you* all the time.' She gave a light, rather hard laugh. 'God, I sounded just like my mother then.'

When he'd gone, Heather unlocked her own car and sat in the driving seat feeling cross. She didn't really like him very much, after all, she decided. He just, as he had before, represented An Adventure. He was being deliberately mysterious, as if it made him more interesting – a sure sign of bloated ego. Instead, she was just confused and cross. He'd gone all *heavy* on her, she thought, reverting appropriately to her teenage vocabulary. It was way after midnight and she was supposed to be tucked up in a cosy bed-and-breakfast place miles from the village. She could wake up the household with an awkward tangle of excuses for an early return, or she could stay in the car all night getting cold and stiff and unnerved by prowling foxes. Eventually she started the car, drove with exaggerated care down the lane and out on to the main road and turned into Margot's driveway, tucking the Renault away on the far side of Margot's BMW. Russell was safely (or not) in Coventry, and she thought of him asleep, satiated from 'Delphine', with his conference name-badge pinned securely to his silk

252

pyjamas. She giggled quietly as she threw gravel gently up to the lighted window, and Margot's make-up-cleaned face as round and pale as a moon, leaned out of the window.

'Oh, it's you. I thought for a minute my prince had come.'

'One day,' Heather promised her, crossing her fingers against the lie.

Chapter Seventeen

Heather woke up feeling stiff from the effort, even in sleep, of keeping to her side of the bed. Margot was probably the last person she'd have guessed she'd be sleeping with. She imagined Margot could have thought of more thrilling bedfellows, too.

'If you don't want the whole village gossiping about the two of us, you'll have to leave before 10.30. That's about when Tamsin and Simon start feeling hungry enough to drag themselves out of bed,' Margot said as she brought Heather an early cup of tea. 'Of course, Simon probably wouldn't actually notice you're here, seeing as he's in training for being a man,' she added, with the kind of smile that told Heather it was only halfway to a joke.

Just after ten, Heather thought it might be reasonable to be on her way home, seeing as she was pretending to have made an early start from the other side of Kettering. She felt slightly queasy, as if all the lies she'd been telling had given her mental indigestion. They'd been unnecessary too, which made her feel as cloyed inside as if she was overstuffed with chocolate cream cakes and guilty regret. *It's my own stupid fault, trying ridiculously to dig up the thrills of the past*, she told herself as she drove out of Margot's gates, looking carefully to the left and right as if she could swiftly hide the Renault behind a tree, should a familiar face come into view. She was just thinking about sensibly (and boringly) leaving teenage kicks to teenagers when she noticed the large white van with blackened windows pulling out of her own driveway. Heather could see

'Private Ambulance' written in red on the side and felt immediate heart-banging panic, knowing, just a hundred per cent certain, that her mother was in it and that something *catastrophic* must have happened. It was unsurprising, really; obviously a punishment. She only wished she'd actually done something thrilling enough to be punished *for*. Trembling, she steered up her drive, sure she was about to be assailed by a tearful Suzy or Kate hurling themselves on her and wailing about heart attacks, broken hip joints, blood on the carpet or strokes. Why didn't they phone, she wondered, and also, since when had her mother been subscribing to anything medical that involved an ambulance flaunting itself as 'Private'.

'Mum, Mum, you won't *believe* it!' Both Kate and Suzy came running out of the house, wide-eyed and worried, towards her as she forced her shaky legs out of the car.

'What's happened? What's happened to Grandma?'

'Grandma? Oh she's here,' Suzy said.

'Oh yes, *she's* here all right,' Kate echoed crossly, 'and not *just* her.'

'Well who was in the ambulance then? Surely not Mrs Gibson?'

'Mrs Gibson went home cross and said she wouldn't do any cleaning, not while Uncle Edward's here,' Suzy told her, with her thumb in her mouth, a sure sign, Heather knew, that she was quite seriously alarmed.

'Yeah he's come to stay, so Gran says.'

Heather strode into the house to confront her mother, hoping at the same time that Edward had at least got his lid nailed down.

'Hello dear, did you have a nice evening?' Delia greeted her cheerfully as she walked across the hallway from the dining-room.

'Not bad. Look, Mother, what's all this about Edward? Kate and Suzy say he's *here*.'

255

'Oh yes, of course. I had him brought home. It's quite usual, you know, the day before the you-know.'

'Well not here, it isn't, and I mean we haven't even discussed it. And where . . . where exactly is he?' Heather looked around the hall nervously, seeing in her own house closed doors that she was too spooked to open. Jasper was running up and down, snuffling excitedly at the bottom of one of them, his little tail frantically wagging with disrespectful curiosity. What would happen if he actually got in hardly bore thinking about.

'On the dining-room table. Don't worry, I made them line up all your place mats under the coffin, so there won't be scratches. It's not as if you use that room very often anyway, is it? You always eat in the kitchen.' Delia started muttering about family meals with proper damask tablecloths.

Suzy did her homework on the dining-room table, Heather was thinking. She'd probably feel too creepy to sit alone in there from now on. She'd need to be talked to. She took her mother's arm and led her gently outside to sit by the pool. 'Look. I know that for your generation it's the proper thing to do,' she began carefully. 'It's just that, well, the girls. *Their* generation don't come into contact with the dead. Come to think of it, neither does mine. They're feeling a bit nervous, scared. Dead people make them think of ghosts at their age. And they weren't expecting it.' Who was? she thought. 'Nothing had been said. You just—'

'It's all right, I get the picture,' Delia said, sniffing and fishing in her sleeve for a handkerchief. 'But perhaps you could explain a few little things to them. Edward is *family*. Just because he's dead and gone, it doesn't mean that his body should stay in that awful anonymous undertaker's chapel among *strangers*. I hope I don't have to. I'd want to come home.'

'But this *isn't* his home,' Heather pointed out, carefully not answering the hint of a question.

'Well he could hardly stay all by himself back in the sheltered housing. Home is where your family is, where last respects can be paid. It's proper to accompany a person to his last resting place,' Delia insisted. 'You don't just say "I'll meet you there" as if you're going to the pictures.'

Heather sighed and surrendered. She hadn't the heart to summon the undertaker and demand the removal of Edward. Part of her understood and agreed about death being a natural part of life, and that it shouldn't be tidied away by people barely different from the specialist collectors who dispose of difficult refuse, like asbestos and old fridges. 'Goodness knows what Tom will say,' she said eventually, hoping to give up and pass the buck.

Later, having showered and changed and had a good think about exactly *when* her mother had made these arrangements, and if it was anything connected, however obliquely, with the presence of Iain, she crept down the stairs and summoned enough courage to open the dining-room door. She hadn't minded Edward being dead at the hospital, that had been such a small progression from his last moments of life. But there was something so creepy, Uriah Heep-ish about having been got at by undertakers, she thought, that it turned death into a quite horribly artificial process, with all its secretive rituals – something similar to the sneaky addition of water and chemicals to bulk out bacon.

Edward was lying in the snug blue ruffled-satin nest in his best suit, which had obviously fitted him several, heavier, years ago. He looked as smart as if he was going to a Rotary Club dinner, with his tie militarily straight and his shoes richly polished. The wrong shade of blusher had been applied to his sagging cheeks and his eyelids were suspiciously bluish. Delia had closed the curtains and lit two pairs of geranium-scented candles in Heather's favourite silver holders, which told

Heather that she must have been preparing this little surprise quite carefully on the sly – even 'Inside Story' didn't stock candles like these, they must have been secretly purchased on the trip to Oxford. The discreet scent brought to mind pot pourri on lavatory window sills. *I'll think of this every time we have people to dinner*, she thought, trying to banish grumpy selfish thoughts and replace them with more humble ones in the presence of death.

Outside the dining-room door, furious whispering was going on.

'I'm not going in there. Not if you paid me a million,' Suzy was saying.

'I wouldn't mind for a million,' Kate whispered back. 'But I'm not going to give myself nightmares just for Gran's satisfaction.'

There was a stifled giggle from Suzy. 'I *dare* you!' she hissed at her sister.

'Dare me how much?'

'The new Blur CD, and Oasis. Simon's got loads of stuff apparently going spare, Tamsin says, and she can get them off him . . .'

'Well . . . maybe,' Kate wavered greedily, faced with a bribe.

'But it has to be at *night*. In the dark, just the candles.' Suzy was pushing her luck, Heather considered, at the same time having a passing thought about what Simon was doing with a load of spare CDs. The idea of crime did not, of course, enter her head. He wasn't that sort of boy.

'So when the noise got too much with all the drunks yelling and laughing, this little chap asks the stewardess for ear plugs and she's too busy and waves him off in the direction of the loo.' Tom paused for breath and sipped his wine. 'Couple of minutes later, back he comes with a

Tampax sticking out of each ear with the string dangling! "You all right, Sir?" she says, and of course the things obviously work 'cos all he says is "Pardon?"!'

Suzy and Kate were spluttering over their chocolate mousse. Delia smiled politely to show no real hard feelings, but Heather saw her eyes turn worriedly towards the direction of the dining-room, as if Uncle Edward, in his condition, should not be exposed to such unseemly conversation. It was no good saying yet again that he couldn't *hear*. Since his arrival, Delia had been ostentatiously tiptoeing round the house, shushing anyone who dared to speak in more than a whisper. Kate had lost her temper and told her that it would take more than a Senseless Things album played at full volume to wake the dead, at which Delia had gone to her room for a new handkerchief to cry into down by the river, where everyone could see her. Kate had apologized, but warily, still smarting from when Delia had been so waspish about her going to the pub with Iain.

Tom seemed so grateful and relieved that, after the Hughie business, Heather allowed him back into the house at all, that he was being determinedly cheerful and entertaining.

'He's being very *wearing*,' Delia complained as she watched Heather making coffee after supper.

'Just glad to be home, I think,' Heather told her. 'I'm glad he's here too,' she added, which she would have done, out of loyalty, whether she meant it or not. Luckily, she realized that she *did*.

'Sorry about the presence of death,' she said to Tom as they got ready for bed, getting in first with the apologizing. It would be his turn soon enough.

'I don't mind. It's not as if he's being any trouble – not like some visitors. And at least we don't have to feed

259

him or listen to endless tales of golf triumphs,' Tom told her from the bed where he was flipping through the TV channels pretending he was trying to find something worth catching up on. 'And if it makes your mother happy.'

'You're being very accommodating.' she commented.

'Yes, well.' He shifted and adjusted pillows, not looking at her. 'Guilty conscience I suppose. Do you want to talk about it?'

Heather fleetingly thought he meant Iain, not Hughie. She only had a guilty conscience about *intent* and couldn't work out where that rated on the Richter scale of marital earthquake. 'Did you honestly imagine I *wouldn't* want to?' she asked him, 'I mean wouldn't most people rate it a fairly cataclysmic event, having your husband's boyfriend call you up from across the world and spill the beans?' Heather's hands were shaking as she folded her skirt, unfolded it and then threw it inaccurately towards the laundry basket in the bathroom. They'd spent the evening play-acting at happy families and now it was as if not just that one performance, but the whole run might be over.

'Not much actually happened, not *actually*,' Tom muttered. 'Things just got ever so slightly out of hand.'

Heather felt ridiculously inclined to giggle like a smutty child at his choice of phrase and put it down to nerves. 'I wouldn't do anything to put you at risk.' he added.

'Oh thank you so much for that. Goodness I *am* grateful.' She resorted to heavy, heartfelt sarcasm. 'Actually I don't know *what* to be at all. There's probably a helpline one's supposed to ring for bloody counselling about this sort of thing,' she said, sitting heavily down on the bed and wondering when they would all be grown up enough to accept that romance was just a shimmering layer on the top of otherwise fairly murky water.

Tom shifted warily towards her. 'God I'm sorry. I'm not surprised you're angry. I mean I would . . .'

Heather got up and paced to the window and back. 'Would what? Be *slightly miffed* if I trotted off for a spot of girls-together afternoon fun with, oh, who? let's say Julia Merriman.' No, let's not, she suddenly thought. Her mouth started twitching into an involuntary smile at the very idea and she turned away to play with the curtain. She accepted that justified outrage at Tom was watered down by her own guilt, but couldn't allow it to be further diluted by an intrusive sense of farce as well.

'No I mean you and well, *anyone* else. Unfair I know.' She heard him sigh and waited for him to move on to explaining.

'It was just rather flattering, at first. But then of course as soon as I'd shown a bit of interest, it was all too intense.' He grinned nervously, as if afraid to gauge her reaction, 'Hughie is simply looking for Captain Right. It couldn't possibly be me.'

'Poor Hughie,' Heather commented, returning to sit beside him on the bed, 'you've hurt him.'

'I've hurt *you*. And I'm sorry,' he said, reaching across and touching the back of her neck carefully as if afraid she'd flinch and recoil. I'd have hurt you, too, terribly badly, if things had gone the way I'd planned, she told herself, but not him. Tom, sensing that his sins might eventually be forgiven, if not forgotten, smiled at her looking, she thought, rather like a grateful child let off a naughty deed by his mummy. But I'm *not* his mummy, Heather thought, wondering if all wives had to put up with an element of this. In some men, she knew, it took the form of boyish little questions like 'Have I got a clean shirt?' or regarding the sharing of domestic chores as 'helping'. In Tom, right now, it was a matter of off-loading guilt – clearing out his emotional toybox and waiting for Heather to tell him he was *such* a good boy. 'Bloody Hughie,' he declared suddenly, as if,

261

confession safely over, blame could now be success-
fully reallocated. 'Why ever did he have to go blurting it
all out to you?'

'Do you mean that simple phrase: "what I never knew
could never have hurt me?" ' Heather asked, feeling at a
loss in the face of such blatant naivety. How new to
deception he must be. In which case, how much luckier
she, with her trunk-load of untidy secrets, was than
Tom.

Tamsin came round to see Suzy about last-minute
arrangements for the night on the island just as she was
getting ready to go to the funeral. Suzy wore a dark blue
pinafore dress which looked, she thought, terrific with a
T-shirt under it, but completely, humiliatingly infant-
school with the white blouse and Peter Pan collar that
her mother insisted she wore. She sulked down to the
hall to talk to Tamsin, who snorted with laughter at her.

'What *do* you look like?' she said. 'You look about
nine!'

'It's only for a couple of hours. Gran thinks being
smart shows respect.' The dress would never feel the
same again, she thought miserably, whatever stunning
little top she wore underneath it. She'd forever associate
it with these awful bulbous sleeves that were just a tiny
bit, uncomfortably too short when the horrible pearl
buttons were fastened.

'Yeah but . . .' Tamsin, in violet leggings and a
bottom-covering Take That! sweatshirt, looked her up
and down as if she'd never seen anything like it.

'Anyway what do you want?' Suzy asked her,
keeping her hovering on the doorstep in case Delia
came and saw her and made a fuss about Visitors at
Such a Time. The cars would be coming any minute.

'You still on for tonight?' Tamsin asked anxiously, as
well she might be, Suzy judged. 'It's all fixed, Simon's

organized it and everything. Don't forget your torch or your lantern and that. And bring some food.' She stopped and giggled slightly. 'Don't come dressed like that, will you? I mean your chances with Simon are already zero, you don't want them to go down to a *minus*.'

Suzy glanced round the hall behind her. No-one was on the stairs, no sign of her gran or parents. 'Look Tam, I've got to go now. Er . . . oh yes, my new lamp and loads of chocolate, they're in here, come in and take them with you now if you like.' She invited Tamsin in, opening the door and listening carefully for household noises. She pointed to the dining-room door, knowing the chocolate bait would be completely irresistible. 'It's all in there, on the table. Bye . . .' And so she was halfway up the stairs before she heard Tamsin screaming and everyone else came running.

'Yes!' she whispered loudly to herself in the safety of her bedroom, punching the air with the satisfaction of sweet revenge.

Heather sat in the back of the Daimler between her mother and Tom, feeling hot and sticky in her navy silk suit. She was aware of the soapy scent of her deodorant, which made her feel as if she was getting clammy under her arms. Delia, in a hat made entirely of bluish feathers that Kate was horribly sure were magpie, glared through the windscreen ahead at the hearse containing Uncle Edward, furious that the cars were too pale a grey instead of the more traditional black. American influence, she assumed. Heather was glaring at the driver – a thoughtful undertaker who, having carefully supervised the removal of the coffin from the house, had polished the dining-room table with what looked disgustingly like a much used handkerchief and left the room smelling strongly of Silk Cut.

Heather turned her unholy thoughts towards Iain, who seemed to have disappeared from her life again. Not a word since That Night. He must have realized she was practically throwing herself at him and gone into hiding. Or just gone – the film people were now in the process of breaking camp. Maybe in the restaurant he'd had a glimpse of the contents of her handbag, caught sight of the lacy black edge of her favourite bedtime-fun knickers and been frightened away. All evening he'd seemed to be on the edge of saying something that needed saying, but hadn't got round to it. Perhaps the word he'd had such trouble with had been 'Goodbye', though she couldn't think why – he hadn't had any problem with it the last time they'd separated.

At the crematorium, only Kate looked as if she was having appropriate soulful thoughts about the sad transience of earthly life. Her face looked sorrowful and pale, and she listened to the short service with her oval face tipped sideways, like a serene Madonna in a holy portrait. Big gruff men in black overcoats and dark suits made up the numbers from Edward's British Legion, along with a bearded gingery warden from his sheltered housing who had brought along several of his neighbours in a mini-bus. Tom was fidgety, and Heather guessed he could hardly wait to get back home to the Test Match on TV. Suzy, she could see, wasn't concentrating at all on the procedures, but was reading the waxy marble plaques dedicated to the memories of the district's worthier citizens. When the awful theatrical moment came, of the purple velvet gold-fringed curtains swishing back and the coffin, whirring and clicking on its conveyor belt, trundled through the doors, Suzy gasped loudly and gripped her mother's hand. Heather put an arm round her and patted her gently for comfort, but Suzy stretched up and whispered to her, 'It looks just like a puppet theatre, doesn't it?'

*   *   *

'Well that's over, then,' Delia announced as Tom unlocked the front door and they all went in, casting off hats and jackets as they went, and gladly abandoning them on the newel post at the bottom of the stairs.

'Drink, I think,' Tom declared, heading for the kitchen.

'Just a small sherry for me, please,' Delia said. 'Then I think it should be the will.'

'Have you got it then?' Heather asked, pulling off her shoes with a sigh of great relief.

'He gave it to me a couple of weeks ago, once he knew.'

'Oh. You never said.' Heather wondered why she hadn't mentioned the will, then realized it was probably because being the trusted possessor of it made her feel important, needed.

'No, well . . .' Her mother was looking shifty, as if she'd steamed the envelope open and taken a sneaky look already. Delia, still in her magpie hat, sat very upright on the sofa by the open French doors and thought that this really ought to be more formal, perhaps gathered round the table in the dining-room, where she was well aware that Heather did not, for the moment, like to be. She fished her reading glasses out of her handbag, opened the large buff envelope, and began to read the complicated formal bits about being of sound mind, followed by a couple of charitable bequests and then '. . . the residue to be divided equally between Katherine Melissa Bellingham and Suzannah Victoria Bellingham—'

'What?' Kate, who had not been showing any signs of listening, interrupted abruptly. 'Me and Suzy?'

'Ssh,' Heather said, 'listen to the rest first.'

Delia took her glasses off slowly, folded the document and said, 'But there isn't any rest. That's it. £5,000 to the

NSPCC, £1,000 to the Lifeboats and the rest to Kate and Suzy. He was fond of children.'

Tom cleared his throat and took a long sip of his beer. 'Clearly,' he said, impressed.

The question that hovered unspoken was eventually asked by Suzy. 'How much exactly does "residue" mean?' she said, scarcely more than whispering.

When Suzy finally escaped from the house and hauled her tent into the rowing boat she felt as if she'd won the National Lottery. 'I've got a hundred thousand pounds. Probably about that anyway,' she told a passing pair of ducks. 'I'm rich.' She wasn't allowed to tell anyone; Gran had said money wasn't for talking about, but she felt a lot more confident about being interesting with Simon. She had a secret, and it was more intoxicating than the sherry she'd been allowed after the funeral.

There was the sound of a lot going on at the island as she rowed along to it. It was getting dark, just, and her mother had said the usual annual thing about nights starting earlier, which was so depressing and made them all think about going back to school and the winter beginning. She looked over her shoulder as she rowed, and could see that there were more than just Tamsin, Simon and Tam's beloved, awful, Shane. She could smell woodsmoke, too, which made her think of bonfire night and being cold enough for gloves. Kate appeared on the bank, at the end of the garden, waving and calling to her, and she had to go back and get her. Kate had loads of money now too, and although Suzy would normally have felt inclined to ignore her and just go on rowing, now she felt linked to her by this peculiar secret and the odd generosity of this uncle they didn't know.

'Why do you think he left it to us?' Suzy asked Kate as she clambered into the boat.

'Don't know. I suppose it's because we really are the

only people in his family. He could have left it to a dogs' home.'

'Margot would have liked that,' Suzy commented.

Kate giggled. 'She would wouldn't she? She's so lovely, old Margot.'

'Funny thing to say. As if you're going to *miss* her or something. You're only going to the sixth form college, not boarding school or the moon.'

Kate trailed her hand in the water and splashed it up and down like a toddler making waves. 'Mmm. Maybe. Perhaps I don't need to now.'

'What about your A-levels?'

'What about them? People get by without them. Specially if they've got money.'

'Dad says it's not *that* much.'

Kate laughed, her teeth very white, Suzy thought, in the dusk. 'Well he would, wouldn't he, in case we get silly and rush out and buy a Mercedes each.'

'I wouldn't want one.'

'I might,' Kate said thoughtfully.

Simon lurked behind a tree on the island watching Kate's arrival. He stepped forward to take her hand and help her out of the boat, hoping she wouldn't realize he'd been hanging around and waiting for her. She looked so fantastic, he thought, all that ripe-corn hair and a silly little black wispy dress that was going to be much too cold for her later.

'You made it then,' he said, cursing himself for stating the stupidly obvious, but continuing to hang on to her hand.

'Hey what about me?' Suzy yelled, furious to be left to deal with the oars and the ropes by herself. 'I'm not a *ferry*,' she complained, while Kate looked blankly back at her as if not quite understanding what her role in the safe mooring of the boat should be.

'Oh I'm sure you can manage,' Kate said with a smile, 'you're amazingly capable.'

'Amazingly stupid,' Suzy muttered, securing the rope to an overhanging branch and stamping off with her tent and bag in search of Tamsin and whoever was making all the noise just beyond the first line of trees. Bugsy was upside-down, swinging from a branch and trying to drink lager from a can. Most of it went down his face towards his forehead and hair, but the over-loud way he roared with fury and frustration told Suzy that he'd probably got quite a lot of it inside his body already. Darren was perched higher up the same tree, chucking twigs at Bugsy and aiming for his nose. Simon and Shane prodded at the little fire that Suzy thought didn't look safe – it looked too spread out, without any stones to mark its edges and stop it spreading over the dried-out ground and the leaves that were already starting to fall. She hoped she wouldn't be the only one who'd keep a careful eye on it.

'Another three boat loads are coming!' Tamsin squeaked with excitement next to her, looking out towards the slipway below the pub just up the river. 'It's going to be a real party. Darren's brought a sound system with loads of batteries so we can have it really loud, and there's stacks of drink.' Tamsin was looking amazingly like Orville the puppet duck in a green fake swansdown jacket. Suzy had a fleeting thought that this might look just like pondweed if it should accidentally happen to get terribly wet.

She felt cross and betrayed, her game, her lovely Swallows and Amazons sleep-out, in ruins. 'You said, you *promised* it would be just us and Shane and Simon,' she accused Tamsin.

'Well, you weren't too happy with that if I remember rightly,' Tamsin replied smugly. 'I'd have thought you'd be *pleased*. Safety in numbers. Anyway, you can always go home if you want to. After that disgusting trick you played on me this morning, you should be glad I even let you come here at all.'

Suzy smirked, remembering Tamsin howling, her face seasick-green and wild-eyed with terror, fleeing from the sight of Uncle Edward's corpse in the murky half-gloom of the dining-room that morning. Her face had been almost the colour of the bizarre jacket she was wearing.

From the terrace outside the pub, Heather, Tom and Delia picked at their salads and watched Lisa Gibson's tightly-skirted bottom waving in the air as she attempted hopelessly to get into a small boat in high-heeled shoes. She shrieked and giggled and fell on one of her friends, who dropped an oar in the water and swore loudly. The boat was leaning and rocking, girls yelled and squealed and laughed, and eventually the overloaded craft pulled away from the pub steps and moved precariously off towards the island and the source of a great deal of unaccustomed noise.

'Call that music!'

'Should someone get the police?'

'Are they *allowed* to have parties over there?'

Disapproving remarks from pub patrons filled the air around Heather, and she could see Delia looking from one speaker to another, her face expressing her agreement with their comments.

'It's only a bit of fun. Better than trashing the village hall,' Tom said softly, collecting glasses and going back into the bar to get them all a refill.

'Your children are out there,' Delia said to Heather, waving her hand vaguely in the upstream direction. 'Surely you don't want them associating with, well, *rough* people.'

'They'll be OK, it's just the village kids. They *should* mix more locally, I've been thinking. And it's not as if it's just Suzy. Kate and Simon are there, too.'

Delia thought for a moment, neatly cut the last piece

of tomato on her plate and said rather pointedly, looking round swiftly to see if Tom was on his way back. 'Well at least Kate is with people more her own age. We should be grateful for *that*.'

Heather bit her lip and stopped herself from responding with something cutting and hurtful. Her mother had had a trying day. A funeral, to Heather and Tom, was still thankfully a rare experience. To Delia and to those elderly dignified men at the crematorium, it was probably increasingly and depressingly the usual social thing.

'I think they've got a barbecue going over there,' Tom said, coming back with drinks. 'I'm sure I can smell sausages. Perhaps it would have been fun if we'd joined them,' he added, looking glumly at the sulky faces of his wife and mother-in-law.

'This isn't really a day for having fun,' Delia reminded him.

Back in their own garden later, Heather and Tom wandered down to the river and looked along the water to the island where they could just make out figures moving in silhouette against the trees and firelight.

'I don't suppose Suzy will want to stay out too long with that lot,' Tom commented, putting his arm round Heather.

'No, I expect you're right. She and Tam would have been better spending the night in the treehouse if they wanted a bit of peace.'

'Peace isn't the kind of thing I associate with Tamsin,' Tom said, making Heather laugh. She was watching a figure rowing from Margot's dock up towards the island. All she could make out was that it was a man, not a teenager.

'Late arrival,' Tom said, indicating the rower, 'unless it's Russell going off to collect Tamsin.'

Heather shivered. 'It isn't Russell,' she said.

Chapter Eighteen

The sharp smell of smoke and the night-rending blare of emergency sirens pulled Heather back to consciousness. Half-dozing, she realized acutely that she wasn't just having a worried-parent dream about something selected randomly from the list of what's most dreadful that can happen to children. It was way after three o'clock, and the party on the island had gone quiet hours ago. She'd done some lying awake, agonizing with Tom as to whether Suzy should really have been allowed to stay camping out with Tamsin as arranged, or be collected and made to come safely home. Her decision in favour of Suzy getting her own way had been, Heather admitted to herself, influenced by the fact that her mother continued to make her own disapproval so obvious as they left the pub the night before.

'What time is Suzy to be home?' Delia had asked.

'You know she isn't coming, she and Tamsin arranged this night out ages ago,' Heather had explained, worrying if her mother's memory was starting to give way.

'But you can't let her out there all night! It's an All Night Party!' Delia had gasped, as horrified as if Suzy was being specially equipped by Heather with a personal supply of illicit drugs.

'It isn't a party, or at least it won't be as soon as they get bored and cold. Tam and Suzy are playing camps, that's all. They've had it planned for weeks,' Heather had replied, trying to bluff away her own misgivings and at the same time prove that *she* could bring up her own children with tolerance and leniency and *still* end

271

up with reasonable, well-adjusted grown-ups at the end of it all. Though when *did* it all end, she wondered, still, at over forty, childishly trying to outface her mother and now cravenly using her own daughter as a weapon to do it with.

Once the party sounds had died down, and Tom and Heather imagined that everyone else had gone safely home to sleep somewhere more comfortable, they'd concluded with relief that Suzy really would be safe enough, with Tamsin and in the company of Kate and Simon. Now Heather sat up fast enough to make her head whirl, sniffed the air and knew she'd been terribly, irresponsibly, wrong. Tom was already out of bed, leaning out of the window, seeing the smoke drifting along the river in the deep grey dawning light.

'I can't see flames,' he told her, as if that would be any comfort. 'And the smoke *might* just be the barbecue fire. The sirens could be a road accident or *anything* – that sort of thing always does seem worse in the middle of the night,' he added, his anxious face belying his attempt to deny his fear, while at the same time he was hurling himself into his clothes. 'I'll whip a boat from the pub and go and check on them. Probably they're asleep and I'll scare them witless.'

'I'll come,' Heather said, reaching into a drawer for her jeans.

'No, don't,' he said. 'What about Delia?'

'I'll see if she's awake. If she is I'll tell her what's happening, and if not I'll leave a note in the kitchen. She *was* exhausted.'

Heather ran alongside Tom to the pub, faster than she knew she could. Her head was full of dreaded 'what ifs', just as she knew Suzy's must be. Suppose the boats had all caught fire and they were all trapped over there? She thought about fire, about how Uncle Edward's body had, that afternoon, been cremated to pale ash as finely ground as powder. It was impossible not to picture that happening to Suzy and Kate, out there under the trees cut off from the shore. It wouldn't have been far to swim if the river had been just a safe and placid lake, but there was a fierce current around the island, and it was treacherously close to the weir. The earliest dire warnings the girls could remember weren't about the danger of strangers but the terrible unguessed hazards of the river. As they ran down the lane towards the water, a fire engine hurtled past, lights flashing. Heather flattened herself against the hedge to let it pass, gasping painfully and her throat burning with the unaccustomed effort of running.

'Wasn't wrong then,' Tom gasped hoarsely beside her, starting to run again behind the fire engine.

Down by the water, where the lights of the pub lit up the scene, Heather thought of old newsreels of the Dunkirk landings. The water seemed full of boats, shadowy, moving slowly and overloaded. Shamefaced, strangely passive teenagers were landing on the bank and clambering silently up the pontoon. A police launch carried a skulking bunch of boys who had jackets wrapped round their heads as if any moment they were ready to hide their faces from accusing television cameras.

'Where's Suzy and Kate?' Tom muttered, then grabbed a boy from the gloom. 'Simon? Where are the girls?'

'Suzy's coming, she's got Tamsin and some others with her. Kate's not here,' he said, before being man-handled away by a police constable with more force than Heather thought, in the circumstances, was appropriate.

'Did you see *that*?' she whispered to Tom. 'You'd think they'd be a bit more gentle – these kids are in shock.'

'Probably thinking they're just a bunch of vandals,' Tom replied. 'I mean, look at the state of the poor island:

not many round here are going to think they're anything else, are they?'

'Mum! What're you doing here?' Suzy yelled from her boat as she and Tamsin arrived at the pontoon. Heather, sick with anxiety about Kate, looked beyond Suzy to where the island's rain-starved saplings and old dead wood were now crackling and blazing like a municipal bonfire night display. She prayed no-one was still left over there. The fire brigade were aiming jets of water that arced over the river and sizzled in the flames. Curious residents, hauled from their sleep by noise and nosiness, were beginning to gather in the pub garden and, seeing that everyone seemed to be safe, commented that it would be neighbourly to reopen the bar.

Tom hugged Suzy so tightly, the girl started struggling to escape and breathe.

'Where is Kate?' Heather demanded. 'I can't see her. Simon says she's not here.' She couldn't have drowned or been burned could she? A little, dreadful, rat of fear chewed persistently – though if the others could get away, Kate could too, surely.

'Kate went off in a boat. Ages ago,' Tamsin informed them as she passed by on her way to see why Simon was being shoved into a police car.

'Oh didn't she come home? I thought she would have,' Suzy said, 'Iain came in Russell's boat to give her a lift. Don't worry about *her*, she's been gone hours.'

'Who the hell is Iain?' Tom asked suddenly.

Suzy looked at him with astonishment, as if, Heather thought, she'd realized for the first time just how much of their everyday lives her father missed by being away so much. 'He's just that man who wrote the film that they've been doing at Margot's. *You* know,' Suzy said, as if she shouldn't have to be telling him this. 'At least, he wrote the book that the film's of and—'

'Never mind that now. What's he got to do with Kate?'

'He got her a part in the film, just a walk-on,' Heather

told him as they started walking back towards home loaded with Suzy's tent, bag of equipment and Tamsin tramping along beside them looking quite enviably snug in her pea-green baby bird coat.

Heather could feel Tom's impatience for a deeper explanation and she wished there was something simple and placatory she could say. She wondered which aspect of 'Who is Iain?' he should be informed of first: that Iain was her ex-husband, a 'friend' of Kate, sworn enemy of Delia, partner in failed adultery. Foreboding that was worse than the moment when she'd woken up smelling the smoke was now taking over her mind. As soon as they got home, she knew Tom was going to demand to know where Kate was now. Heather knew with quite shattering, awful, certainty exactly where she was. No wonder there'd been something Iain had found impossible to tell her over dinner. She could picture all too painfully the pretty dovecote room and the brass bed containing her smoothly naked child nestled beside the well-worn body of Iain. For only the first time since she was Kate's age herself, she could understand how sorrow could be described as *stabbing*, and as she walked along the path to her house, she rubbed at the area where her heart was, trying to ease the dread and the hurt.

Margot was unaware that she was interrupting anything more than a late breakfast when, at a more civilized time that morning, she came bustling into Heather's kitchen, full of the awfulness of what Simon had done. She didn't notice the sleepless, worried faces of Heather and Tom, the array of used coffee cups lying around on every surface.

'Arrested! Charged! The police found stolen goods all over the village. They've had the cottage upside down! God knows what Russell will have to say about it.

Though if he was around a bit more to take notice—' She stopped and bit her lip, conscious that she might have touched a nerve with Tom. Tom, however, was looking blankly out of the window, staring down to the river as if expecting to see Cleopatra's barge come floating along at any moment. 'Sorry,' she muttered.

'It's OK,' Heather reassured her, feeling as if she was conversing on an unreal, automatic level. 'I am sorry about Simon. Are they sure he did it? I mean he's not—'

' "Not the sort", you mean,' Margot said with a short sardonic laugh. 'No such thing as not the sort, I think. Anyway the good news is we heard from the school in the post this morning, and they're willing to have him back, just like I said they would. Can't afford to let good fee-payers out of their grasp. So he's going back there in September, no question. If he stays around here there'll just be more trouble, I can see it coming.'

'What will happen to Shane and Darren, do you think?' Heather asked.

'Something custodial, the police think, this time.' She smiled sadly. 'They didn't think Simon would get more than a caution. It's being middle class, you see, isn't it? When *our* kids are a problem we just pack them off to boarding school and let someone else sort them out. A quite socially acceptable equivalent of putting them into Care.' A flurry of noise came from the hallway and Margot turned to see what was happening. 'Good grief, you're looking pleased with yourself!' she said to Kate, who appeared in the kitchen doorway, radiant as an angel.

Heather felt furious – how dare the girl come swanning in like that, looking as if she was walking six inches above the ground? The very air around her was practically alight in post-sexual glow. The pain in her chest, the awful knifing of sexual jealousy, started up again and she lunged forward and slapped Kate's face with all the angry, irrational strength she could gather.

Tom grabbed her arm before she could inflict more damage – the urge to keep slapping, to pull all that golden hair and watch her howl with pain was horrendously powerful.

'Er, I'll be off now. See you later,' Margot said, backing out of the door and tactfully bolting for home.

'What was that for?' Kate screamed at her mother.

'What do you think it was for?'

'Heather, for heaven's sake calm down, let Kate tell us herself why she thinks it was all right to stay out all night.'

'God, Tom, stop being so *reasonable*.'

'You *knew* I wouldn't be home. I was going to stay out with Suzy!' Kate wailed, rubbing her face.

'But you didn't, did you? I know where you went, *and* who with!'

'Heather, don't you think it would be more helpful if we just sat down and discussed this *sensibly*?' Tom was saying, pulling her gently into a chair and removing her to a safe distance from Kate.

'*Sensibly*? No. No I don't,' Heather said, glaring at him.

'Look, let's not over-react,' he said. 'What's she done? She's stayed out all night with a man. OK, not one's first choice, having your daughter sleep with someone about as old as her own father, who happens to be one of her mother's ex-boyfriends. It's bizarre, probably something deeply Freudian, but it'll pass,' he said to Heather, stroking her hair.

'No it won't. I'm going away with him,' Kate stated sullenly, staring intently at Heather. 'He's asked me to go to Bermuda, and I've come home to pack.'

Delia waited outside the kitchen door, listening to Kate make her announcement. *They're lucky*, she thought, *at least their daughter is telling them before she goes, rather than phoning them two days later*. 'Well doesn't history have a strange way of repeating itself?' she announced to Heather as she walked into the kitchen.

'Does it?' Tom asked, perplexed.

'Kate, you can't possibly go. What about A-levels?' Heather argued, falling back rather feebly on education as a reason for staying.

'School! *You* never thought about school!' Delia commented as she filled the kettle.

Heather looked at her mother, watching her calmly going through the motions of preparing herself some breakfast while coming out with remarks she must have been saving up for twenty-five years. It was turning into a truth session – family therapy without a counsellor to do the safe refereeing.

'Am I missing something here? What exactly are we talking about?' Tom said. 'Isn't this supposed to be about Kate and this mysterious Iain character?'

Kate stood fidgeting, waiting for them all to get back to discussing *her*. Her grandmother, she assumed, was going dotty, referring back to the past the way old people do, remembering more, probably, about what happened thirty years ago than she did about the previous week. Iain wouldn't get like that, she just knew. He would be permanently *not old*.

'You can't go with him. He's too old, you're too young – he's . . . he's *evil*,' Heather said with a shudder, trying not to cry.

'How did you know where I was?' Kate suddenly asked, sitting opposite Heather at the kitchen table. 'How did you know? Who told you?'

'Because she went there herself. Didn't you? With him.' Delia had a look of self-satisfied foreknowledge, as if she'd long ago put two and two together and should now be congratulated on announcing that it made four.

'Be quiet, Mother. This is *my* business,' Heather said coldly. 'Yes, I went to the Manoir the other night. With

Iain. For dinner.' She looked at Tom, 'Just dinner,' she repeated. They were all looking at her, waiting.

'I knew,' Delia chipped in. 'I could tell. You had that look, like you used to get back then. And you still haven't told Tom have you?' she said to Heather, as if Tom, being just a husband, could hardly be counted as being in the room.

'Back when? Told him *what*?' Kate demanded.

'When I was your age. When we, when I went out with Iain. Look, you can't go off with him, you just can't.' Heather got up and started bustling around, loading cups into the dishwasher and trying to dissipate the nervous energy that was collecting in her. She could feel tears welling. They were all looking at her, waiting now; all of them, not just Delia, knew there was some old truth to be told. Tom should have known years ago. He could hardly complain now, he being an absolute master at expecting the past, even if that constituted a brief last-week flingette, to *be* the past. If she told them, she decided, Kate wouldn't, couldn't go. She leaned against the dresser feeling trapped and flattened, feeling their expectancy squashing hard against her.

'He wasn't just a boyfriend. Iain and I were married for a little while when I was only sixteen and silly, like you,' she began. Upstairs, Suzy broke their silence with her new Blur CD. The thought of Simon in police custody flashed through Heather's mind. If Kate had been caught stealing instead of *this* – what a small, easy thing it would have seemed by comparison. She took another breath and told them the rest as flatly as if she was reading from a script, talking about someone else. 'We went up to Scotland and I lived in Iain's castle with just him and a murderous old nanny. I got pregnant and Iain didn't want the baby. He wanted the nanny to abort it with a knitting needle. I refused, so he decided everything had been a ridiculous mistake and took me to the station and put me on a train to London. He liked little girls as toys, not as wives, not when they reminded him that deep down they were women. Doesn't look like he's changed. I didn't see him again till Margot's party, when you jumped in the pool,' she told them. 'So you see, Kate, now you know the truth, you can't possibly go off anywhere with him.'

There was a small, tense silence, then Kate, rubbing the painful side of her face, said simply, 'Yes I can.'

Heather sat alone by the river watching the magpies terrorizing the songbirds, and thought about her dead baby. One for sorrow, two for mirth, she thought about the older, more sinister version of the rhyme, which said, seven for a babe that's buried in the earth. She'd never known if it was a boy or a girl; it had been treated as a growth, clots, something distasteful to be wrapped up and disposed of like bits of cancer or amputated limbs. 'There's no place in here for girls like you!' the staff-nurse had hissed coldly when Heather had woken in the night, shivering with fever and pain. The way they'd handled her, she might as well have had the knitting needle treatment.

She thought about the journey from Scotland, about the hot and itchy plush red seats of the train, and how she'd realized that she wasn't sweating, but bleeding, browny-red into the browny-red material. She'd felt paralysed by fear and shame. Blood from *there* was blood to be hidden, menstrual blood that was to be disguised with pads so thin, tampons so discreet. She remembered the pink-and-white quasi-medical adverts for the products, Dr Whites, Lillets – all, back then, so coy and so hinting that a period was only one step away from a sexually transmitted disease. Women went about in fear of anything *showing* – the bulge of a pad, a shadow of a stain on a pale skirt. A friend's mother had whispered that she shouldn't wash her hair at such a time, the blood would go to her head and the clear implication was that this sinister stuff was dangerous enough to do *damage*. On the train she'd borne, silent with the terror of embarrassment, excruciating waves of pain till just before King's Cross she'd passed out and had to be taken from the train by ambulance. Semiconscious, she'd simply been relieved that she hadn't had to get up and walk and expose the dreadful trailing blood, humiliated, like girls at school who started to bleed out on the games field.

'Well at least the truth's out.' Delia sat heavily on the bench next to Heather and handed her a cup of tea.

'Yes, but what good did it do?' Heather said.

'In the end, it's probably better. *I* should have been more honest,' Delia told her. 'Running off seems to be in the family.'

'Did you . . . ?'

'No, not me. Your father.' Delia gazed at the ducks battling over food on the opposite bank.

'You always said he died. Something he picked up during the war.'

Delia smiled wryly. 'What he picked up during the war was a little red-headed Wren, stationed down on the south coast. She was married, too. They couldn't make up their minds, or at least he couldn't. He kept coming and going for years. Didn't go for good till you were born and I was safely tied down. He didn't like to think of me being as free as he was. They went off together and died together, crashing her car.'

'Why did you never say?' Heather asked in a whisper.

Delia's cup was trembling in its saucer, and she had to put it down on the bench. 'Because I didn't want you to think I hadn't been able to keep him,' she said. 'By the time I'd realized he wasn't *worth* keeping, it was far too late to tell you.'

'Another of those moments that pass,' Heather murmured.

'Yes. Well it wasn't all awful, your Uncle Edward was very comforting.'

'Good grief! Was he?' Heather looked at her mother and saw a spark of happy memory in her eyes.

'Oh yes. Did you really think your generation was the one that invented sex?'

'Kate's probably thinking *hers* is.'

'You shouldn't have hit her. She might not have gone. Now you've left her no choice really, have you?'

Up in her room, Kate packed a small bag with flimsy summery clothes, sun-tan lotion and beachwear. Her face didn't hurt any more and she gently touched the place where her mother had hit her. In the mirror she could see the red stripe had started to fade, so she rubbed at it to make it come back. What did her mother mind about most? Her or Iain? She decided to think it was Iain, far more convenient at the moment than having to face the responsibility of her mother loving her. Her GCSE results were due in a week, she noticed from the calendar on the wall. How important they'd seemed only a few weeks ago. Now she thought she'd probably not even ring home on the day to find out how she'd done. She also knew now why she'd felt so different from her friends, couldn't stand the girly chumminess of school. She *was* different. Imagine Annabelle, she thought with a giggle, ordinary, nice, everyday Annabelle with her huggy-buggy family, even *thinking* about a relationship with someone more than a couple of years older than herself! *She'd* probably get as far as a fling with an Australian surfer during the statutory year off, marry a nice Environmental Science graduate that she'd meet at Exeter and spend the rest of her life mothering him and moaning at him.

Kate, meanwhile, pushed her toy panda into the corner of her bag and hugged herself at the knowledge that she was *treasured*.

'Kate? Can I come in? What's happening, why's everyone so cross and peculiar?' Suzy appeared in the doorway and Kate felt an unexpected rush of sorrow. Suzy looked bewildered and frightened. She wanted to hug her, but was afraid they'd both cry, and she didn't want that – she wanted this to be a triumphant outgoing, no invading, painful, conscience in the way. 'I'm going away for a while Suze. Just like a holiday, but maybe for a bit longer.'

'You're going away with Iain?' Suzy's voice was small, but sure of the facts.

'Did you guess, or did you know?'

'The way he looked at you, right from the time he pulled you out of Margot's pool. I didn't think I could be right though because he's—'

'Don't say it.' Kate put her hand gently over Suzy's mouth. 'I've heard it enough from *them*. I don't want to hear you say it too, not you. Get Mum to tell you the whole thing.' She screwed up her nose. 'It's all a bit tacky.'

'Taxi's here!' Tom called as he came up the stairs. 'Shall I carry your bag?'

'It's OK, I can manage. Why are you being so nice?' Kate felt she might cry in spite of being so determined not to.

Tom grinned at her. 'I want you to know that you've got someone to come back to. I'm old and I love you too, but I'm allowed to, I'm your dad,' he told her as they went down the stairs.

'Why is she off to Heathrow in a cab? Why didn't he just drive her there? How gutless can you get?' Heather agonized tearfully as she felt the impact of Kate's absence the moment the taxi disappeared down the drive. The house felt instantly too big, as if the walls had suddenly moved outwards because Kate had left behind great silent echoing hollow spaces where she had been. When Edward's dead body had been parked in the dining-room, the house had seemed to contract around them, making them whisper, making them aware of the small space between themselves and the presence of death. Kate left great, aching spaces echoing with the phantom of her energy.

'She said he told her to meet him there,' Tom said, opening a much-needed can of lager from the fridge. 'I suppose he could hardly saunter up to the front door and say "Excuse me, I've come to steal your daughter." ' Tom's voice wobbled with the effort of trying to stay in control.

'Oh, he arranged that, did he?' Delia said with interest. 'Then I think you'd better get in the car,' she told Heather. 'After all, what makes you think he'll be there?'

It was like admitting that Kate, who was so special, could possibly have been just someone to be used, Heather thought as she drove through the village. She was ashamed of her lack of faith in her own daughter's lasting attraction, no trust that Kate could keep Iain interested for any longer than she herself had. Perhaps it had been for as little as that one night. Heather thought of the last, agonizing chapter of *Peter Pan*, the one she'd found impossible to read aloud to the girls, where Peter returns years later to claim Wendy's daughter. She'd looked at their little clean pink faces in their beds as she'd tried to read, imagining with painful foresight, just how Wendy must have felt, having to let her child go. Iain was the very last Peter she'd have then imagined Kate flying with.

The traffic through the village was horribly slow. Trucks and vans were leaving Margot's driveway and

284

forming a slow and ramshackle convoy that rumbled along in a tired procession, like a broken-down fairground at the tail-end of the season. Along the pavement where the shops started, Heather, crawling along with her windows open, could hear the conversations of people who stood around gossiping about the previous night, about the awfulness of young people, the undoubted influence of drugs. Julia Merriman with her dogs was in the thick of the gathering, smiling and full of purpose, looking as if she was relishing the fact that the village had some common cause for concern at last. Perhaps trouble and problems were really the only thing that could link the community, now that no-one could summon up much interest in the church organ fund or the cricket tea rota.

The airport was stifling and dusty, and reeked of oily fuel and overheated cars sweltering in lines trying to get past building works to the central terminal areas. Heather drove around the perimeter road as fast as she dared, and parked opposite Terminal Four, scanning the car park as she drove for the scarlet Mercedes and not finding it. She wanted very much to take that as a sign that Iain wasn't there and wasn't going to be there, but intrusive reason told her he'd probably left it somewhere else or taken a taxi like Kate.

Once she'd parked and locked her car, Heather came suddenly to the point at which she wasn't sure what to do next. Down on the pavement, with all the terminal entrance doors in view, all she could do was find somewhere to wait. She paused, feeling that her hesitation made her conspicuous. Baggage-handlers eyed her for suitcases that needed carrying, traffic wardens shied away in case she was going to ask them for change or for directions. Suddenly she caught sight of a man climbing slowly out of a black hire car, accepting the help of the driver's arm. It was Iain, suddenly, recognizably on his way to overripe old age. He was alone, moving strangely slowly and awkwardly like someone who wasn't bothering to disguise a bout of rheumatism. She noticed his hair was looking unusually thin and stringy, clinging limply round his head as a result of the heat. There was something pathetic about him, an ageing fool still chasing young girls who were so much more easy to flatter and charm than mature, wise, questioning women. Now she watched Iain's stooped figure counting out cash for tips while baggage (expensive, soft leather) was unloaded from the car boot and stacked on a porter's trolley, then taken through the automatic doors into the building. Kate must be somewhere just beyond those doors, noticing the same things, she thought. If she doesn't now, she will later and she'll wonder what on earth she's done. In case it was *now*, and praying to all available Gods that it might be, Heather found an abandoned trolley and sat on it in the shade watching the doors till her eyes blurred, prepared to wait for her daughter, either here or at home, for as long as it took.

THE END